FOX DRUM BEBOP

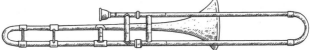

Published by Kaya Press (Muae Publishing, Inc.)
www.kaya.com

14 15 16 17 18 01 02 03 04 05

For information about permission to reproduce selections from this book,
please write to permissions@kaya.com.

Book design by spoon+fork
Cover and interior illustrations by Rui Tenreiro

Distributed by D.A.P./Distributed Art Publishers
155 Avenue of the Americas, 2nd Floor, New York, NY 10013
800.338.BOOK   www.artbook.com

Library of Congress Cataloging-in-Publication Data
Oishi, Gene, 1933-
Fox Drum Bebop / by Gene Oishi.
pages cm
ISBN 978-1-885030-17-7
1. Japanese Americans – Fiction. I. Title.
PS3615.I85F69 2014
813'.6--dc23
2014011888

Printed in the United States of America

This publication is made possible by support from the USC Dana and David Dornsife
College of Arts, Letters, and Sciences; the USC Department of American Studies
and Ethnicity; and the USC Asian American Studies Program. Special thanks to the
Choi Chang Soo Foundation for their support of this work. Additional funding was
provided by the generous contributions of Lisa Chen & Andy Hsiao, Floyd Cheung,
Douglas Choi, Susannah Donahue-Negbaur, Sesshu Foster, Prince Gomolvilas,
Thea Gray & Jeanine Mattson, Lillian Howan, Qing Lan Huang, Keesoo Huh &
Jisun Suh, Helen Kim & Stephen Lee, Juliana S. Koo & Paul Smith, Bill Lee & Corey
Ohama, Whakyung & Hong Yung Lee, Ericka Mattuck, Minya & Yun Oh, Lily So &
Tom Beischer, Duncan Williams, Amelia Wu & Sachin Adarkar, Anita Wu & James
Spicer, Amy Zeifang, and others.

GENE OISHI

FOX
DRUM
BEBOP

KAYA PRESS

LOS ANGELES
NEW YORK

EDITORIAL NOTE

This novel is fiction based on memories that have been reimagined and embroidered in the story making. The "kabuki" stories are childhood impressions and are probably not authentic in many details. The same should be said of the father's "joruri" chanting, which would be from bunraku, or classical puppet theater, an offshoot of kabuki that my own father was fond of. The camp described in the novel is a fictional composite of three camps—an "assembly center" in Tulare, California, and two "relocation centers" in Arizona, one on the Gila River Indian Reservation and the other at Poston, near the California border. In its entirety, it does not match any camp that I know of or personally experienced.

CHAPTERS

THE OKIE

1940 - 1941

The boy was barefoot. He had dirt on his face. His overalls were patched and shredded. His dirty blond hair covered his eyes like a sheep dog's.

Hiroshi thought he might be an Okie. He knew about Okies from his older brother Isamu, who said they were people made poor by a bad drought in Oklahoma. The drought had happened a long time ago, but Okies were still coming to California, riding boxcars like tramps and hobos.

"You an Okie?" Hiroshi asked.

"Naw. I ain't no Okie. We come from Texas. You can call me Tex if you like. You Chinese?"

"Japanese!" Hiroshi said, clenching his fists.

The two boys stood at arm's length, silently taking each other in.

Toward town, a few lights were beginning to flicker on. To the west, a pasture stretched out, dark blue in the fading light. Somewhere in that emptiness lurked a bull. It usually hid at the far edge of the pasture, where the woods began. The late afternoon sun glittered through the trees, turning them black. The wind had come up and the trees were beginning to wave back and forth. Soon they would begin to whistle.

"Ya wanna fight?" Tex said.

"Sure."

Hiroshi looked at Tex's bony hands, at the chafed and cracked skin over his knuckles. The queasiness he felt in his stomach made him almost wish the fight would start, but Tex remained loose.

"Shucks, I'm just joshing," Tex said, breaking out into a grin. Then he dug into his overalls and took out some coins.

"You steal it?" Hiroshi asked.

"Naw, my Pa give it to me."

"You better give it back."

"Aw," Tex groaned and spat on the ground with a look of disappointment. But he recovered quickly. "Hey, you wanna flip pennies?" he asked. "Come on, I'll lend ya some."

It was wrong to gamble, but it would have been stupid to say that to Tex. So Hiroshi sat down and flipped pennies with him. When one boy won them all, they would divide them up and flip some more. Hiroshi began to enjoy himself after a while. Tex was like a character out of a storybook, what with his long yellow hair, blue eyes, and freckled face, not to mention the way he said, "I reckon," "ain't," and "shucks."

"Maybe I'll go snitch some of my Pa's tabbaky," Tex said, "and we can have us a smoke."

"Yeah," Hiroshi said. Just for the fun of it, he added, "I reckon that'll be real keen."

Tex looked at him quizzically.

Then, from a distance, barely audible, it came.

"Hee-ro-sheeee." His sister Sachi.

He ignored the call, but it came again and again, each time a little closer. "Hee-ro-sheee. Hee-ro-sheee."

Then Sachi was upon them, hugging her cardigan sweater with both arms against the chill and looking put out with her pinched nose, pursed lips, and squinting eyes. She was 15; she didn't have time to chase after her brother who, at eight, was old enough to find his own way home.

"You're gambling!" she shouted.

"So long, Tex," Hiroshi said. "I gotta go."

"Aw," Tex said. As Hiroshi ran off, Tex called after him, "So long, Hee-row."

Hiroshi hurried, hoping that if he managed to get home so that he was at the table before his sister, she wouldn't mention what he'd been doing. The chances of that were next to nothing, but he ran anyway.

He hurried down Main Street toward the Mexican cantina and the sound of guitar music. As he passed the swinging doors, he was hit by a strong blast of tobacco smoke mixed with beer and whisky fumes. The force of it nearly made him stumble into a fat lady with painted lips and no eyebrows who was coming out of the cantina.

"Hey, watch out little boy," she said. "Look where you're going."

At the China House the next block down, a waiter sitting in the doorway glanced idly up from his Chinese newspaper at Hiroshi as he ran past.

Hiroshi's family lived in what his father insisted was the finest house in Hacienda. He had bought it from the boss of the sugar company who, like all rich hakujin, had moved years ago to Santa Marguerita, ten miles to the east. Santa Marguerita was where all the best stores were. It was where Hiroshi's mother bought the hot-house lilies that suffused the entrance to their house with their milky sweet fragrance. The flowers billowed out of a large porcelain vase set on a curved-footed mahogany table below a gilded mirror.

Arriving out of breath, Hiroshi hurriedly took off his shoes and placed them in the rack, which he saw was already full. He put on his house slippers and announced his return, shouting "Tadaima!" to the empty living room. The logs were still flickering in the fireplace. A portrait of the Emperor dressed in a military uniform and bedecked with medals graced the wall above the mantel. Hiroshi always thought the Emperor looked a little sleepy and slightly baffled behind his steel-rimmed glasses.

The family was already sitting at the dinner table. Father had his coat unbuttoned, but, as usual, his tie was neatly knotted below his chin and his vest remained securely fastened up to the top button. He was sipping hot sake and scarcely seemed to notice Hiroshi as he rushed in. To his father's immediate right was Hiroshi's oldest brother Yukio, in khaki work clothes. Next to Yukio came his next eldest brother, Isamu, in his wheelchair, then Mickey, home for the Christmas holidays from the university. Mother was ladling misoshiru from the soup urn that Masako-san, their housekeeper, held for her.

"Hiroshi," Mother said, frowning. "Go wash your hands. And your face. Look at your clothes. What have you been doing?"

No sooner had Hiroshi washed and taken his seat when Sachi rushed into the dining room, her face flushed from having chased him through half the town.

"He was gambling!" she said in Japanese, making it clear that she was addressing Mother and Father. "With a hakujin boy!"

Mother placed the ladle in the urn and nodded to Masako-san, but Masako-san remained standing where she was. Hiroshi sank in his chair and hung his head. He didn't dare look up, but he felt his father's stare.

"With a hakujin boy?" Isamu echoed in English.

"One of those Okie boys," Sachi replied, also in English.

Hiroshi stiffened and looked up. "Unh-uh," he countered. "He isn't an Okie. He's from Texas." Hiroshi thought for moment that he ought to repeat himself in Japanese, but it wouldn't have made a difference. He wasn't even sure it made a difference in

English.

"With a hakujin boy," his father said finally. He did not speak loudly, but the room had grown quiet; Father's voice was like thunder striking the earth. "You are Japanese," Father said. "Such boys are below you. What if someone saw you? What would people think? It's a black mark on the family."

His father's voice was beginning to rise. Hiroshi began to understand how careless he had been in allowing Sachi to see him with the white boy.

Mother went to Hiroshi. "He won't do it again," she said softly, putting her arms around Hiroshi. "Say you won't do it again. Ne? Ne, Hiroshi?"

"Hai!" Hiroshi said as loudly as he could. "I will not do it again."

"Unh," Father grunted, relaxing the stern expression on his face.

"That's a good boy," Mother said and smoothed Hiroshi's hair.

Masako-san returned to the kitchen with the soup urn; the children bowed and murmured "Itadakimasu" and started to eat. Father began talking to Yukio about the price of lettuce and the work that needed to be done at the packinghouse. All was well.

Dinner was sukiyaki. Slices of beef and onions sizzled in the thick iron skillet that had been placed over a gas-fired burner on the center of the table. Around the skillet, mounds of crisp, chopped vegetables had been arranged alongside mushrooms, tofu, yam noodles, raw eggs for dipping, and a thinly sliced pile of well-marbled beef. Father insisted on eating well, but food in such great abundance seemed to bring out feelings of guilt in Mother.

"We must be grateful," she said softly. "We are so fortunate. In Japan, even the most wealthy do not eat as we do."

When school reopened in the new year, Tex was in Hiroshi's third-grade class. He wore overalls as before, but now he had shoes as well—though they were high-tops, which no other kid, not even farm boys, would ever think of wearing to school. The sole on one of Tex's shoes was so loose that you could see his toes.

The white children persisted in calling Tex an Okie and would have nothing to do with him. Even the teachers were cold toward him. Like other white boys, Tex didn't play with Mexicans, so instead he hung around the Japanese boys, who tolerated him.

One Saturday, when Hiroshi and his friends were poking at old tires behind Mr. Shimada's garage, Tex came walking toward them across the vacant lot next to the garage. He was carrying a stick on his shoulder with a small bundle tied to one end the way hobos did in comic books. He was rubbing his eyes, and the dirt on his face was streaked with tears.

"What's the matter, Tex?" Hiroshi asked.

"I'm running away," Tex said. "My Pa whupped me, and I ain't takin' it no more. I'm hoppin' a freight train, goin' to Los Angeles maybe."

"Whatcha gonna do in Los Angeles?" Albert Yamada wanted to know.

"I'll get me a job. I'll be all right."

"You know anybody in LA?" Eddie Nakano asked.

"Naw, but I'll get by. I ain't afraid."

"You got anything to eat?" Hiroshi asked.

"Yeah," Tex said, grinning through his tears. "I snitched a can of sardines and a can of soup," he said, pointing to his bundle wrapped in a red bandanna. "Got me some crackers, too. My old man's gonna have a fit. Look, I got his tabbaky," he said, taking a bag of Bull Durham from his pocket. "You wanna have a smoke?"

"Naw, that's all right," Eddie Nakano said, backing off. All the Japanese boys murmured agreement.

"You better save it," Albert Yamada advised. "Maybe you can sell it if you need money."

Minoru Sawada, who had been silent up to then, spoke up.

"You got any money?"

"Naw," Tex shook his head. "I don't need none. I can get me a job real quick in Los Angeles. I hear you can get a job just like that over there," he said, snapping his fingers.

Minoru dug into his pocket and brought out fifteen cents. The boys were surprised to see so much money. They were even more surprised when Minoru handed it to Tex.

"Maybe you should have some money," Minoru said. "You might need it before you get a job."

"Gee, thanks," Tex said.

The other boys dug into their pockets. Albert came up with a nickel. Eddie had seven cents and some rubber bands. Hiroshi knew he had no money, but he stuck his hands in his pockets anyway. He found two pieces of caramel, which he handed to Tex.

Tex shook hands with all the boys. They wished him luck. As Tex walked away, they watched him go with admiring eyes.

If Tex had disappeared for good, he would have become a legend among the Japanese boys, but a few days later, he was back in school. When Albert Yamada asked him whether he still had the money, Tex said he had spent it all in Los Angeles, but he would pay them back as soon as he got a job.

"I bet you didn't even go to Los Angeles," Albert said. "You're a liar."

"I'll pay you back, honest," Tex said, but nobody believed him.

As usual, Minoru Sawada didn't say anything. He kept his head down and peered at Tex now and then from the corners of his eyes.

After the Los Angeles episode, the Japanese boys were suspicious of Tex, but they still let him hang around.

"I ain't no Okie," Tex would assure them. "We come from West Texas, near the neck of the panhandle." He spoke as if he expected them to know where West Texas and the panhandle were. "My Pa had a cattle ranch there."

"You mean you were a cowboy?" Albert Yamada said with a sniff. "I'll bet you don't even know how to ride a horse."

"I do, too," cried Tex. "I used to help out with the roundup all the time. Pa had five hundred head of cattle, Texas longhorns."

"How come you're not still in Texas, then? What're you doing in California?"

"The bank come and took away our ranch."

"You're a liar," Albert said, "I bet you're lying."

Tex's father went off shortly after the family arrived in Hacienda, so Tex was left with only his mother. They lived in a shack belonging to the railroad that was used by work crews to store equipment. The crews would sometimes even spend the night there, but it hadn't been used for a long time.

Other families had lived in the shack before, but none had lasted more than few weeks before Sheriff MacAffrey kicked them out. After the last family was evicted, Tex and his parents moved in. Sheriff MacAffrey didn't bother them for some reason— maybe because Tex's father left soon thereafter, leaving Tex and his mother all alone, or maybe because he was busy with other things.

Hiroshi and his friends were familiar with Sheriff MacAffrey. He was often seen rousting drunken Mexicans at the cantina or passing late afternoons in Peroni's Saloon, an elbow on the bar and a glass of whisky cradled in one of his big gnarly hands. The children were all scared of him, but Tex and his mother probably hadn't seen him yet.

Tex told the boys his father had gone up north to find work, and as soon as he did, he would send for them. "I wanted to go, too, but Ma said I had to go to school. She used to be a schoolteacher in Texas 'fore she married Pa."

"Yeah," Albert Yamada said. "Just like you used to be a cowboy."

"It's the truth!" cried Tex. "She went to college in Lubbock."

"Where?"

"In Lubbock."

"Yeah, in the panhandle, I'll bet," said Albert with a sneer.

"Yeah, that's right," Tex said, looking perplexed.

Hiroshi and his friends passed Tex's place on their way to and from school, and sometimes they saw his mother boiling clothes in a washtub over an open fire or hauling water from the tap outside the jailhouse nearby. Tex was never there when the boys walked by. After school, he would dawdle by the tracks until the boys were well past his home. He didn't want anybody to know where he lived, even though Hiroshi and his friends knew right from the beginning.

Tex must have realized this, because one Saturday afternoon, when he and Hiroshi happened to meet near the railroad tracks, he invited Hiroshi to come home with him.

It was getting dark already, and a kerosene lamp cast big, flickering shadows on the walls inside the gloomy shack. It was cold outside, but inside it was so hot that Hiroshi's cheeks flushed. A fire blazed in the wood stove, and Tex's mother was cooking what looked like a thick soup or vegetable stew in a chipped enameled pot. She was a tall, skinny woman with light brown, straggly hair. Her face was pale and bony, and her blue eyes were so sunken that she frightened Hiroshi at first. But when she smiled, her face seemed to soften.

On the table to one side of the room were two bowls, two spoons, a few slices of white bread, and two apples. The shack was so small that most of the family's possessions had to be piled on top of one another to fit. Two small beds that had been squeezed together took up nearly half the space.

"Ma, this is my friend, Hiroshi," Tex said. "You can call him Hiro. That's what everybody calls him."

"Well, how do you do, Hiro," Tex's mother said. She spoke with a soft lilt that sounded like someone from a movie.

Hiroshi didn't know Tex's last name, so he replied with what Tom Sawyer might have said. "I'm just fine, Ma'am."

"It's nice of you boys to be so friendly to William."

"Tex, Ma. My name's Tex."

"Oh, all right," she said, smoothing her boy's hair. "Back home, you're William or just plain Bill, but in California, you're Tex."

"Ma, can Hiro stay and eat with us?"

"Well..." Tex's mother looked down and stirred the pot on the stove. It was a small pot, hardly big enough for two portions.

"Oh, I can't stay," Hiroshi said quickly. He couldn't have stayed even if there had been enough. Mother would never have allowed it, and his father would have been furious.

"You're sure now. We don't have much, but you're welcome to share what we have."

"Yes, Ma'am. I have to go home. It's getting pretty late already."

"Well, if you have to," Tex's mother said. "You come back real soon, you hear?"

After that, Hiroshi often spent time with Tex on weekends. They would explore the junkyard not far from Tex's shack, making hideouts and forts inside the wrecks of abandoned cars. They would pretend they were outlaws on the run or cowboys surrounded by Indians.

Hiroshi had played cowboys and Indians before with his Japanese playmates, but Tex's imagination opened up a world found only in books and movies. Unlike Japanese boys, Tex was bold and reckless. He did indeed have a stash of tobacco that he kept hidden from his mother. He taught Hiroshi how to roll a cigarette using pages torn from a Sears Roebuck catalogue, which Tex said was just the right kind of paper. He even taught Hiroshi how to hop a freight train.

It was a dangerous business, running alongside a train as it moved out of the depot, grabbing the iron ladder at the end of the boxcar, and hoisting themselves up. The stationmaster would yell at them and threaten to call the sheriff, but Tex would only laugh. Getting off was the scariest part. The train would be picking up speed so they couldn't wait too long. "Jump!" Tex would shout. If they were lucky, they would land on a grassy spot, but most of the time, they would roll onto crushed stone and gravel. Afterwards, they would lie on their backs, wide-eyed, breathing hard, and laughing like maniacs.

Near the depot was a hobo camp. Tex would walk up unafraid to the unshaven men with torn clothes and dirty hands and faces to ask them about his father.

"Jake Canfield from West Texas," he would say. "He was going to Fresno up north."

Usually the men would scratch their heads and say they couldn't help him. One man seemed to recall meeting someone by that name a few weeks back in Salinas, but he'd only known him a short time. They'd been crating lettuce, he said.

These were scary men. Hiroshi's mother often warned him about tramps and hobos; they would steal clothes off of wash lines and rob you of your money if they had a chance. But Tex was at ease with them.

"This here's Hiro," Tex would say. "He's my friend."

"What are you?" one of the men asked Hiroshi. "A Jap? A Chink?"

"His name's Hiro!" Tex shouted.

The man looked amused.

"Okay, kid. Just asking," he said, and that was sufficient to bring Tex and Hiroshi into this ragged and ever-shifting band of drifters who would share even their food with them. They would cook a stew over an open fire in whatever pot or bucket they could find. Pieces of meat or chicken, potatoes, assorted vegetables—whatever they could buy, steal, or scavenge—would go into the mix. When the stew was done, the men would sit around eating it out of tin cups and plates. Tex would get his portion in a tin can, which he'd share with Hiroshi.

Hiroshi's time with the hobos was a dark secret that he would never divulge, not even to his friends. His parents would have been appalled if they had seen him sitting among these men whose tattered clothes were nearly falling off their bodies and who gave off a stinging smell of sweat and grime. The language of these men was coarse, laced with curse words that Hiroshi barely recognized, but used so casually that they hardly seemed bad, maybe because of the sadness in the men's voices. They would take long, slow breaths as they hung their hands between their knees and stared at the ground, talking about family and home, people and places Hiroshi had never heard of.

In many ways, Tex's mother, or Mrs. Canfield, as Hiroshi now called her, was a lot like these men, even if she didn't talk like them. When the boys came upon her unexpectedly, she looked weary and lost in sadness, though she would brighten quickly when she saw them. She was always pleased to see Hiroshi, and she would make the two boys peanut butter or jam sandwiches, or cut an apple in two. She worked weekends at Bruner's Restaurant washing dishes and sweeping the floors. Tex said they hardly paid her anything, but she was allowed to take leftovers home. What little money she did get, she was saving up to go north to join Tex's father. Tex admitted that he had handed over the money Hiroshi's friends had given him to his mother. "I told her I found it," he said.

Mrs. Canfield would often ask Hiroshi about his family, about his brothers and sister. She wanted to know what his father did for a living and when he had come to America. She was always polite and friendly.

One day, in early spring, Hiroshi lingered too long at Tex's place as he often did when engrossed in play. Mrs. Canfield, who had already begun preparing dinner, called to Tex to fetch water from the jailhouse. Waiting for Tex to return, Hiroshi sat at the table where Mrs. Canfield was peeling potatoes. It was chilly outside but getting warm in the shack with the wood stove burning red-hot. Through the open door, he watched the horizon turn from orange to a dark red; the marsh on the other side of the railroad tracks was a murky stretch of deep purple.

Sitting alone with Tex's mother, Hiroshi got the courage to ask, "Mrs. Canfield, were you a schoolteacher in Texas?"

"Yes, Hiro, I was a teacher for a year before I married William's father..." Then she stopped, swallowed, and looked out the door toward the sunset. "Those were good times," she said. Her voice was so soft Hiroshi couldn't be sure she was talking to him. "It was a long time ago, a different place, a different time." She turned to Hiroshi. "Why am I saying these things to you? You wouldn't understand."

"I do, Mrs. Canfield," Hiroshi assured her. "Tex told me about your ranch. How rich you used to be."

Tex's mother looked into Hiroshi's eyes and smiled. She seemed happy. "You're a good boy, Hiro," she said.

When Hiroshi finally started for home, cold and darkness had already begun to set in, and he knew he would be late for dinner. He'd stopped to zipper his windbreaker when he saw Sheriff MacAffrey's car approaching. It stopped in front of Tex's place, and the sheriff got out. Hiroshi ducked behind a pile of railroad ties some twenty yards away and watched the big man with his long legs and bulky arms walk toward the shack. The sheriff banged on the door with his nightstick. When the door opened, the light from the kerosene lamp and the wood stove inside made eerie flickering shadows on his face.

Tex's mother was at the door, wiping her hands on her apron. Hiroshi saw Tex stretching his neck around her to peek at the intruder. The sheriff was gesticulating with his nightstick. Hiroshi couldn't hear clearly what he was saying—something about "railroad property" and "trespassing"—but soon he and Tex's mother were shouting at one another. Tex's mother began to cry. Hiroshi lowered his eyes as Mrs. Canfield began to howl and scream. Tex pushed her aside and charged the sheriff, pummeling his massive chest with his fists.

"You leave us alone!" Tex shouted. "You leave my ma alone!"

Sheriff MacAffrey put his nightstick under his arm, lifted Tex by the shoulders, and tossed him back into the shack like a rag doll.

"Twenty-four hours!" he said, "You got twenty-four hours. That's it! This time, I mean it. I'm fed up with you goddamn Okies."

Then he returned to his car and turned it around. The sheriff was looking straight ahead, so he didn't see Hiroshi as he drove by the railroad ties not ten feet away from the road.

The door to the shack was closed again, but Hiroshi thought he could still hear Tex's mother crying. Sheriff MacAffrey's car made the left turn onto Guadalupe Street and went past the jailhouse. Hiroshi watched until he could no longer see the tail lights. Then he broke into a run.

On Main Street, storekeepers who were preparing to close for the day stopped to look at the boy running down the street, then glanced behind him to see who might be chasing him. Sheriff MacAffrey's car was parked in front of Peroni's Saloon, so Hiroshi dashed across the street to avoid it, running right in front of a pickup truck. The Mexican man driving the truck slammed on his brakes and shouted, "Hey, look where you go!" followed by a string of Spanish cuss words.

Hiroshi ran even faster. When he got to the graveyard, he stopped to catch his breath. He had meant to cut through the cemetery as he often did, but in the darkness, the gravestones looked like giant fingers poking out of the ground. They seemed to be moving, beckoning to him. The eucalyptus trees at the far end were towering shadows, waving and groaning in the wind.

He stayed on Main Street, and as he turned onto Hidalgo Street, he slowed to a walk. His home was at the far end of the street. The lights from the dining room windows were blazing.

His father's black Chrysler was parked outside, as was Yukio's Chevrolet coupe and one of the pickup trucks used in the fields.

He was late for supper, but he felt no hunger. He'd be scolded, but he didn't care. Sachi, who had no doubt been sent to find him, would be pouting and glaring at him, but that didn't matter either. He tarried outside the house in the shadow of the front porch. He was cold and the wind was picking up as it always did when night approached. But he was not ready to enter his house. He sat on the ground with his arms crossed and his hands tucked in his armpits. With his knees bent, he rocked back and forth, bumping the back of his head against the stone pillar that supported the porch.

He heard the front door open and someone step out. It was Mother coming out to look down Hidalgo Street for a glimpse of him. She stood against the porch railing; if she had looked down and to her left she could have seen him. Her face, illuminated by the porch light, was worried, but tender and beautiful. Hiroshi wanted to call out to her, but he kept perfectly still. After she went back into the house, he made himself wait a while longer. Then, wiping his face and squaring his shoulders, he marched in to take his scolding.

THE EMPEROR'S BIRTHDAY

May 1941

Hiroshi watched his brother Mickey and Mickey's friend Shig Matsumoto put up flags above the entrance to the Young Men's Association hall.

"The old men aren't going to like the American flag," Mickey said.

"It's okay," Shig assured him. "I already explained it to them—to your father anyway. Things are different now. The hakujin will take it the wrong way if we only put up a Japanese flag."

"You're right," Mickey said. "I told you about the FBI guy."

"We need to talk more about that later," Shig said, lowering his voice.

"Which way do the flags go?" Mickey asked.

"Cross them. The American flag facing right, the Japanese one to the left, the pole of the American flag on top."

"They're not going to like that."

"The old men aren't going to notice unless you tell them. Besides, I looked it up. That's the way it's supposed to be."

Mickey laughed. "Where'd you look it up? In your Boy Scout handbook?"

"If you'd read it more, you might have made Eagle Scout," said Shig, eliciting a dismissive flop of the hand from Mickey.

The hall was being decorated to celebrate the Emperor's birthday. On April 29th, the Emperor had turned forty. In Japan, the day had been declared a national holiday, and huge celebrations had taken place throughout the country.

But not in Hacienda, California.

From listening to Father and Mother talk, Hiroshi knew there'd been some grumbling about this, but his brother Isamu was the one who'd explained what was going on. Isamu was always reading everything he could get his hands on, be it in English or in Japanese, so he could always be relied on to know what was what. This year, Isamu explained, the Emperor's birthday had fallen on a Tuesday. But the local farmers were still busy with their spring plantings, and store owners in the area were unwilling to lose a day's worth of business by closing their shops in the middle of the week. As a result, at least in Hacienda, the Emperor's birthday was being celebrated five days after the fact, on the first Sunday in May.

Mickey had come home from the university that weekend, though not to celebrate the Emperor's birthday. Still, since he was around, he was told to help with the preparations. "Bad timing," he grumbled as he carried boxes from Shig's car into the hall. Even Hiroshi had been recruited to pick up trash and empty wastebaskets.

The birthday celebration ceremony began promptly at two

o'clock. Inside the hall, a big Japanese flag was stretched out behind the podium, and the stage was decorated with red and white bunting. Shig had wanted to add a touch of blue as well, but in the end had thought better of it. The large portrait of the Emperor that usually hung over the fireplace in Hiroshi's house had been placed on an easel on the stage, surrounded by bouquets of lilacs.

A crowd of more than 300 people streamed into the hall: the men in dark suits, the women in black dresses and veiled hats, and the girls wearing their best homemade dresses. The entire Kono family was there as well. Father wore a black three-piece suit, while Mother looked elegant in a black silk dress with a white collar and a plain black hat with white trim. Sachi's new spring dress, with its flowery blue-and-white pattern and accompanying new pair of stylish white pumps, made up for the dreary rituals and speeches she would have to endure. Yukio, Isamu, and Mickey were attired in their best suits, complete with white shirts and properly quiet ties, while Hiroshi, too young for a suit, squirmed in the itchy woolen trousers he was made to wear on solemn occasions.

The Rev. Tsutomi, the local Buddhist priest, delivered the benediction. This resulted in some sour faces in the crowd because he didn't mention the Emperor's divine origin. Rev. Tsutomi was a Buddhist, after all. In Japan, a Shinto priest would have presided over the occasion, but in Hacienda, people had to make do.

Mr. Sakamoto, who was sitting behind Hiroshi, grumbled, "This is the Emperor's birthday, not the Buddha's."

The speakers who followed more than made up for Rev. Tsutomi's omissions. Not only was the Emperor divine, the crowd was assured, so was the entire Japanese race. So was every man, woman, and child sitting in the hall on this glorious day. Yamato damashii, the Yamato spirit, was invoked over and over.

Hiroshi's father was the principal speaker of the day, as he was at nearly every community event.

"The Yamato spirit is what drove us," Father said. "We came over in steerage, eating wormy rice and drinking stagnant water. We made our way in this strange land by washing dishes, sleeping on kitchen floors, working the hakujin's fields from dawn to dusk. But we survived; we rose because of what we are and what we will always be, the people of Yamato."

From stories that he'd heard over and over at the dinner table, Hiroshi knew that his father had in fact shared a stateroom with only one other passenger and had drunk wine with his dinners. The only problem his father had had with the food was that instead of rice, he'd been served potatoes with overcooked vegetables and undercooked meat. It was true that once in America, his father had started off working on a fruit-picking crew, but soon thereafter he'd begun organizing Japanese work gangs. The English he'd managed to acquire while attending business college in Japan had been enough to negotiate a contract with the sugar company. After that, he'd never done another day of physical labor. Now, thirty-seven years later, he farmed more than a thousand acres in the Santa Marguerita Valley and was co-owner of a packinghouse that shipped ice-cooled vegetables to the East Coast.

The men in the hall, most of whom still labored in the fields, knew the story of Hiroshi's father and were inspired by it. Together with everyone else in the hall, they rose in unison and joined Father in singing the "Kimigayo," an anthem that wished for the Emperor's reign to last eight thousand generations "until pebbles turn to boulders lush with moss."

Hiroshi knew the words by heart, having sung them so often, but they were so poetic and obscure he scarcely understood them. At the end of the song, everyone shouted "Banzai!" to the Emperor and raised their arms high above their heads. Like all the other children, Hiroshi joined enthusiastically in the group salutation, even though he had no idea what it meant. The one thing he and all the other children knew for sure was that the gesture marked the end of the ceremony.

As people left the hall, members of the Hacienda Kabuki Association took off their suit coats and began preparing the stage for the evening's performance. As it so happened, this too would feature Father, this time as the legendary warrior Sato Tadanobu.

Hiroshi helped Mickey carry the various items belonging to his family to Shig's car. They had just brought the Emperor's portrait outside when Mr. Kubota and his wife walked by. As the principal of the Japanese School, Mr. Kubota was the final arbiter on protocol and decorum in Hacienda. When he saw that Shig was about to put the Emperor's portrait in the trunk of his car, he became alarmed.

"Shigeo!" he shouted. "You mustn't put the Emperor in the trunk! What are you thinking?"

"Oh, Kubota-sensei," Shig said. "I know, but you see there's no room in the back seat with all the junk I have there. And Hiroshi has to sit there, too."

"Then put Him in the front seat," Kubota insisted.

"Mickey is sitting there, sensei."

Mickey said quickly, "That's okay, Shig. I'll walk." Then turning to Kubota, he elaborated in Japanese, "It's not far, sensei, I can walk."

"Unh," said Kubota-sensei with a nod of approval.

Shig put the portrait on the front seat, but when Mickey started to walk away, he whispered, "Wait, Mickey. Just wait."

They stood talking until Mr. Kubota and his wife got into their car and drove off.

"Okay, Hirohito-san," Shig said. "Back you go in the trunk. It's not the Rolls Royce you're used to, but it's a good ole American Chevy."

When they got home, Father and Mr. Ryono, the kabuki coach from Los Angeles, were already busy at work in Father's study. Some of the furniture had been moved, and the big rug had been rolled up to provide a clear space.

"*Ah, shan shan rin sha,*" the two men sang in unison as Father pulled Mr. Ryono toward him.

"*Shan shan rin sha,*" they sang as Mr. Ryono pulled away.

Hiroshi had witnessed this scene before. He knew they were imitating the sound of the shamisen that Mr. Ryono would be playing to accompany the action of "The Enchanted Flute," the piece they would be performing that evening. Hiroshi was familiar with the story as well. Sato Tadanobu, the vassal of the Lord Yoshitsune, needs the blood of a pure maiden in which to bathe his flute, which would then be used to lull to sleep the men defending the enemy's castle. Tadanobu, disguised as a peasant, finds such a maiden, only to fall in love with her. Even so, duty requires him to sacrifice her.

Mother was in the bedroom preparing the kimono Sachi was going to wear that evening for her performance with her dance group. She listened to Father rehearsing with Mr. Ryono with a look of resignation on her face. Mother, too, was a lover of kabuki. She often talked about how as a girl in Japan she had looked forward to the annual arrival of the traveling kabuki troupe. Her family would take along a picnic, she said, and spend nearly the entire day at the outdoor theater set up on the grounds of the Shinto shrine.

"The performances were so exciting," she said. "You would have been amazed." Now, listening to her husband chant his kabuki lines, she shook her head from side to side and said, "He practices and practices, but he never gets it quite right."

In the living room, Shig and Mickey were putting the Emperor back on the wall above the fireplace. Yukio, Hiroshi's oldest brother, sat on the sofa reading the *Rafu Shimpo*, a Japanese language newspaper from Los Angeles.

"Your father needs to get rid of this thing," Shig said, nodding to the portrait. "You know, there's going to be trouble with Japan."

"We're not going to go to war," Mickey said. "Roosevelt promised to keep us out."

"Then why did the FBI agent come to see you?"

Mickey looked nervously at Yukio. "I don't know, but I told him I wasn't going to spy on my own father. Besides, he already knew more about Father than I do. He knew about his speeches and his letters to the *Rafu Shimpo*. He even knew about the money Father sent to the Japanese War Fund."

"Somebody else talking to the FBI," Yukio said. His heavily accented English was not fluent, but he continued in it nevertheless. "It your Loyalty League. Loyalty League! It is League of Spies, League of Traitors!"

"We're Americans, Yukio-san." Shig spoke in Japanese now. He could have spoken English and Yukio would have understood him perfectly, but Shig worked for Yukio's father, and as the chonan of the family, Yukio was his superior. "Excuse me for saying this, but you are also American. That is why your father ordered you back from Japan. You were a student at Tokyo University—Tokyo University! But he wanted you home because he did not want you fighting in China. Your father and I talked about this. He was so proud when you were accepted at Todai."

"There was no danger of conscription," Yukio said, finally speaking in Japanese. "Father was paying the deferment tax to keep me out of the army. And he calls himself a patriot."

"He is a patriot," Shig said, "but what he cares about more is his family. He brought you home because he heard the government was ending the deferment tax. And the rumor turned out to be true. You could be fighting in China right now."

Yukio was silent for a moment. Then, when it seemed the discussion was over, he burst out suddenly in English: "If you so American, why you working bookkeeper for Father. You went Stanford University. Why you not working for sugar company? For Bank of America? For General Motors?"

"Well, that's another story," Shig said in English.

Dinner had to be rushed because of the evening's festivities, so Masako-san had prepared a cold collation of sushi and beef teriyaki. Afterwards, the family gathered at the Young Men's Association Hall, which had been transformed. Dark curtains were draped over the windows and unseen lights gave off a soft glow, transforming the hall into a hidden cavern. Pounding and the screech of scenery being pushed across the stage could be heard from behind large white curtains that had been painted with famous kabuki characters: a fierce, white-eyed samurai in armor; an oval-faced courtesan in a flowing orange robe; and a war-like monk wielding a stanchion that bristled with steel knobs.

The hall was filled to capacity. The crowd was much larger than the one that had attended the afternoon's event; people had driven in from the countryside and from other towns, some as far away as Lompoc and San Luis Obispo. They sat on wooden benches. Hiroshi and the other children occupied the front two rows or sat on the floor; a few were perched on judo mats rolled up along the sides of the hall.

The first part of the program consisted of singing and dancing, mainly by the students of Osho-san, the local Hacienda dance and koto teacher. Sachi hated her Japanese dance lessons— she only took them because, as a compromise, Mother also allowed her to take up tap dancing. Hiroshi thought she looked good in her kimono.

At last, Mr.Yatsushiro, chairman of the Hacienda Kabuki Association, came on stage. The lights in the hall went off and the stage lights came on, making the painted figures on the curtain shimmer and come alive. Then these lights too were dimmed and a lone spotlight shone on Mr. Yastushiro. He spoke in the elaborate manner of an impresario.

"Honored members of the audience, lovers of kabuki, patrons of the flowering Hacienda stage, renowned throughout the vast Santa Marguerita Valley and beyond. You know the featured attraction, a special treat for kabuki lovers young and old, a tale of high drama, of heroism and sacrifice: the story of Sato Tadanobu and the Enchanted Flute!"

As Mr. Yatsushiro walked briskly off stage, the traditional clatter of wooden boards started up and the curtains began to part in small, jerky, tantalizing motions. Slow at first, the clatter increased in tempo until the curtains hissed and opened fully with a whoosh.

The spotlight revealed a ferocious figure dressed in black. His face was powdered white, and his lips were painted a bright red. His eyes, enlarged with blue-black greasepaint, were ablaze with crimson,

"The crescent moon climbs o'er Izumi Fort," the figure chanted.

Yaaach! Mr. Ryono's voice chimed in from off stage. With his shamisen, Mr. Ryono had the daunting task of providing the entire musical background for the performance; on a real kabuki stage, this would have required a minimum of three musicians. He was also responsible for filling in much of the narrative chanting.

The boys in the front row were aghast. They couldn't understand a word the frightful figure was saying, since he was speaking in classical Japanese. Only Hiroshi, long accustomed to his father's nightly rehearsals, had any notion of what was going on. The apparition before them continued:

I, Sato Tadanobu, vassal to Lord Yoshitsune,
Disguised in rude attire, alone I come.

Hiroshi grew stiff with apprehension, knowing bloody work was afoot, but Father's Tadanobu groaned on and on—interminably it seemed—until finally a young maiden came trippingly onto the stage.

It was Okuni, played by Reiko Yatsushiro, the star of the Hacienda stage.

"Sanji, Sanji, where are you," she sang out, feeling her way through the darkness of the stage, her hands outstretched.

From the way she walked and her frantic expression, it was

clear that she couldn't see Tadanobu, who was standing only a few feet away. Her desperate groping in the dark became a prolonged dance to the strumming of the shamisen. Okuni would come ever so close to Tadanobu, then suddenly turn in a new direction, threatening to tumble off the stage. The audience collectively drew in their breaths, but Tadanobu appeared oblivious to Okuni's presence until at last he suddenly exclaimed:

She calls to me! As Sanji I am known among the peasants here.

Oh, Sanji, Sanji. It is I, Okuni.

Uuuuuooorchi! Mr. Ryono played a dramatic run on his shamisen as Father switched to the role of the narrator. Normally Mr. Ryono would have been responsible for all of the narration, but Father had insisted on sharing those duties.

The battle armor 'neath my raven cloak
Weighs heavy on my breast and prods
My warrior's heart by love unmanned.

Tadanobu struggles desperately with himself. He needs the lifeblood of the woman he loves, the pure maiden's blood in which to bathe his flute, the enchanting sound of which would place the enemy in yonder castle under its somnolent spell. Sweet, innocent, and loving Okuni must he slay, or commit the unthinkable act of betraying his lord. Would he, or would he not?

Mr. Ryono's guttural cries and the vacillating rhythms of the shamisen underscored Tadanobu's anguished moment of decision. Until finally:

Okuni, here beneath this ancient pine I stand.

Okuni gives a start, recognizing Sanji's voice. She runs to him.

Oh, Sanji!

Yaaaaach! The fevered and rapid strumming of shamisen foretold the inevitable climax.

Behold! I am Satooo Tadanobuuuu!

Tadanobu moved his right arm in a half circle over his head while stretching out his left arm. At the same time, he twirled his head slowly, coming to a dramatic halt with his profile to the audience in a classic kabuki pose. As he did so, his peasant clothing fell away as if by magic, revealing bright red armor interwoven with gold and silver threads. "Aaaaaah," the audience gasped. Hiroshi was amazed. He could scarcely believe that that was his father on stage. Where had the armor come from? He had never seen it at home. It was fantastic, like a storybook come to life.

The scene that followed, the life and death struggle between Tadanobu and Okuni, was the high point of the drama. This was the scene that Father and Mr. Ryono had been practicing that very afternoon.

Mr. Ryono was playing wildly now, doing double, triple duty, and accenting the deadly action on stage with throaty bursts: *Yuch! Ooch!* It was a dance of death. Tadanobu would pull Okuni toward one end of the stage, then Okuni would resist, and the two would totter toward center stage again. Back and forth they moved to the rhythms of Mr. Ryono's shamisen, his grunts and yelps reflecting the agony and passion of the death struggle. Mercifully, the fatal blow was struck offstage. Hiroshi was cold with fear when Tadanobu reappeared. In his hand was a drawn sword drenched in gore.

The shamisen played very slowly and sadly now. *Yuuuuoooorch.*
Be still, soft maid, and wait upon the morn,
I'll join thee 'fore this day is through.

With that, Tadanobu raised his sword and did a hopping half run off the stage while the stage manager clapped the wooden boards on the floor, heightening the dramatic effect.

The applause was boisterous and long, and the men in the audience shouted their approval. Father was smiling as he and Reiko reappeared on stage, but because of his makeup, his countenance remained fierce. "Wow, that's your father?" the boys exclaimed again and again, as if in need of reassurance.

As the crowd filed out of the hall, many stopped to

congratulate Mother. Mrs. Okamoto patted Hiroshi's head and said, "You must be very proud, Hiroshi-chan. Your father was magnificent."

The rest of family left together with most of the audience, but Mother and Hiroshi waited for Father to change. When he came out, his face still bore traces of makeup, but he looked like himself again. He was laughing. "It went well, don't you think?" he asked.

"Yes," Mother said. "Everyone was very impressed."

"Yaaaa, it went well," Father said. "The critical moment, when the peasant robe falls away, I was afraid the threads would not break just right, or they would break too soon. But the timing was perfect. Ryono was ecstatic."

"Yes, it went very well," Mother repeated.

"I have to wait for Ryono. We'll stop by the Nikoniko, but I won't be long. And take this sword home for me."

"Can I carry it, Father"? Hiroshi asked.

Father looked doubtful.

"I'll be careful, Father. I won't drop it."

"You'll hold it with both hands?"

"Yes, Father. I'll be careful. I promise."

"All right, then," Father said with a laugh. "You carry it and protect Mother."

Main Street was dark at that hour except for places such as the Nikoniko, the Japanese bar/restaurant where the waitresses dressed in kimono. The China House was also open, its windows misted with smoke and steam that carried the scent of herbs and noodles frying in pork fat. As they approached Juanita's, they could hear the strains of one of those Mexican love songs that to Hiroshi sounded like a man plaintively calling to a girl named Cora-san.

Rodriguez, one of Father's foremen, stumbled out of the cantina, his eyes glazed and his face fixed in a moist grin. "Hallo, Señora!" he called out.

"Buenos noches, Rodriguez," Mother said, and as Hiroshi slowed to get a peek into the cantina through the swinging doors, she grabbed his arm and pulled him along.

Outside Nakano's Pool Hall, Filipinos lined both sides of the sidewalk, leaning against the walls and fenders of parked cars. Their long black hair was slicked back with sweet smelling pomade. They wore garish silk shirts, sharply creased gabardine slacks, and Florsheim shoes that shone like jewels. The Filipinos were hard workers, but they didn't have any women—none were allowed into the country—so they were said to be "girl crazy." Hiroshi and his mother quickened their steps, and were not unhappy to see Sheriff MacAffrey coming out of Peroni's Saloon.

When they got home, the others were having tea with the sweet buns that Mr. Ryono had brought as a gift from Los Angeles.

"The old man was in his glory tonight," Yukio said with a laugh.

"Yukio," Mother said. "Don't be disrespectful. It went very well."

"That's what I meant," Yukio said with a shrug. "Ah, Hiroshi. The sword. Bring it here."

"Father gave it to me to put back."

"Never mind that. Bring it here."

Hiroshi reluctantly gave Yukio the sword, and Yukio immediately drew it out of its scabbard. Hiroshi shuddered when he saw that it was still flecked with blood.

"That's what I thought," Yukio said. "Hiroshi, get me the dish towel."

"But Yukio," Hiroshi hesitated.

"What?"

"There's blood on it."

Everyone laughed.

"Hiroshi," Mother said. "You know better than that; it is just catsup. They usually use red dye, but Father thought catsup would look more like real blood. Mr. Yatsushiro was very upset because he thought it would make a mess on stage."

"That's the old man for you," Yukio said. "But I have to say, his hopping off the stage was good. I'll bet Yatsushiro didn't like that either, but you saw how the crowd responded."

Hiroshi had wondered about that. "Why did Father hop off the stage?" he asked.

"Ah," Yukio said. "You don't know about Sato Tadanobu. He was a fox, but I'll tell you the story later. First get me the oil from the pantry."

"Why, Yukio? Why do you need the oil?"

"The blade needs to be oiled so it won't rust."

"Is that what samurai do?"

"This isn't a real samurai sword," Yukio said, as he held the blade up to the light. "I brought it home from Japan. I couldn't afford a real samurai sword. This is an imitation they make for tourists. It looks like the real thing, but the blade isn't tempered steel, so it'll rust unless you keep it oiled."

Hiroshi brought the oil and Yukio proceeded to put a thin coating on the blade. By the time he had finished with the sword, the conversation around the table had already turned to other matters.

Hiroshi was in his bed still awake when Mother as usual came in to see that he was properly covered. Most of the time, Hiroshi would either be asleep or pretending to be so that Mother would pull the covers over him and quietly slip out the door. But this night, the events of the day were still troubling him. When his mother turned to leave, he called out, "Was Tadanobu really a fox?"

Mother laughed. "Hiroshi, it's just a story."

"Was he really a fox? Can a fox turn into a samurai?"

Hiroshi was aware of tales in which animals, raccoon dogs, cats, and especially foxes changed their form to play tricks on people. But Sato Tadanobu was a famous samurai. There were many stories about his heroic exploits.

"Tell me, Mother. Was Sato Tadanobu really a fox?"

"Well, that is the tale. Tadanobu is a fox who turns himself into a samurai. He serves Minamoto Yoshitsune, who owns a drum made out of the skin of his mother."

"His mother? His mother was a fox?"

"Of course," Mother said. "And Tadanobu serves Yoshitsune to be close to his mother."

She went on to tell Hiroshi that the drum was called Hatsune, and whenever it was beaten, Tadanobu would be irresistibly drawn to its sound, even if he had to leave his lord in the pitch of battle.

"Is that why Father hopped off the stage at the end of the play? Did he hear the sound of the drum?"

"The drum plays no role in that particular play, but everybody knows about it so Father thought the hopping would amuse the audience. You heard how they all laughed."

"But, Mother, foxes don't hop."

Mother put her hand over her mouth like she did whenever she found something immensely funny.

"That's just the way they do it on the stage," she said. "It's supposed to show that he's not really human."

"Is the Emperor human, Mother?"

"Hiroshi! What a thing to ask! We were talking about Sato Tadanobu."

"Father was saying today that the Emperor came from heaven and that all Japanese people came from heaven."

"Yes," Mother said, suddenly turning very solemn. "The Japanese people are very special, and most special of all is the Emperor. Now go to sleep, Hiroshi. It's getting very late."

It took a long time for Hiroshi to fall asleep. The horrific image of his father resplendent in full samurai armor was still fresh in his mind. But as it turned out, the sword his father had wielded so fearsomely was counterfeit and smeared not with blood but with tomato sauce. The armor was no doubt also phony, probably made of bamboo, not steel. That was just the sort of trick a fox would play. And it had all taken place as part of the celebrations for a birthday that was not the actual birthday of an Emperor who wore steel-rimmed glasses and looked more befuddled than divine. Shig had even made fun of the Emperor as he crammed him into the trunk of his car like a piece of worn-out luggage. As Hiroshi brooded over the day's events, sinking his face into his down-filled pillow, he thought he could still hear Mr. Ryono strumming his shamisen, grunting like a bear and yelping like a wounded coyote as his father hopped off the stage.

KUROMBO BOY

December 8, 1941 - July 1942

On Monday morning, Hiroshi was told he didn't have to go to school, so he was still in his pajamas when he went to the kitchen for his breakfast. Sachi was the only one there, poking at a bowl of mush.

"Look at what they did," she said, pointing to the wall telephone next to the swinging door. The line to the receiver was severed and the other end dangled close to the floor like a broken clothesline.

"Who?" Hiroshi asked, puzzled.

"The FBI. When they came to arrest Father."

Hiroshi stood silent. He had slept through the night and didn't know what Sachi was talking about. He went from room to room until he found Mother huddled with Yukio and Isamu in Father's study. Listening to them, he gathered that all the important Japanese men of Hacienda had been arrested: Father;

other rich farmers and businessmen; the Buddhist priest; Mr. Kubota, the Japanese school teacher; even Mr. Yatsushiro, chairman of the Kabuki Association. No one knew where they had been taken.

On Tuesday, when Hiroshi went to school, everything seemed unusually quiet. His teacher, Mrs. Abernathy, took her Japanese children aside and told them they didn't have to worry. Mr. Nash, the principal, had called an assembly on Monday to announce that he didn't want to hear the word "Jap" used in the school. "The Japanese children are Americans just like all of us," he had said.

"If you have any trouble," Mrs. Abernathy said, "you come straight to me. Do you understand?"

The Japanese children remained silent and nodded their heads.

Much to their alarm, Mrs. Abernathy then hugged each of them individually. She was ordinarily a stern disciplinarian, so such unwonted tenderness made the children apprehensive. But nothing else out of the ordinary happened at school that day.

More than two weeks passed before the family finally got a letter from Father. Parts of it had been cut out with a razor so that Mother could hardly read it. She had to lay it flat on the dining table so that it wouldn't fall apart. "They killed him," she concluded.

Yukio and Isamu said that that wasn't the case, that Father was still alive. Mickey, who was home again, having graduated from the university that year, agreed. The American government would never do such a thing, he insisted. This was a democracy. There were laws.

"Look, look what they did to his letter!" Mother said. "They cut the telephones, opened all the drawers, pulled books off the shelves. They threw everything on the floor—clothes, photographs, letters. And they wouldn't let me pack anything for him. They woke everybody up. Sachi's bed was wet through; even the mattress was soaked."

"It wasn't, it wasn't," Sachi protested, looking as if she were about to cry.

That was the first time Hiroshi had ever heard of Sachi peeing in her bed. Had he known earlier, he would have gotten even with her for constantly teasing him and telling on him whenever he did something bad. If he wasn't punished as severely as she thought he deserved, she would call him a "Mama's boy." Worst of all, she teased him for being so dark. "Kurombo boy," she called him.

"They found you on the beach when they went fishing," she once told him. "Ask Yukio. He'll tell you. They said, 'Hey, look at the kurombo boy lying in the sand.' Then they brought you home."

"That's a lie!" Hiroshi shouted. He went to Yukio. "Tell Sachi that's a lie."

Yukio just laughed.

When he'd gone to Mother, she'd smiled absently and said, "Saah," which is what she always said when she wasn't paying attention.

"Kurombo boy! Kurombo boy!" Sachi had continued taunting until he started to cry. Only then did Mother tell him, "I drank too much tea when I was pregnant with you. That's why you're so dark."

Had Hiroshi known that Sachi peed in her bed, he would have taunted her until she was the one crying. But by the time he found out, it was too late.

The day Japan bombed Pearl Harbor, Father had been late for dinner, which was unusual for him. When he got home, he seemed slightly tipsy. He said he and his friends had gotten together at the Japanese Farmers Association office and listened to the Japanese news reports on a short-wave radio. Then they had celebrated, toasting the occasion with sake.

Mother told him that it was a foolish thing to have done, and she was right. The FBI came to arrest him that very night.

Until his letter arrived, Mother feared he had been shot or hanged. Even after, nobody knew for sure what would happen to him next.

Three months later, in March, Sheriff MacAffrey came to the house. The Japanese called the sheriff "mah-ke-fu-ri," which everyone thought was funny, because it meant "Lose-and-Shake." A huge man, the sheriff filled the doorway, casting a pall over the living room as he entered. When he removed his Stetson, Sachi began to giggle and ran into the dining room. Hiroshi followed and found her laughing so hard she was in tears. "He's bald! Lose-and-Shake's bald!" she said.

When Hiroshi returned to the living room, the sheriff was sitting in the wingchair next to the fireplace. Above the mantle, on the wall once graced by a portrait of the Emperor, now hung a richly embroidered silk tapestry that depicted a hazy mountain lake seen through the branches of a gracefully bending pine tree.

Mother and Yukio were hunched on the sofa opposite the fireplace, while Isamu, sitting in his wheelchair at the far end of the room, played with the fringes of the brocaded draperies that bordered one of the tall casement windows.

Sheriff MacAffrey was talking to Yukio, who, as the oldest son, was now in charge of the family.

Mother sat next to Yukio, nodding her head and frowning as her son translated what the sheriff said.

MacAffrey said he was visiting Japanese families of his own accord. He rubbed his bald pate with the flat of his big hand as if wearied by his long years of service. He reminded Yukio and Mother that he had been the sheriff for more than twenty years. The Japanese, he said, were good people who had never given him any trouble. He wanted to make sure that the evacuation went smoothly, that no one harmed them or gave them any trouble. Then he repeated that he was doing all of this on his own time.

Mother called to Masako-san, who was standing by the dining room door, and told her to bring out the whisky.

Yukio thanked the sheriff for his courtesy and asked if he was visiting all the Japanese families.

"All the important families," the sheriff said. He looked about the living room, his eyes moving like shifting gun sights pointed at the dark walnut paneling and the matching waist-high porcelain vases that stood on either side of the stone fireplace.

"You folks have done pretty well in this country. I remember when I was a boy in Hacienda—that was a long time ago—and you people were working in the beet fields like Mexicans, doing stoop labor."

Hiroshi, standing by the entry to the dining room, found it hard to imagine Father as a field laborer, even though he did sometimes talk about working on a fruit-picking crew when he first came to America.

Masako-san brought out a bottle of whisky with two crystal goblets. She'd also filled an elegant porcelain bowl with macadamia nuts from Hawaii, which were reserved for important hakujin guests. Masako-san never needed to be told how to do things.

"Perhaps you will join me for a glass of whisky," Yukio said.

"Well, maybe just a drop," MacAffrey said and laughed.

Yukio said in Japanese, "I think he wants money."

Mother tried not to show how frightened she was. "How much do you think he will take?"

Yukio said to the sheriff, "I tell my mother we must be grateful to you." Then he said in Japanese, "Twenty dollars should be enough."

"He might be offended by so little," Mother said. "Perhaps we can write him a check."

"He won't take a check," Isamu chimed in.

"Isamu is right," Yukio said. "He won't take a check."

"This is good whisky," the sheriff said. "I usually drink

bourbon, but Johnny Walker. That's good whisky. You Japanese people have good taste. I'll say that for you."

"Please have more," Yukio said and poured more whisky into the sheriff's glass. "We don't drink whisky often. My father, you know, prefers sake. You ever have sake?" Switching to Japanese, he murmured, "How much cash is there in the house?"

"What you say? Sackie? You mean sackie?" MacAffrey said with a broad grin. "Naw, I've never had sackie, but I heard that stuff will knock your head off."

"I have a hundred dollars," Mother said. "I will put it in an envelope."

"That should be enough," Yukio said. Switching to English, he said with a smile, "You know, sake weaker than whisky. Sake just wine, rice wine. But very good hot."

"That's too much," Isamu cried out in Japanese. "That's too much for this crook."

MacAffrey looked at him with a quizzical expression.

"Isamu, be quiet," Mother said.

"My brother, Isamu," Yukio said, squeezing and rubbing his leg to convey his meaning, "he has pain. He often has great pain."

"Yeah, I'm sorry, kid," MacAffrey said. "Terrible thing, just terrible."

Three months later, in June, two hakujin came by with a truck. The fat one pointed at the piano. "Twenty dollars, mama-san. Okay?"

Yukio was out, so Mother told Hiroshi to fetch Isamu. "Wait, Wait," she told the men. "My son come."

Isamu came quickly, declining Hiroshi's help, furiously spinning the wheels of his chair. He could move with amazing speed when he needed to. After consulting in Japanese with Mother, he said: "One thousand dollars for everything," Mother pointed to the piano, the sofas, chairs, tables.

"Two hundred. No more," the man said. He got his wallet

out of his back pocket, counted out the bills, and thrust them at Mother.

"Don't take it, Mother," Isamu said. He's trying to cheat us."

Mother hesitated, pressing her lips together tightly, then took the proffered bills.

"I'm sorry, Isamu," she said, "but we can't take the furniture with us. Everything is lost whatever we do."

"Oooh," Isamu said in a tone of utter despair. "Mother, you should not have."

After the men loaded the furniture onto their truck, they came back and, without asking, went into the basement. Hiroshi watched from the top of the stairs while the men looked around. The tools had been packed away, but the vise was still on the workbench.

"Take the vise," the fat man said.

As his partner unscrewed it, the fat man looked up at Hiroshi and said, "Where's the toilet around here?"

When Hiroshi didn't answer, the man shrugged. Turning his back, he unbuttoned his trousers. Hiroshi watched as a stream of urine formed a frothy puddle on the concrete floor.

Upstairs, in the living room, the dark, fruity smell of the hakujin lingered. Mother stood in the middle of the empty room rubbing her hands together. Her narrow, delicate face was still framed by carefully coifed ringlets, but her hair was now streaked with grey and her silk dress hung loosely on her thin frame like borrowed clothing. When she saw Hiroshi, she turned her head away.

For months, an ominous new word had been bruited about in the community. Evacuation. What it meant became clear to Hiroshi when on a sunny day in late June all the Japanese of Hacienda and environs gathered at the train station.

They'd been told they were going to a desert, so people had bought straw hats, pith helmets, canteens, boots, sunglasses, and the like. Soldiers with rifles patrolled the platform and guarded both ends of the railroad cars. Like all the others, the car occupied by Hiroshi and his family was packed with people. The Kono family numbered only six now. Father was gone, and Masako-san, whom Hiroshi had always thought of as a member of the family, was also missing. Shortly after the evacuation order was issued, she had gone north to Fresno to be with her aging parents.

The Kono family occupied the rear of the car because Isamu's wheelchair had to be stored in the luggage space next to the doors. Isamu sat with Yukio in the first two seats. Mother, Mickey, Sachi, and Hiroshi arranged themselves in the seats across the aisle.

The overhead racks, the space under the seats, and even the aisle overflowed with scuffed and battered suitcases, cardboard boxes tied up with old clothesline, and lumpy bundles made of sheets and tablecloths. It was late morning, and the car was getting hot, but the windows remained closed, the shades drawn. The air was odorous and so heavy that Hiroshi had to pull it into his lungs in small tugs.

Someone farted. Sachi pinched her nose and pointed toward Mr. Nakashima in the seat in front of them. He already smelled of whisky.

"How do you know?" Hiroshi asked.

Sachi cupped her hands over Hiroshi's ear and whispered: "He has a stomach ache. He said so. I heard him."

They both ducked their heads down, laughing under their breath and holding their noses. Mr. Nakashima suddenly stood up with an angry look. Hiroshi froze. Mr. Nakashima was a bachelor and a drunkard who was known for doing crazy things. He once sat on the sidewalk in front of Mr. Nakano's pool hall for two days because, according to the sign he carried, the gambling room in the back was "sucking the blood of the Japanese people." It took a committee of community leaders to get Mr. Nakashima to end his protest.

When Hiroshi peeked up, he saw that Mr. Nakashima was glaring not at Sachi or him, but at the guard in Army uniform who was stationed at the other end of the car. His shoulders squared and his head up, kicking bundles and boxes out of his way as he went, Mr. Nakashima walked up to the guard and began shouting. The soldier looked down at him with his lips curled, then said over Mr. Nakashima's head to everyone in the car: "Nobody's allowed out of the car or in the toilet until the train is out of the station."

"Very well," Mr. Nakashima said in clear English. "Then I will take care of the matter here."

He opened up the newspaper he had rolled up under his arm and spread it neatly on an open space in the aisle. Then he lowered his trousers and squatted. There was a big gasp. Everyone sucked in their breath as if on signal. The silence was total. There was a sound of something falling on paper.

"Oooo," everyone said as one. It was a groan, a cry of shared pain. Slowly, an acrid, fishy odor wafted through the car. Hiroshi was tempted, but he didn't dare stand up for a better look. He heard only the shuffling noises made by two women who got up to clean up the mess.

"Jesus Christ," the guard kept saying, "Jesus Christ." Meanwhile, Mr. Nakashima, triumphant, returned to his seat. Hiroshi looked across the aisle and saw Isamu and Yukio with their hands over their mouths. Their shoulders were shaking. Finally they broke out into laughter. All the young people, even straight-laced Mickey, began to laugh as well. Only Mother and the other older folk kept their heads bowed, silent and rigid with shame.

The soldiers insisted on keeping the window shades drawn throughout most of the trip. They didn't want the Japanese looking out or the white people on the outside looking in. It wasn't until the afternoon of the following day, when the train had entered the Mojave Desert, that the shades were finally allowed to be lifted.

Looking out, Hiroshi saw an exotic wilderness filled with gnarled trees that had needles for leaves. Cacti, the likes of which he had never seen before, bristled like angry, ill-natured dwarfs. The landscape was like a jigoku from one of his storybooks, a netherworld inhabited by horned, crab-red demons with bulging eyes that nearly burst from their sockets.

They didn't enter Arizona until the morning of the third day. The landscape was still a menacing wasteland bristling with sagebrush. Giant cacti—thick, pudgy forks—poked the sky. Buttes erupted like angry boils out of the grit of the vast horizon. The guards finally allowed the windows to be opened to get the stale air out, but the heat that came back in from outside felt like blasts shooting out of a furnace.

Japanese volunteers, wearing blue armbands, came through the cars dispensing salt pills along with the usual box lunches of baloney, cheese, or jelly sandwiches. The children got milk, but it had soured in the heat, and most refused to drink it. Those who did vomited afterwards.

It was midday before they finally arrived in a city. There, they were loaded onto buses and taken to their final destination on what looked like a newly constructed dirt road. Moving in a column, the buses churned up clouds of dust that forced everyone to close their windows once more despite the stifling heat.

When they arrived at last at the camp, weary and exhausted, they were directed to sordid rows of foul, tarpapered barracks that stood on broken ground stripped of even the barest traces of desert life that had been visible from the train. Cast down into gloom and inexpressible despair, everyone walked about as if in a daze.

Mother fell ill after a week and was put in the camp hospital set up in segregated barracks. They said she had desert fever. Nobody was allowed to visit her.

They said the sickness was in the dust. Hiroshi could smell

it; it was everywhere. When people walked, dust puffed up around their feet. Inside, it seeped through the cracks in the floor. Hiroshi could write his name in the dust on the window. The sun cooked the oil in the tarpaper, and that smell, too, was always in Hiroshi's nose, even when outside. His head hurt, and his throat felt scratchy.

The camp was not yet finished, and Negro men were still digging ditches here and there.

"Look, they're looking at you," Sachi said to Hiroshi, stubbornly clinging to the pointless game. "They're thinking, 'Hey, what's that boy doing in here. The kurombo think you're one of them!"

Everybody was afraid of getting dark in the sun, especially the women. But it was so hot indoors that people couldn't stay there during the day. Outside, the only shade available came from the tarpapered barracks, which reeked like burnt rubber. The men wore straw hats and pith helmets, the women broad-brimmed sun hats. Those women lucky enough to have them carried umbrellas.

Soon after arriving, Mickey said that everyone in the family, even Hiroshi, had to write letters to the Justice Department asking them to give Father a parole. Sachi thought this was a good idea. She liked to write, and she always got good grades in composition. Hiroshi said he didn't want to and left the barracks.

"What's the matter with you?" Mickey shouted after him. "Don't you care about Father?"

Hiroshi wasn't sure if Father was dead or alive. All he knew was that he was gone. He had seemed to Hiroshi like a god, but the FBI had come and whisked him away as if he were a fly. Now Mother, too, was gone.

He went to the edge of the camp and sat below one of the empty barracks. The guard on the tower manning a machine gun could see him, but paid him no attention. Neither did the soldier who was patrolling the area between the barbed-wire fences.

Looked straight ahead, his rifle on his shoulder, the perimeter guard walked slowly and deliberately as if marching in a funeral. Beads of perspiration dripped down from his helmet, which was strapped tightly to his chin, and the back of his khaki shirt was drenched with sweat. As Hiroshi watched, he ducked under the shade of the guard tower, removed his helmet, and drank from his canteen. Then he poured some of the water on his head, and, mopping his face with the sleeves of his shirt, began to curse loudly, using words Hiroshi had never heard before. The soldier on the guard tower laughed.

In the distance, Hiroshi heard the clanging of the iron slab that hung outside his mess hall, but he remained sitting. After he had waited for a bit—just long enough to avoid having to sit with his family—he made his way to the mess hall. They were serving boiled potatoes and gravy with small, sinewy pieces of sharp-smelling meat that curled the tongue. The jello had melted into the gravy. Hiroshi ate it all, sopping up the gravy-jello mix with a slice of bread.

That evening, they showed a movie. A makeshift screen had been built at the foot of a low hill. The brush had been removed from the hillside to make room for the audience, but the area was still strewn with small, jagged pieces of rock that people had to clear away in order to sit. While waiting for the movie to begin, boys passed the time by throwing rocks at a huge saguaro cactus that stood near the top of the hill like a giant sentinel.

The feature that evening was a war movie, but at the beginning of the story, it was still peacetime. The soldiers on the screen were dressed in khaki, and, like the soldiers guarding the camp, they wore helmets held down with chinstraps, ammo belts, and heavy boots. Then the war started, and the Japs came. As the American soldiers lay wounded in their foxholes, the Japs bayoneted them. The Japs laughed as they machine-gunned Americans parachuting out of burning planes. When the Marines landed and began killing the Japs, the teenagers began to clap and cheer, so Hiroshi and his friends began to clap and cheer, too. This somehow made Hiroshi feel better. Back in Hacienda, posters in the post office had urged people to buy war bonds by depicting the Japanese as snarling monkeys and rats. Newspaper cartoons even showed them as insects that needed to be exterminated.

After the movie, as people began to disperse, Hiroshi picked up a rock and hurled it into the crowd.

Shouts echoed from down below, about where the stone would have landed. Hiroshi ran down the hill to where the commotion was and looked around cautiously. A man had picked up a small girl, four or five years old, and was carrying her. Someone had tied a handkerchief around her head. She was crying, her face glistening with blood in the moonlight. "What happened?" people were saying. "She's okay, she's okay," the man said. "Get a doctor!" someone shouted. Hiroshi edged away from the crowd, and when he was far enough away, he broke into a run. When he reached his barracks, his stomach began to churn, and he vomited.

The next day, Yukio took him to the hospital. They said he had desert fever and put him in the isolation ward, where nobody could visit him. The nurse, a young Japanese woman, came and said, "There's a Mrs. Kono in the women's ward. I think she's your mother."

"No, she's not," Hiroshi said.

"I think she is," the nurse insisted. "Would you like to see her?"

"No!" Hiroshi shouted. "I hate her!"

He swung at the water pitcher on the bedside stand and knocked it to the floor. He buried his face in the pillow, his shoulders heaving.

The nurse put her hand on his back to comfort him, but soon removed it. Perhaps she was fearful of contagion. Or maybe it was because he was a kurombo boy, getting darker and darker like a fish left lying too long in the sun.

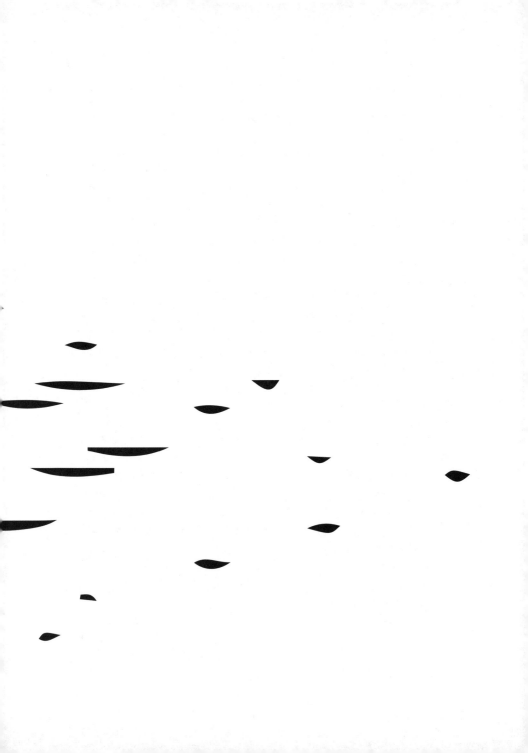

BREAD CRUMBS

1942 - 1943

When Otsui Kono first arrived at the camp with her daughter and four sons, barbed-wire fences still separated them from the desert world beyond—the pale and dappled green of the sagebrush, the hard-packed sand, the giant forks of saguaro cacti, the buttes rising like tiny volcanic eruptions frozen in time on the flat, expansive surface of glittering sand and gravel.

The camp was divided into more than 30 blocks separated by streets or firebreaks; each block consisted of 14 barracks, a shower house/latrine, a laundry room, and a mess hall. The Kono family, among the last to arrive, found themselves in Block 72, which bordered the desert.

With little to occupy them, her children each went their own way after the morning meal, and Otsui usually found herself alone in their cramped 20-by-20 foot room. It was early summer and by mid-morning, the desert would already be shimmering with heat. As the sun rose higher, Otsui was forced outside by the stifling air inside their small cell. She would sit in the sliver of shade afforded by the barracks, breathing in its oily stench and gazing out at the desert landscape, which melted into a blur of greens, browns, and grays until it was nothing but a broad mix of colors that wavered in the lazily shifting air. Even the soldiers patrolling the camp with their rifles and bayonets seemed like creatures of the desert that slid and scuttled about in the vast wilderness.

After a while, Otsui stopped seeing the desert at all as her thoughts turned inward. She felt like a widow. Only the spirits knew where her husband Seiji might be. He could well be looking down on her at that very moment from the spirit world as she sat sipping lukewarm tea she'd made in a tin can scavenged from the mess hall.

At home in Hacienda, Otsui had led an active life, puttering around the house with Masako-san, tending her flower garden, modestly showing off her flower arrangements to friends who'd been invited for tea, and doing community work with the Japanese Women's Association. Then the war had come, destroying everything she and Seiji had built over a period of three decades.

From where Otsui liked to sit, she could see the corner of the mess hall. A large iron slab hung from the roof like a yellowtail tuna drying and hardening in the heat. At mealtimes, a cook would come out to beat it with a steel rod. Beyond the mess hall, she could see a narrow section of the fence that ran between the barracks. Time was measured by the sentry who came and went in and out of her span of vision, walking mechanically in regular steps, holding the butt of his shouldered rifle with one hand and swinging the other by his side like a pendulum.

The barracks themselves had been completed the week of their arrival, but debris from the construction still lay strewn about, and water and sewer lines remained uncovered in their trenches. People seemed afraid to move for fear of stirring the dust that lay baking on the ground and on the floors and windowsills. The dust was everywhere—outside, in the barracks, in the very air. Its musty odor, mixed with the heavy smell of tarpaper, was always in her nostrils.

It should not have been a surprise that the FBI arrested her husband on the first night of the war. Seiji was the leader of the community, and he had a position to uphold. Kifu, it was always kifu—for the Japanese school, for the Buddhist church, for the annual community picnic, the kabuki association. "Kifu, kifu, kifu, it's going to be my ruin," he used to grumble. He might have been right. Not only was he the biggest contributor to the Japanese war relief fund, he was chairman of the drive. When Japan attacked Pearl Harbor, Seiji said he was proud. He and his friends had gathered at the farmers' association where they had drunk sake and shouted "Banzai!" to the Emperor. They had done so to show each other their spirit. That's how men were. It was a foolish, reckless, heedless thing to do, but they couldn't help themselves.

And now Seiji was gone. People were saying that the men who'd been taken away would be executed, shot as spies. It would be just like Seiji to get himself shot out of pride. That was fine for him; he didn't have to deal with the sheriff or the man from the bank who wanted the loan paid or the awful men who came to the house to cheat them of their belongings. Otsui didn't know how she'd survived those months, all the worrying, getting their finances in order, paying the bills, packing. A week after she arrived at camp, she had collapsed.

By the time she was discharged from the camp hospital, her face had shrunk, and the skin along her jaw and under her chin had drooped and withered. Her eyes, shadowed by weariness and care, had lost their light. Only a few months before, her hair had been black. She used to collect rainwater to wash her hair so as to give it luster; she would carefully pull out any white strand that appeared. Now, at forty-nine, she was turning gray. And what did it matter anyway? She was amazed that she and her children were still alive. Why had the American government brought them to this desolate wilderness, hidden and out of sight, if not to be rid of them?

Out of the hospital, the only one of her children she saw regularly was Isamu, who couldn't wander far from their barracks in his wheelchair and so rarely went beyond their block.

Yukio, who had joined the Seinin-kai, a group of Japanese-speaking Kibei like himself, was hardly ever home.

Mickey had been a member of the Loyalty League even before the war. Now he was talking against Japan. The constant quarrelling between him and Yukio made it unpleasant for either to spend much time with the rest of the family. One particular point of contention was that Mickey had begun volunteering to make camouflage nets for the Army. When Otsui found out about this, she tried to warn him. It would be difficult for him after the war if it were discovered that he had aided the American war effort. Mickey just smiled and said, "It'll be all right, Mother. Don't worry," as if she were a child. How could she help but worry when she overheard him arguing with men outside their barracks. Some were Yukio's friends, members of the Seinen-kai, and they often spoke a rough mix of Japanese and English. Mickey would often respond in pure English, seeming to anger them further. "Inu!" they would shout at him. They were calling Mickey a dog—a spy, an informer. One day, after a particularly heated exchange, one of them said, "If you weren't Yukio's brother, I'd beat your head in!"

Sachiko did everything she could to keep clear of such unpleasantness. She was almost always with her high school friends, and rarely to be seen.

But what pained Otsui most of all was the absence of Hiroshi. True, he was already nine, but he had still been close to her at home. At the camp, he seemed to be avoiding her. She would catch a glimpse of him only now and again during her long, lonely days. Still, when Hiroshi returned to their small room, Otsui never asked him what he had been doing, and he never volunteered any information. She'd begun to hear complaints about a group of boys that would run like a pack of wild dogs from mess hall to mess hall, eating twice or even three times per meal, and she wondered if Hiroshi might be one of them. If so, she would not have minded; she might even have encouraged him. He needed to eat, after all, to survive.

It was Mr. Nakashima who started Otsui thinking about survival. He said he had brought a short-wave radio into camp with him. He wouldn't show it to anyone because he feared it would be confiscated, but he reported regularly about what he heard on the Japanese newscasts. Japan, he said, was winning victory after victory in the Pacific. As for the American fleet, what had survived the Pearl Harbor attack was already at the bottom of the sea. Japanese forces were preparing to mount a major invasion of the American mainland.

"When that happens, Kono-san," Mr. Nakashima told Otsui, "that will be our time of greatest danger. The Americans will be running for their lives. They will abandon us here in the middle of the desert. Food shipments will stop. Until the arrival of the Japanese troops, we will have difficulty surviving."

That was when Otsui hit upon the idea of bread crumbs.

She decided she would eat only the two slices of toast she got at breakfast and save all the bread she was served at other meals. It would have been difficult to not eat the breakfast toast; sometimes there was nothing else to eat, and she feared she would be refused even that small portion if they saw her saving what she'd been given.

The kitchens in the camp were self-run by the Japanese, who were very careful with food. They gave women smaller servings than men and large people more than skinnier ones—at least so it seemed to Otsui. But everyone got two slices of bread and the same amount of sugar at every meal. The girl who doled out the sugar would scrape the top of the serving spoon with a knife to make sure each portion was level.

Otsui liked her coffee sweet, so she asked for only a half a cup of coffee to go with the single teaspoon of sugar. When the girl scraped out half the sugar from the spoon, Otsui tried to explain, but the girl was young and her understanding of Japanese was poor.

"One cup coffee, one spoon sugar; half cup, half spoon, Oba-san," the girl said in childlike Japanese. Otsui didn't argue. Thereafter she drank a whole cup of half-sweetened coffee for breakfast. But the stupidity of it nearly made her weep.

Every day, Otsui would stash the two slices of bread she got at the midday and evening meals in her blouse. After returning to the barracks, she would toast the bread on a hot plate or on the oil heater and crumble it into empty flour sacks. Her children thought she was being silly.

"Nakashima-san does not have a short-wave radio," Yukio said. "Everybody knows that. He's just making all that up."

"How can you say such a thing, Yukio, you of all my children? You were educated in Japan. You know about the Japanese spirit."

"The Japanese spirit is one thing," Yukio said. "Nakashima-san is another. He's a disillusioned Marxist. He's just angry because the FBI didn't arrest him when the war started. He says he was the real danger to America, not capitalist bourgeoisie like Father and his friends. Now he's hoping for Japan to win the war because he thinks it will hasten the downfall of American imperialism."

Mickey was even harsher. "Mother, you have to stop listening to Nakashima-san. He's crazy. Japan is losing the war. It has no chance against the United States. They already lost half their ships at Coral Sea and at Midway. They're losing, Mother.

You have to be prepared for that. Japan is going to lose the war."

For Sachi, the sacks of bread crumbs that lined the walls of their barracks were an embarrassment. She wanted to cover them up with blankets because she didn't want her friends to see them, but Otsui wouldn't let her. The crumbs needed to be aired lest they got moldy.

Only Hiroshi showed any interest in his mother's bread crumbs. He said they would make good desert food and could be used to catch mice. When she asked why he would want to catch mice, he said one could eat them, or use them to trap larger animals.

"Hirano Oji-san caught a wildcat in his trap," Hiroshi said. "He cooked it on his stove."

Otsui laughed. "Hiroshi, you're making that up."

"No, Mother. It's true. He gave us some. It was good. And we ate rattlesnake, too. We killed it ourselves. A big one." He stretched his arms out wide. "We cooked it in the desert with potatoes."

"How did you cook it?" Otsui asked with a broad smile.

Hiroshi was becoming angry. "We did! We did!" he shouted. "We packed the meat and potatoes in mud, and we put it in a fire. It was good. It tasted like chicken."

Otsui was taken aback by her son's ferocity.

"Hiroshi, I don't want you to go hunting snakes. It's very dangerous," she said.

"It's not dangerous. We know how to do it. Hirano Oji-san showed us."

Mr. Hirano was a savage-looking man with little red pig eyes, disheveled hair, and several days' stubble on his face. His children were just as unkempt and wild looking as he. They probably did eat wildcat. Otsui wished that Hiroshi wouldn't play with them as often as he did, but how could she stop him?

With the onset of winter and its near freezing temperatures, the family would sometimes gather around their oil heater as darkness fell. This provided some solace to Otsui, who enjoyed having her children with her once more even if their cramped, dimly lit cell made her think of a family of bears huddled in a cave.

An eight-foot high plasterboard partition separated the Kono family from their neighbors. On one side were Mrs. Kubota and her four daughters. The father, Kubota-sensei, had been arrested the night of Pearl Harbor along with Seiji and the other community leaders. A cultivated and refined family, the Kubotas tried hard to be considerate, but everything they said came over and through the thin partition: every whispered admonition of Mrs. Kubota and her oldest daughter Kazuko, every whimper of the younger children, their giggling, coughing, sneezing, and blowing of noses.

On the other side was a constantly quarreling couple whose private lives, filled with lies, insults, betrayals, and failures, soon became intimately known to the entire barracks. Keiko had been a waitress in one of the more disreputable bars in the Little Tokyo quarter of Los Angeles. No one could figure out much about Keiko's husband Sukie despite the clues they got through the partition.

"You have brains in prick, Sukie," Keiko would often shout, her screeching echoing along the length of barracks. "You like all men. Fucking, drinking, gambling. You a fucking, drinking, no-good prick-head!"

Judging from other sounds they made, the two usually made up their differences late at night.

When Mickey complained, Sukie said, "Hey, don't complain me. Complain government. What the hell but nookie in this goddamn place?"

Otsui's own family added its share to the ambient noise as well. Yukio and Mickey were constantly quarreling, and Hiroshi and Sachi were often at each other's throats over one thing or another.

Mediating over all of this chaos from his wheelchair was Isamu. Crippled by polio since the age of 17, he found solace in books written in both English and Japanese. He was the intellectual of the family. Like his brothers, he had no problem staking out a position and staying with it, but he looked at the war, with all its contradictions and fallacies, in the context of history.

When Mickey insisted that everyone in the family write to the Justice Department to have their father released, Isamu refused. "It's a waste of time," he said. "Our father is a Japanese patriot. They have solid proof of that. That's different from being a spy or a saboteur, but that's the kind of fine distinction our government isn't capable of making right now."

Sachi's Americanism was less political than cultural. On the wall next to her bed was a photograph of a young American movie star clipped from a magazine, and she and her friends were constantly singing the popular songs of the day that they heard on the radio. They took extraordinary pains to dress in white bobby sox, plaid and pleated skirts, and white blouses with prim collars. Most precious of all were the knit cardigan sweaters that they would wear unbuttoned, the sleeves pushed up to their elbows. This was thought to be as smart and fashionable as was possible. It pleased Otsui to see Sachiko give her cardigans, at least, the care they needed—the gentle washings, the careful drying on paper, the cautious, delicate smoothing and patting with an iron.

One evening, Sachi and two of her friends were rehearsing a number for a talent show. One of the girls had brought a phonograph to play a record of three hakujin women singing in harmony. The girls sang along with the record, shuffling their feet, swinging their hips and arms, snapping their fingers. "Don't sit under the apple tree with anyone else but me, anyone else but me, 'til I come marching home…"

Otsui sat on her bunk knitting a sweater while Isamu

watched from his wheelchair, his face changing gradually from mild amusement to exasperation and finally to despair.

"Sachi," he said, "stop copying the hakujin. To them we're just Japs. That's not going to change. They're just going to break your heart."

"Sammy," Sachi said with pity in her voice, "I don't even know what you're talking about. Why would you say something like that?" Her friends stood by, smiling uncomfortably and looking embarrassed.

"Why am I saying this? Can't you see? Look around. We're in a concentration camp!"

"Oh, Sammy," she said.

Isamu took a deep breath of resignation. He reached for a book and tried to read.

Otsui agreed with Isamu: Sachiko's singing and dancing and the picture of the hakujin boy on the wall were grotesqueries. She said nothing, though, and focused instead on her knitting. Poor Isamu seemed to be the only sensible one left. The others were out of control. If Seiji were there, he'd be able to talk some sense into their children. He would have imposed some discipline on Yukio, Mickey, Sachi, and especially Hiroshi. But she was alone, abandoned and powerless.

This had happened once before, when her father had suddenly died, leaving her alone at fourteen. A low-ranking samurai, her father had always felt that his greatest failure was not having died in the great rebellion of 1877 with Saigo Takamori. Instead, he'd lived on even after the death of his wife. Clinging to the tattered remains of impecunious gentility, he taught for many years at a school and sold off his family heirlooms one at a time. In the end, he died drunk and consumptive, but nobly, by his own hand, much as Saigo and his followers had done more than twenty years earlier.

Before her father died, he had arranged for Otsui to live in the home of Goto, the village wine merchant. Otsui was never told what he had paid Mr. Goto, but she suspected it was the proceeds from the sale of a sword that had been in the family for 12 generations, an object of value that her father had managed to retain through years of poverty and hardship. Even so, she'd been treated no better than a maid in the Goto household. She'd slept in an alcove next to the kitchen and was always the first to get up in the morning to start the fire for the morning tea.

One year, at the annual kabuki festival on the grounds of the Shinto shrine, Mr. Kono, the fish merchant, came over to chat with the Gotos. As he sat with them on the straw matting, he seemed to be studying her intently.

"What is your name, child?" he asked.

"It is Otsui."

"Otsui," Kono mused. "I observed you watching the earlier performance. You appear to understand the play very well, its nuances and complexities. How old are you, child?"

"I am seventeen years old."

"Never sick a day in her life," Mrs. Goto chimed in, "and strong as an ox. As for being clever, you know what children are like nowadays, Kono-san, but this one, I must say, is a big help."

Otsui was astounded. She had never before heard such fulsome praise from Mrs. Goto. She attributed it to the sips of sake Mrs. Goto had been taking from her husband's gourd.

The following month, Mr. Yamasaki, the owner of the noodle shop, came to visit, bringing with him a photograph. He explained that Mr. Kono, the fish merchant, was hoping to arrange a marriage between Otsui and his son in America. Seiji Kono was 26 years old, had been in America for seven years, and was a highly successful farmer.

The photograph was handed to Mr. Goto, then to Mrs. Goto, and finally to Otsui.

Mr. Kono's son looked exotic, not so much because of his Western clothes, but rather because of the way he stood with his legs crossed, his left arm bent at the elbow and resting on the back of an ornately carved, upholstered chair. The pose struck Otsui as too casual, unserious. His hair, which was unusually long, was parted on one side in the western fashion.

"The groom is prepared to bear all the expenses," Mr. Yamasaki said, "including a proper wardrobe for the bride and all items necessary for the passage to America. She will travel first class."

"Maaa," Mrs. Goto said. "He must have done marvelously well in America."

"He is an established farmer and a respected leader of his community," Yamasaki said. "And all at the age of 26! But when I say farmer, don't imagine that he mucks around in a miserable rice paddy. Why, in America, you could put this whole village on a single farm."

"Hooooo," the Gotos gushed in amazement. "How can one man work such a large farm?"

Yamasaki laughed heartily.

"Goto-san, you don't understand. In America, the farmer does no work whatsoever. He is like a lord. He has work crews of fifty, a hundred men. And horses. Seiji Kono wrote his father saying that he owns eleven horses."

After a pause to allow the Gotos to take in all they had heard, Mr. Yamasaki said, "But of course you will want time to consider the offer."

"Time?" Mrs. Goto said. "Why should we need more time? Of course, Otsui will accept."

And, of course, Otsui accepted.

Otsui sat in the rear of the car with the luggage while her new husband Seiji sat in the seat in front of her. They had come upon Hacienda without warning after a six-hour train ride through the heartland of California. Having been dazzled by San Francisco's massive buildings, streetcars, and horse-drawn carriages, Otsui was underwhelmed by the appearance of the town in which she was to live. There seemed no obvious reason for establishing a settlement there in the middle of what appeared to be a flat, unending wasteland.

A horse and buggy driven by a Japanese man named Taneda took them through Hacienda's Main Street. Otsui was appalled at the shabbiness of what looked like makeshift buildings on both sides of a hard-packed dirt road. Though they appeared to be places of business, they swayed and creaked with every gust of wind.

The town itself was full of people, both dark and white skinned. The Chinese were recognizable because of their queues, but the Japanese looked strange in their Western clothes and close-cut hair. Most of the dark-skinned people, Seiji said, were Mexicans, the original inhabitants of the land.

At the edge of town, the horse made a right turn and proceeded down a narrow dirt track. Now Otsui could see that the land was indeed being cultivated, though farmers in Japan would never have allowed such slovenly fields. The rotting residue of the harvest was scattered as far one could see—perhaps even as far as the mountains, whose dim outlines were only barely perceptible as night fell.

As the horse plodded on, she wondered where her new home might be. She had seen pictures of Western cities and towns in Japan, and the houses in San Francisco had been tall with gabled roofs and ornate porches supported by decoratively carved pillars. Anything like that was sure to stand out in this flat landscape, but all she could see was bare land.

"We will be there soon, Oku-san," Taneda said, addressing her as an honored lady of the house. "The camp is right around that stand of trees there."

When they arrived, Otsui saw that what Taneda had called "the camp" was made up of several buildings, all made of rough, unpainted pine boards that had been burnt to a reddish hue by the sun. Next to the main building, Taneda pointed out structures that he described as the mess hall, kitchen, and bathhouse. The outhouses and stables were set slightly apart from the rest of the camp; next to them, overlooking the entire complex, were a windmill and a water tower.

"Is the house nearby?" Otsui asked.

"The house? It's over there," Seiji said, pointing toward the main barracks. "My quarters are on the far end. I've had it partitioned into two rooms and a kitchen. The kitchen has running water," he said proudly.

After the luggage was unloaded, Seiji said he would take care of the horse and buggy himself while Taneda helped Otsui settle in. "You will soon be looking after the horse yourself," Seiji said to Otsui. "This horse and buggy are yours. You will need them to go into town for supplies."

Otsui looked at the huge red beast that snorted and rattled its harness. She swallowed hard and said nothing.

After Seiji was out of earshot, she asked Taneda, "Does he really have eleven horses?"

"Oh, more than that. He has ten horses here and ten more at another farm he just leased."

"And does he really have a hundred people working for him?"

"Sometimes more than that," Taneda said. "Right now, there's nobody here but me, but at the height of the season, there will be at least fifty workers living here."

"In such a small building?"

"Oh, you know, we're all bachelors. We don't need much space."

So what Mr. Yamasaki had said was true. He hadn't lied. Still, it would be many more years before Otsui's vision of life in America came close to what she had imagined it would be.

After the third month of internment, Otsui got a job as a dishwasher. This occupied her time and paid sixteen dollars a month. Plus, the mess hall was where one could hear about everything that was going on in the camp, from what official from Washington was visiting to what Mrs. Okubo's hakujin lover had sent her that month. It was through her job there that Otsui first heard about the Loyalty League's efforts to get Nisei into the American Army. She quailed at the thought. Mickey was involved; he had to be.

One evening, as she left the mess hall, she noticed that the door to the storage shed had been left open. She started to go close it, but stopped short when she saw a boy running out with a potato in each hand. Two others followed, also carrying potatoes. One of them was Hiroshi. She thought of shouting at him, but kept silent. In her blouse, after all, were six slices of bread that the cook had allowed her to take.

By winter, Otsui had two flour sacks full of bread crumbs. It was about that time that she experienced her first desert storm. Otsui was visiting her friend Mrs. Okamoto some blocks away. For December, the day was unusually warm and the atmosphere oppressive, but no one expected rain. The suddenness and fury of the storm stunned them. The sky darkened and the temperature dropped as if a huge hand had grasped the sun. Lightning ripped the air with frightful crackling and tearing sounds followed by explosions of thunder. Rain crashed down as if the sky had suddenly split, and wind lashed the walls of the barracks. Before Otsui and Mrs. Okamoto could close the windows, rivulets of water were streaming across the floor.

Otsui paled. She apologized, saying she had to leave, and ran out into the downpour despite her friend's urging that she wait out the storm. Nearly blinded by the heavy rain, she struggled across a firebreak, her head down, her eyes on her feet. She was midway across the open field when she saw to her amazement and horror that the swirling water was rising above her shoes. Looking up, she could scarcely believe what she saw: the firebreak had been transformed into a rippling, muddy lake. The entire camp was standing in a sea of roiling water.

Not a soul could be seen anywhere. The barracks looked strangely deserted, as if its occupants had been swept into the desert by the raging flood. Otsui continued on, but her progress was slow. The water now reached above her ankles, and in some places, came almost to her knees. Lightning flashed in the distance, followed by low rumbles of thunder. Rain pelted her face and heavy gusts of wind threatened to knock her into the choppy water.

Otsui finally managed get to where the road should have been. Hoping to reach higher ground, she forged ahead. Suddenly, the ground beneath her dropped away and she found herself submerged entirely in cold, murky water; she had forgotten about the drainage ditch at the side of the road. Though the water wasn't more than waist high, she couldn't get to her feet in the swift current and was carried to the crossroad, where she caught hold of a sluice gate at one end of the culvert. She hung there for some moments catching her breath. By the time she was able to clamber up to the road, the full fury of the storm had abated, but the rain continued to blow in her face as she stumbled, exhausted, back to her barracks.

When she got there, she found the room empty. The others had made no attempt to return. As she had feared, the windows had been left open, and the floor was awash. The bread crumbs were drenched. She fell to her knees and wept. She didn't care if anyone heard. In tight, choking barks, she screeched out her anger against the steady, dense rattling of the rain and the low moaning of the wind. How could she have been so stupid, so careless?

That night, she tried to dry the crumbs over the oil heater, but they were ruined and already beginning to smell of mold. The flour sacks were still salvageable, though. She would have to start over again.

Near the end of the second year of camp, Father was allowed to rejoin the family once more. When he saw the sacks of breadcrumbs hanging from the rafters, he asked about them, and Otsui told him what they were for. He didn't laugh as he might have in the past. Instead, he smiled and said, "Unh, that was a good idea. You don't know this—you never had to deal with him as we did—but Nakashima is a radical; you can't trust him. But it was a good thing what you did. It was a brave thing."

Otsui was filled with warmth toward her husband; she felt close to him in a way she'd never experienced before. A week later, to make room, she began throwing out the bread crumbs. By the end of the month, they were gone.

BROTHERS

1943

Sammy sat in the mess hall at the end of one of the long tables that, in another time and place, might have been used for picnics. At the other end, his brother Mickey sat with two of his friends, both college graduates like himself and members of the Loyalty League.

For many in the camp, the League gave off a bad odor. It had cooperated with the government in organizing the mass incarceration, and now some of its members were doing clerical chores and serving as interpreters for the hakujin camp administrators. The open profession of American patriotism trumpeted by the League grated on the nerves of even those who might have been in agreement with its policies and goals. Beyond that, rumor had it that the League was helping camp administrators create a list of "troublemakers"—men like Yukio and his Seinin-kai buddies who were openly bitter about the camps. Whereas the League was made up of mostly young, college-educated Nisei, the Seinin-kai attracted older men, often Kibei who had been born in the US but educated in Japan. These men were contemptuous of what they took to be the craven posture and actions of their younger brethren. Some would hurl insults at League members using tough street talk they had acquired in Japan. "He's got the smell of a dog," they would snarl whenever they saw someone from the League. In the tense and perfervid atmosphere that developed in the camp, the hateful epithet "inu" was heard over and over again, whether whispered in hushed tones or shouted in ugly confrontations.

Sammy generally preferred to keep his distance from his younger brother and his crowd, so it was only by chance that he happened to be at their table in the mess hall. Though he didn't necessarily believe the rumors swirling about the League, he found their hyper-Americanism naïve and cloying. It was difficult for him to refrain from butting into their conversations with bits of sarcasm and even ridicule.

Mickey was poking at the mutton stew they'd been served for the third time that week with a disgusted look. The meat was tough and stringy, the broth greasy and lukewarm. "It smells like horse manure," Mickey said, grumbling loudly enough for all to hear. "I'm hungry, but this stuff is making me sick."

A man sitting at the next table turned and glared at Mickey. He was a stranger, new to the block, and hadn't said a word to anybody since his arrival. Now he spoke in a voice that could be heard at the far end of the mess hall: "What the hell do you expect in a concentration camp? Fried chicken?"

Sammy broke out in laughter. This earned him a smile and a wink from the stranger. A tacit alliance of sorts was formed.

The newcomer was a big man with shoulders like a bull. He had an American eagle tattooed on his right arm, which piqued Sammy's curiosity. Even more intriguing was the rumor that he'd been brought to camp in handcuffs by two policemen.

The next day, Sammy was sitting in his usual spot next to the shower house, a good place to observe the comings and goings of the block, when the stranger walked by in a ratty bathrobe. Sammy smiled at him and waved.

The man stopped and asked his name.

He told him, and the man said, "Sammy? You mean Isamu, don't you?"

Sammy nodded.

"I'll call you Sammy, if that's what you want. I was Hideo as a kid, but my friends call me Jack."

After that, Jack always made it a point to stop and talk to Sammy, even inviting him to his narrow, cell-like room in the barracks reserved for bachelors. Jack, it turned out, wasn't the aloof and crusty misanthrope he made himself out to be. One day, when the two were talking and smoking cigarettes in Jack's quarters, he said, "You know, I was in the Army during the last war."

"You're kidding." Sammy said. "I thought they only took hakujin."

"Usually, but Japan was an ally in the last war, so they took me. I thought if I joined the Army, I could be a hundred percent American. I didn't want to be a goddamn Jap all my life."

At first, Sammy had trouble understanding what Jack meant by this. From his own narrow perspective, being Japanese had never been such a hardship, at least not until the war had started. But Jack's meaning became clearer as he ranted on.

"I didn't want to be like my old man, doing stoop labor, saving pennies, dreaming about going home to Japan. This is my home, for chrissakes. I was born here. I went to school here."

The Army had made Jack a cook. He had wanted to be in the infantry, fighting in the trenches "like a Yank," but the kitchen had turned out to be just as hazardous. He showed Sammy a white scar that went up his right calf like a zipper. The boiler had blown, he said, nearly costing him his leg.

Jack was like no other Nisei Sammy had ever encountered. With his curly hair and light complexion, he didn't even look that Japanese. But what really made him different was his demeanor and the way he talked. Jack seemed to be in his 50s, which meant he was old enough to be of Father's generation, but his speech was laced with cuss words that only hakujin used; when he got worked up, he sounded like a rowdy, drunken sailor.

As it turned out, Jack's experience as an Army cook had gotten him a job working in the galley of a merchant steamer. It was mostly "shit duty," he said, but as he talked, he would get a dreamy look on his face.

"Those were good times. I saw a lot of the world: Hawaii, Manila, Hong Kong, Singapore; the bars, the women."

Some of Jack's stories were hard to believe. He said he once landed in a Tokyo jail for insulting the Emperor. "I was drunk, for chrissakes. I didn't know I was supposed to bow when that big black limo went by. I thought it was a fuckin' funeral. A guy from the American Embassy came and bailed me out. Believe me, I was plenty grateful, but that's the only good thing the goddamn government ever did for me."

"Your life as a sailor doesn't sound so bad," Sammy said. "And the Embassy could have left you in Japan, rotting in jail."

Jack gritted his teeth, then shook himself like a dog shedding water. "You know, after Pearl Harbor, I tried to join the Navy, but they said I was too old. I believed that at first, but then I found out they weren't taking Buddhaheads. Not the Navy, not the Army, nobody. The Merchant Marines told me to my face: 'No Japs.'"

When Jack had joined the American Army, he had given himself to his country body and soul. There was nothing Japanese left in him. He was, at least by his lights, completely American. But America had rejected him, casting him out as a foreigner and locking him up in a prison camp as if he were an alien spy.

The stories people had been telling about Jack were true; he had been in jail before being brought to the camp.

"They said I tried to kill a cop. Bullshit. Trumped up charges. I just told the cop I had the right to be in any goddamn bar at any goddamn time, just like any other goddamn American. I was drunk, so I might have pushed him. I don't remember."

"Didn't you know about the curfew?" Sammy said, getting into the spirit of things. "You don't have the same goddamn rights as every other goddamn American. You should've been home where you belonged and in your bed by 8 o'clock."

Jack laughed. "You bustin' my balls now, Sammy? But you know, you're right. US citizenship ain't worth the fuckin' paper it's written on. I don't know about you, but from now on I'm a one hundred percent Jap. Tell that to your brother Mickey and his kiss-ass Loyalty League."

Mickey, twenty-four years old, was Sammy's younger brother by three years. His name was Mikio, but soon after he started elementary school, everyone started calling him Mickey. This was more than just another Americanization; it stemmed from his inability to sit still. His teacher at the time said he was like a mouse—darting about, scurrying from one corner of the room to the other. His friends began calling him Mickey Mouse, and the Mickey had stuck.

For most of his adolescence, Mickey's teachers considered him a problem child. He wasn't inclined toward schoolwork, and he was always getting into fights. Not only was he quick and agile, he was unusually strong. His Japanese schoolmates admired him because he stood up to Mexican bullies, but his teachers, accustomed to well-mannered, docile Japanese children, thought him an incorrigible ruffian.

Once he got to Santa Marguerita, where all the children from Hacienda went to high school, Mickey's pugnacity, overabundance of physical energy, and what turned out to be exceptional athletic ability became huge assets. Not only did he have the audacity to try out for the football team—Japanese kids generally avoided calling attention to themselves in that way—he made varsity. The coach could hardly believe this remarkable find. Mickey could run the hundred-yard dash in ten seconds flat carrying a football and in full uniform. He was physically aggressive, mentally tough, and endowed with unusual agility and balance. By sixteen, he was five-feet-eight—bigger than most of his friends, even if the hakujin still considered him small. They called him a scat back, one of those runners who could cut and weave, then reverse his field, leaving behind a wake of fallen tacklers. By his junior year, Mickey was being scouted by USC, Cal, and Stanford.

Mickey's status as an athlete made high school tolerable for him, but things were different at the Japanese school, which was conducted in the monastic atmosphere of the Buddhist church every weekday afternoon. The hour Mickey was forced to spend there under the stern, hovering presence of Kubota-sensei was agony for him. Unlike Sammy, Mickey had no interest in reading or writing Japanese. His spoken Japanese was broken and childlike, and he frequently had to resort to English words and phrases, even when talking to his parents. So when Father happened to see a picture of Mickey in a football pose—one knee up, right hand extended stiffly—in the Santa Marguerita *Gazette*, it was to Sammy that Father had gone for an explanation.

Father was stunned when Sammy explained that Mickey occupied a unique place in the hakujin community. He was a football sensation not only in Santa Marguerita but also in the three-county region. Hearing this, Father decided to go the following Saturday to see for himself what this game of football was about. Yukio and Sammy were to go with him—Sammy to explain the game and Yukio to help Sammy in and out of the car.

Santa Marguerita was being pegged as a contender for the championship that year, so the bleachers were jammed by the time the Konos arrived. It was a chilly autumn day. Dressed in a suit and tie covered by a dark woolen overcoat and sporting a gray fedora, Father, who didn't own what one would call casual wear, looked utterly out of place. Yukio and Sammy, who wore pea coats with woolen caps pulled over their ears, might have done a better job of fitting in were it not for Sammy's wheelchair. All in all, they made an odd-looking trio.

The Santa Marguerita side of the stands was already full, so they made their way to the opponents' side, which was less densely packed. Father and Yukio carried Sammy halfway up one end of the bleachers, where a group of older couples who looked like parents made room for them.

"My boy, Mikio, he play for Santa Marguerita," Father said to his neighbor, a middle-aged, crinkly eyed hakujin.

"We," the man replied, pointing to himself and the woman next to him, "are from Paso Robles." He spoke slowly and clearly, as one does to foreigners. Father smiled and nodded to indicate he understood, so the man continued: "Our son," again pointing to himself and his wife, "plays for Paso Robles. There," he said, pointing to the visitors' bench. "Are you related to Mickey Kono?" he asked.

"Unh," Father said. "Yes, Mikio Kono my son."

"You must be very proud," the man said. Father made no response.

Santa Marguerita won the coin toss and elected to receive. Mickey was the kick returner.

"There," Sammy said, pointing to him, "standing alone in the back. Number 22, Father. He'll be the one who catches the ball."

Mickey received the ball on the 15-yard line, and after weaving to the left and then to the right, he seemed to be running free; the stands on the Santa Marguerita side of the field erupted in wild cheers. But when Mickey was subsequently trapped by a gang of opposing players, who pummeled him to the ground in a mound of flaying arms and legs, the crowd on their side rose to its feet and cheered. Even the friendly man and his wife joined in. Father was horrified, but he remained silent, as he did through most of the game, only occasionally asking, "Where is Mikio now?"

Santa Marguerita played the single wing, and Mickey was the tailback, but those were details beyond Father's understanding or concern, so Sammy simply said: "He's the one in the back, Father. The one who gets the ball."

For the rest of the afternoon, Father's brow remained fixed and furrowed, his jaw clenched, his hands clasped together in a tight ball at his waist as he watched hulking, leather-hardened boys ram, butt, and throw his son to the ground. Mickey would run, as if for his life, but he would inevitably be caught and knocked down, whereupon two, three, or even four others would pounce upon his fallen and helpless body. Then, having crushed Mickey, his opponents would bounce back up triumphantly, celebrating their savagery by slapping one another's backs and buttocks as the barbarian couple sitting beside Father clapped and shouted encouragement. The few times Mickey managed to evade his pursuers and return to the safety of his teammates, the couple groaned while the Santa Marguerita side roared with happiness and pleasure.

"It is barbaric," Father said when he got home. "I will not allow it. It is not a sport for a Japanese boy. All they do is knock each other down. They run and throw their bodies full force into one another. One boy had to be carried off the field. He might have been killed. No, no, it is no sport for Mikio. It is not a sport for a Japanese boy."

Mother had not seen the game, but was shocked all the same. "Why did we not know?" she said, looking accusingly at her husband. "Why were we not told? Mikio must not play such a dangerous sport. Why do the Americans allow such things?"

The evening meal that Saturday was unusually quiet, but Mickey didn't notice. After the excitement and exertion of the game, he was hungry and still flushed from the afterglow of his two touchdown runs.

Masako-san had prepared fresh sea perch in her usual way with soy sauce, sugar, and ginger. There was also steamed tofu with bonito flakes and the usual assortment of pickled cabbage, cucumbers, and radishes. Mickey preferred to eat meat, but he ate heartily nevertheless, using his chopsticks to shovel rice drenched in fish sauce into his mouth. He had a distant look on his face as he chewed

"Mikio," Father said. "I went to see you play football today."

Mickey no doubt heard the edge in Father's voice, but he still had not made the transition from the world of football to the family table. He looked up, half-expecting the usual congratulatory praise.

"I did not know that football was such a brutal sport," Father said. "If I had known, I would never have allowed you to play. I have told Isamu to call your school on Monday to inform them that you will no longer play the game."

Mickey looked at Sammy as if betrayed.

Sammy and Mickey had never been close. Before Sammy was crippled by polio, he'd excelled in school and in his Japanese studies, and his parents had constantly held him up as a model for Mickey to emulate. "Why can't you be more like Isamu?" they would say. But ever since Sammy's illness confined him to a wheelchair, Mickey, the athlete, was embarrassed by his invalid brother, preferring to pretend he didn't exist.

"You can't do that, Sammy," he shouted. "Tell him you can't do that. We're going to the league championship this season. They're counting on me. Tell him you can't do that!"

"Tell him yourself," Sammy said. "You speak Japanese."

"You talk of your father in his presence?" Father exploded. "Speak to me directly if you have something to say. Speak Japanese. You are still a member of this family. You are Japanese. Speak Japanese."

"Father, there is no danger," Mickey said in his broken Japanese. Even Hiroshi spoke better. Mickey had trouble explaining his importance to the team. He tried "number one" in English, then "ichi-ban," its Japanese equivalent. When that didn't seem to get across, he tried "taisho," which meant great leader or general, a ludicrous overstatement of his importance to the team.

He stumbled valiantly on, trying to explain the league and state championships, but the more he talked, the more he realized that none of what he was saying had any meaning for Father. "Sammy," he finally said in desperation. "Explain it to him. Please, Sammy."

Sammy knew it was futile, but he did the best he could for Mickey. "Father, if Mikio stops playing, it will reflect badly on all Japanese. If he doesn't play, the hakujin will say that he was afraid. The hakujin like football because it is dangerous. They need it to prove their courage. If Mikio refuses to play, they will call him a coward."

As Sammy had expected, Father was not impressed by such convoluted logic. He went straight to the point. "Mikio will stop playing not because he is afraid, but because I will not allow him to play. We will make that clear. I will ask our lawyer to write a letter to the school so there can be no misunderstanding."

Mickey opened his mouth to speak, but Sammy told him with a glance to shut up. Both knew that when Father made up his mind about such matters, arguing further was not just useless, it was dangerous.

Mickey's football career ended that evening.

Without the daily football practices, Mickey managed to improve his grades enough to be accepted to Stanford University. He didn't get an athletic scholarship, but Father, who didn't know about such things and wouldn't have cared even if he had, was delighted. Mickey would be the first of his sons to attend an American university, and the cost was of little concern to him.

"You must work hard, Mikio. Study hard. Do not shame your family," he said. He then concluded his speech with that powerfully obscure exhortation that all his children had heard since earliest childhood: "Remember, you are Japanese."

At Stanford, the Japanese students lived in a rooming house sponsored by a Christian missionary organization. Theirs was a life apart. Contact with the hakujin was so infrequent that it was remarked upon whenever it occurred. Mickey tried out for the football team, but was consigned to junior varsity. The other athletes, scholarship players, lived in special dorms and were treated like royalty; crowds of students would part to make way for them whenever they appeared. Mickey, on the other hand, was just another one of those queer looking Asians who spoke English surprisingly well and sat with others of their kind at the back of the lecture hall.

In the end, Mickey didn't play a single game at Stanford. He hurt his knee in practice trying to make a 90-degree cut at full speed on wet grass and never fully recovered. He didn't even try out his sophomore year.

Still, far from making him resentful of America and Americans, Mickey's experiences in high school and at Stanford instilled in him a driving need and determination to be fully recognized as American. He joined the Stanford chapter of the Loyalty League and converted to Christianity. All the energy he had previously channeled into football he henceforth directed at becoming an exemplary, flag-waving, allegiance-swearing, law-abiding citizen and patriot. It turned out Mickey was Japanese after all—the mirror image of his patriotic, nationalist father. This was an irony only Sammy could appreciate.

Father, of course, was so pleased and proud that one of his sons was attending a prestigious American university that he either didn't see or chose to ignore the widening gulf that was growing between Mickey and the family. It was Sammy who saw from the isolated perch of his wheelchair that Mickey was evolving into an outlier—resentful, if not ashamed, of his alien home and family.

When Yukio returned to Hacienda after a 14-year absence, he too felt as if he were returning to a house full of strangers. It was awkward for him to be with his parents, whom the years had changed considerably; they were not simply older, they had also become oddly Americanized in their speech, dress, and mannerisms—especially Father, who now wore tailored suits, smoked cigars, and seemed unaware that he salted his Japanese with English words. The wooden shack in the country where Yukio had grown up was gone, replaced by a palatial house in town. Even the food, now frequently eaten with knife and fork, had changed.

Of his siblings, the only one he vaguely remembered was Isamu, now crippled by disease. Isamu had been four years old when Yukio had been sent to Japan at the age of six. Isamu was supposed to follow his older brother to Japan two years later, but for reasons that were never made clear to either of the brothers, their parents had changed their minds. As for the rest, Mickey had been but an infant when he'd left, and Sachiko had been born while he was away. Then, much to his surprise, a newborn had appeared in the house—a boy with the given name of Hiroshi.

After Yukio returned from Japan, Father had given him the summer to get acclimated to his new surroundings. Once fall came around, however, he'd insisted that Yukio enroll in high school to improve his English and get an American diploma. It was humiliating for Yukio, formerly a student at Japan's most prestigious university, to sit in a freshman high school class with students six years his junior. Yukio had taken courses in English in Japan, but his spoken English was incomprehensible to American ears. As a result, teachers and students alike treated him as though he were simple-minded. Mikio, already a sophomore and a celebrated athlete, avoided him entirely, a snub that Yukio never forgot.

In those difficult first years back in the US, Yukio found himself relying more and more on Isamu for companionship. Not only did Isamu speak fluent Japanese, he had no problem understanding his older brother's exotic Japanese English and gladly became Yukio's in-house English tutor.

Sammy was a voracious reader of books, magazines, and newspapers, but he now had little actual contact with the world outside his home. Both his and Yukio's view of America thus came largely from the movies. The brothers both loved and distrusted the uncanny ways in which the shimmering, larger-than life images were able to touch their own secret, inexpressible longings. For Sammy, the housebound invalid, and Yukio, the foreigner, movies became a window to the outside world.

Sometimes, after watching a movie, Yukio and Sammy would go to the Mexican section of town to buy a pint of whisky. When the moon was out, they'd drive to a dirt road half-hidden by an embankment next to the graveyard, and Yukio would park under a small grove of eucalyptus trees. From there they could look out over the neat rows of grave markers dappled with shadowed moonlight like a little stone village. Though eerie, the spot was quiet and secluded—a perfect place to sit, drink, smoke cigarettes, and talk.

One night, after watching a particularly glitzy Hollywood romance filled with glamorous women in long gowns and men in top hats, Yukio was visibly agitated. "The world isn't like that, Isamu," he said. "What they show in the movies is all fantasy."

"How would you know? You grew up in Japan. You don't know anything about America."

"I know that that's not how people live, not even in New York."

Sammy signaled his agreement by softly blowing cigarette smoke out of his nostrils in a manner he thought worldly and mature.

The only movies Yukio trusted were gangster movies; they at least depicted the dark underbelly of American life, showing American society the way it really was. His favorite actors were George Raft and James Cagney, tough anti-heroes who smacked people around, even women if they got too cheeky. Yukio said George Raft and James Cagney were like samurai. "A samurai values honor more than life. He has purity, Isamu, the kind of purity that Americans don't understand."

Still, despite his rants, Yukio liked America more than he would care to admit. He liked the abundance of food—the whole fish and meat served in hunks fit for savage carnivores, the chickens Masako-san would roast two at time, the sake and beer that he, as the chonan, was allowed to indulge in from time to time. He liked the suits his father had made for him in Los Angeles, the fine shoes, the Chevrolet coupe he'd gotten for his twenty-first birthday. And despite himself, he was attracted by what he saw in the movies—the cocky, brash Americans succeeding against the odds, winning the beautiful, clinging girl and ending up with wealth, power, fame, and glory. That was the American dream. It tantalized him, but he knew it had little to do with him. Mickey, the high school football hero, could delude himself into dreaming such dreams, but not Yukio, nor Sammy for that matter.

If the three brothers had anything in common, it was that they all admired Kazuko, the eldest daughter of Kubota-sensei. Unlike other schoolgirls her age, Kazuko kept her shimmering black hair long and straight, framing the perfect oval of her face and setting off the pearly whiteness of her skin. Her lustrous eyes and her distinct but delicate features gave her an aristocratic look.

The Kubotas stood on equal footing with the Konos at the top of Hacienda social ladder, but they ranked above the Konos culturally. Both the father and mother had been college educated in Japan, he at a university and she at a women's teachers college.

They took great care to ensure that their four daughters were well trained in etiquette and spoke proper and refined Japanese. Kazuko so excelled in Japanese that she served as an assistant to her father at the Japanese school.

Mickey thought Kazuko the most beautiful girl in town, and like many other boys his age, had a pubescent crush on her. If Japanese school had any appeal at all for him, it was the thrill of Kaz leaning over his desk to correct his scribbled attempts at penmanship.

Kazuko, being three years older, looked on Mickey as a child. Sammy was the one to whom she felt particularly close. As classmates from the beginning of school, they were as close to being childhood sweethearts as the Japanese community would allow. In the early years of high school, they had been constant companions, doing their schoolwork together at the Kono house while Mickey stole envious glances. Their friendship was altered tragically when Sammy contracted polio at the beginning of their senior year of high school. This ended not only Sammy's academic career, but also his intimacy with Kaz. Embittered by his fate and unwilling to burden Kaz with a cripple, he eventually withdrew completely from the friendship, refusing to see her when she came to the house to visit.

Shortly thereafter, Yukio returned from Japan. Even though Yukio was young enough to be Kubota-sensei's son, Kazuko's father welcomed him as almost a peer from the very beginning. Honored in Hacienda as a man of great learning, Kubota hungered for intellectual companionship in a rural village populated by farmers, shopkeepers, and barely literate field workers. Yukio had been a student at Tokyo University, the crown jewel of Japan's educational establishment—even if it had only been for two years. He quickly became a frequent guest at the Kubotas. He was even enticed into assisting at the Japanese school, where he came into nearly daily contact with Kazuko.

It had not been Mr. Kubota's intention to find a match for

his oldest and favorite daughter, but not having a son of his own, it began to dawn on him that he might want to bring Yukio into his family, not simply as a son-in-law, but as his adopted son. The war intervened before his plans could be realized, but unbeknownst to him, Yukio and Kazuko had already fallen in love and were making plans of their own.

In camp, with the Konos and Kubotas occupying not just the same barracks, but adjacent rooms, they could hear each other's voices coming over the partition or through an open window.

One evening, as Yukio was putting away some books, he heard Sachi urging Kazuko to write to the Justice Department to petition for the parole of her father, much as Sachi herself had done. The two had come back from somewhere and were lingering outside the barracks before going into their separate rooms.

"Oh, I don't know, Sachi," Kaz said. "I've been so busy, I haven't had time to even think about it." Kaz was trying to avoid the subject, but she was too honest to stop there so she added: "The government is going to do what it wants to, Sachi."

Suddenly, to his surprise, Yukio heard Mickey's voice.

"The government's going to do what, Kaz?"

"I was just telling Sachi that I didn't think writing to the Justice Department would have much effect," Kaz said, choosing her words carefully. "But I don't know much about these things. I may be wrong. I've just been so busy. I've had so many other things to think about, Mickey."

"Too busy? Too busy to think about your father?"

"Oh, Mickey. I've done nothing but think about Father. I worry about him all the time."

She then switched to Japanese as if actually addressing her father and murmured a prayer for his well-being and safe return. This kind of refinement was typical of the Kubotas, though some mistook it for snobbery.

Mickey was not impressed by such mannerisms. He did

however retain some of his adolescent yearnings for Kaz. He was now old enough to know better, but like a perverse and awkward schoolboy, he channeled the attraction he felt for her into bullying.

"You can't just think about yourself, Kaz," he said. He should have been more deferential, since she was three years his senior, but he went on: "You have to think about the common good. The Loyalty League is trying to convince the government that putting us in this camp was the wrong thing to do. We need to convince them that we're loyal to America."

"Oh Mickey, you should know it's not that simple. My father is Japanese. He believes in Yamato damashii—it's a religion to him. I can't write to the government and lie about him. He would never forgive me."

"Don't talk that way!" Mickey said. "What we're trying to do is convince the government that we're all Americans."

"Maybe you're an American, Mickey, but my father is Japanese." There was an edge to Kaz's voice, which was unusual for her. "So is your father. And maybe I am too. How do you know that I'm not?" It was clear that she was angry.

"Kaz!" Mickey hissed. She had caught him by surprise. He should have known that she wasn't someone he could browbeat. "You don't mean that! You can't let people hear you say stuff like that."

Yukio stood up abruptly. From the expression on his face, Sammy could tell there was going to be trouble. He tried to stop Yukio, but Yukio brushed him aside and went to the door.

Stepping outside, Yukio said in heavily accented English: "She say what she want! Mikio, you leave Kazuko alone. She say what she want. She think what she want. You don't tell her what to think. You don't tell her what to say."

Then, tenderly, speaking in Japanese, he said to Kaz, "I understand you, Kazuko. I understand you very well. Your father is a great man. You must honor him, honor what he believes in, no matter what happens, no matter the consequences. I understand you well, Kazuko."

"I know you do," Kaz replied, also in Japanese.

"Bullshit!" Mickey cried.

That was not a word he should have uttered, but he seemed determined to press on in his reckless course. Sammy quickly wheeled himself to the door.

"You're talking like a bunch of Japs," Mickey shouted. "No wonder they evacuated us. Maybe you belong here!"

"Japs?" Yukio said, switching to English again. "You call us Japs? You Jap, too, Mikio. To US government, we all Japs. You understand?"

"Don't call me a goddamn Jap," Mickey said. He was beginning to advance on Yukio when Sachi, who had stood by terrified, shouted, "Stop it, stop it!" She broke into tears and ran into Kaz's arms. Sammy tried to roll his wheelchair down the ramp, but in his haste, a wheel went off the edge and he went crashing to the ground. As he lay there dazed, Sachi began crying hysterically. "See what you did, Mickey?" she said accusingly. "See what you did?"

Lying on the ground, Sammy saw Mrs. Kubota and her other children come running out, as did their other neighbors. Everyone had heard the row between Mickey and Yukio, and others now took up the argument, which broadened and moved seamlessly amongst the crowd. Mickey started toward Sammy to help him up, but was interrupted by a neighbor, Mr. Kishi, who began to lecture him on what it meant to be Japanese.

"You must be true to Japan, your true home, Mikio," Mr. Kishi said. "You have Yamato damashii within you. Do you think the lazy, spineless, pleasure-seeking Americans have a chance against Yamato damashii? If your father were here, he would tell you the same thing."

Mickey did his best to listen respectfully to the much older man, but his patience and polite, home-bred Japanese manners had been strained beyond their limits.

"To hell with it," he exclaimed in English, then walked off muttering "Bullshit, bullshit, bullshit." Mr. Kishi was aghast.

By then, Mother had come out of their barracks. She bent over Sammy, agitated, and kept insisting that Yukio take him to the hospital. Even Hiroshi, who had heard the commotion from a distance, came running, yelling "What happened? What happened?"

Sammy was finally able to convince his mother that he was all right, and Yukio helped him back into his chair, then pushed him up the ramp and back into the barracks.

Some months later, in late January, the Loyalty League, supported by the camp administration, called a public meeting. This created much fear and alarm throughout the camp. Some urged support for the meeting, others favored a protest or boycott.

On the day of meeting, Yukio and Kaz wandered off together after the evening meal. They were alone outside; it was too cold for most people to be walking about. Both wore heavy woolen coats, scarves, and knitted caps that they pulled low over their ears.

"Don't go to the meeting," Kaz said. "What good will it do? It's only going to lead to trouble."

"I won't speak. I just want to hear what they have to say. People are coming from Salt Lake City, Loyalty League people. They want the government to draft us into their Army. It's crazy. I won't fight in their Army. I'll refuse."

"I know, I know. Why can't they just leave us alone? But they'll send you back to Japan if you refuse. Is that what you want?"

"No."

"I would go with you."

"Don't be silly. You know Japan is losing the war. There's no future there."

There was a long pause. Neither said anything. Then Yukio said, "You know, when I went to school in Japan, they wouldn't write my name in kanji? They used katakana, as if my name wasn't Japanese."

Living in Japan had not been so bad when Yukio was still young, even though the other children had teased him at first about having an "America stink." His bad memories came mainly from his high school years, which were spent not with relatives but with strangers in Tamana, where his school was located.

"They treated me as if I were Chinese or Korean," Yukio said, "But I showed those bastards. Only two students from Tamana passed the examination for Tokyo University, and I was one of them."

Yukio and Kaz walked to the gazebo that the men from their block had built next to the men's shower house. There they sat huddled together against the cold, looking out at the pale shadows of cacti and sagebrush that were slowly fading with the approaching darkness.

"Much good it did," Yukio continued. "The old man pulled me out after my second year."

"It was because of the conscription."

"I was still exempt at the time. The old man thinks of himself as a loyal Japanese, but he didn't want his son in the Japanese Army. Ironic, isn't it?"

"It's different when you're dealing with your own children."

"What do you think the old man would say if he heard that Mickey wants to fight in the American Army? What would he think about the American government conscripting us for military service? It's almost funny, isn't it?"

"No. I don't think it's funny," Kaz said, her voice breaking. She began to sob as Yukio held her in his arms against the cold wind that was beginning to blow in from the desert.

Back at the barracks, Sammy waited impatiently for Yukio, who'd promised to take him to the meeting.

He sat brooding by the window. It annoyed him to see Hiroshi tuning the radio to the Green Hornet and his once Japanese but now Korean sidekick Kato.

"Turn it off!" Sammy said.

Hiroshi was startled. It was not like Sammy to shout at him. "Why?" he asked.

"Because it's a stupid show. It's just war propaganda. Don't listen to that junk. Turn it off."

"But I want to find out what happens."

"Well, okay," Sammy relented, feeling foolish. "Go ahead and listen then. But they're just filling your head with a lot of junk."

Sammy was fond of Hiroshi, a skinny nine-year-old, burnt brown by the desert sun even in winter. He was sorry he didn't see more of him, confined as he was to the barracks where Hiroshi rarely lingered. Even in the dead of winter, Hiroshi would be out climbing over or ducking under the fences and exploring the desert. Every once in a while, though, Sammy could entice Hiroshi to stay with him by reading from a volume of poems that Hiroshi had stolen for him. Hiroshi and his friends had broken into the storeroom next to the school through an unlocked window and had helped themselves to the donated books they'd found scattered on the floor.

Hiroshi liked the poems by Whitman and Poe best. He would go about declaiming, "But O heart! Heart! Heart! O the bleeding drops of red. Where on the deck my Captain lies, fallen cold and dead," reciting the words with great feeling but without fully understanding them. Hiroshi imagined that the poem was about Father, even though he knew by now that Father had not been shot but was being held prisoner in Montana.

Seeing Hiroshi listening to the Green Hornet with his ear to the radio made Sammy think of other young boys doing the same in their bedrooms or living rooms, lying on rugs in front their family radio consoles. But the world was no longer the same for

Hiroshi, nor was it for Sachi and her friends, who jitterbugged in bobby sox to boogie-woogie tunes on the radio. They were in a concentration camp where boys and girls with enemy faces were behaving like Americans. It was probably merciful that Hiroshi and Sachi couldn't see the paradox in their existence, even if Sammy feared that a perilous future awaited them.

Things were different for Mickey and Yukio. They each saw their situations clearly and had chosen radically different paths. Mickey, like his friends in the Loyalty League, was fervently and aggressively American. In much the same way that Sammy's friend Jack was one hundred percent Jap, Mickey was one hundred percent Yank. For Sammy, the intellectual, the only way to be so absolutely sure about anything was to suppress one's inborn intelligence. He couldn't decide whether the Loyalty League was basically craven and sycophantic or courageous and loyal. He thought they might have all those characteristics. But Sammy's primary sympathies were more with Yukio than with Mickey. Since early childhood, Yukio had been tossed from shore to shore, leaving him no place to call home. Was he Japanese or American? The government had made that decision for him, and now it was about to ask him whether he would fight in the American Army. Sammy, too, would be asked. The question for him was purely academic, but he nevertheless struggled with it.

The mess hall of Block 32, near the administration buildings, was nearly full by the time Yukio and Sammy got there. They were able to squeeze in, but those who came later had to stand outside. The windows had been left open so everyone could hear; as a result, it was as cold inside as it was out. The men all wore heavy coats with woolen caps. Those in front sat on the benches that were attached to the tables, while those in the back sat or stood on tabletops, their shoulders hunched, jostling one another and blowing into their hands or sticking them deep into their pockets. As Yukio wheeled Sammy to the front of the hall, people made way for them. After finding a spot for Sammy with an unobstructed view, Yukio went to the back of hall to join his friends. Looking around, Sammy spotted Jack, who was also in the back. He was standing on a tabletop with his arms crossed over his chest and a scowl on his face.

Mickey was sitting with the other officers of the Loyalty League at the front of the hall facing the audience.

As the local chapter president, Mickey was responsible for opening the meeting. When he got up to speak, a small group at the rear began to chant "*inu, inu, inu, inu, inu.*"

Loyalty League members and supporters began to clap to drown out the chant.

"Quiet! Let Mickey talk!" they shouted.

"You'll all get a chance to talk," Mickey said. "I'm Mickey Kono, Chapter President." That started another round of chanting.

"We have Ken Sakai here, Loyalty League National President from Salt Lake City." That quieted the crowd. Even the protesters were curious to hear what Sakai had to say.

Sakai was a short, stocky man dressed in a dark gray, pin-striped suit, a navy blue overcoat, and a gray fedora. Sammy thought he looked like J. Edgar Hoover, a comparison Sakai would probably not have been displeased to hear. But for his Asian face and skin tone, he might have been white and Anglo Saxon. Beyond that, he was patriotic to the point of fanaticism. It was said that early in the war, he had proposed an all-Japanese American suicide battalion, but the War Department had turned him down, saying the American Army did not send soldiers on suicide missions. He had then proposed that alien Japanese be put in labor camps and used as cheap farm workers and road builders to help with the war effort.

Sakai began speaking slowly in a carefully cultivated baritone voice. Sammy mused that if he closed his eyes, he might well think he was listening to a hakujin; he had heard that Sakai claimed as a point of pride that he did not speak Japanese.

Sakai started off by giving an account of the League's negotiations with top Washington officials. "The evacuation of Japanese from the West Coast to relocation centers," he said, "could not be avoided. The government deemed it a military necessity. It was..."

"A goddamn crime! It was a goddamn crime!" someone shouted.

Sammy knew instantly that it was Jack. He looked back and saw him still standing on his tabletop, shaking his fist. Where everyone else saw anger, Sammy saw the pain in Jack's eyes. Jack was pounding away helplessly at some vision in his head. "What the hell do you mean, Sakai?" He wasn't talking to the crowd. He was talking one American to another. "We weren't evacuated. We were arrested. We were rounded up. This is a goddamn concentration camp, for chrissakes. Don't you see that? A goddamn fucking concentration camp!"

That brought the crowd to its feet. Some shouted encouragement and support for Jack, but most were angry. "Sit down!" they shouted. "Let's hear what Ken has to say."

A stern looking man, somewhat elderly, pointed a finger at Jack and said, "Watch your language," as if Jack were a schoolboy, prompting a loud outburst of approval from the crowd.

Sakai remained calm. He seemed used to such chaos. He raised both arms in the air to quiet the crowd. "Okay, okay," he said. "I've got some real news for all of you, if you'll let me finish."

He waited for the ruckus to subside before he continued.

"I was in Washington last week for discussions with the War Department. We met with the top officials there, with Secretary of War Henry Stimson and Assistant Secretary John J. McCloy. I've got good news for you. Very good news!"

He paused for effect. The hall had suddenly grown quiet—not a sound could be heard, not even the sound of breathing.

"The government has agreed to the creation of an all-Nisei combat battalion," Sakai said. Grinning broadly, he waited for a response. When there was none, Mickey and the other Loyalty League officers got to their feet, clapping and shouting "Hey, great! Great news!" But only a smattering of applause came from the crowd. Most of the listeners looked bewildered.

"The unit will be open to volunteers from Hawaii and the mainland. This will be the first step toward reopening the Selective Service System for Japanese Americans," Sakai said with an air of exaltation. "Our rights as American citizens are being restored and honored."

It took some moments for Sakai's announcement to sink in.

"They're going to let us go home?" a young man wanted to know. "They're going to let us out of here?"

"That's something we're going to have to work out," Sakai said.

"You're getting your goddamn suicide battalion!" It was Jack again. "You want them to draft us? Out of a concentration camp? How much are they paying you?

The crowd erupted. Shouts of "*inu, inu, inu*" rang out while others pointed angry fingers at Jack.

"Who is that guy?" one man shouted.

"Get him outta here," Sakai said.

"That's Yamasaki," someone else replied, "the hundred percent Jap."

Part of the crowd surged toward Jack while others rose to stop them. Men started throwing punches wildly, scarcely knowing whom they were hitting as they scuffled on the concrete floor. Somebody shouted, "Get Sakai!" and a group of men started toward him. Just then, the front door burst open and helmeted military policemen armed with batons rushed in. Those standing outside shouted, "Police! Police!" A line of soldiers armed with rifles had surrounded the place.

The lieutenant in charge of the detail shouted, "All

right, everybody. This meeting is over. You will leave this hall immediately. This meeting is over. You will evacuate this building immediately!"

Yukio got to Sammy, and they joined the crowd streaming out the doors. Some leapt out the windows.

"That bastard Sakai brought the Army with him," a man said.

After Yukio got Sammy back to their barracks, he went out once again. He said that the Seinen-kai had called a meeting.

It was past midnight before Mickey came home. He looked tense. "They got Ken Sakai out of the camp," he said. "He's okay."

Sachi and Hiroshi finally went to bed, but Mother, Mickey, and Sammy stayed up waiting for Yukio. Just after two o'clock in the morning, they heard a loud knock on the door. Mickey put his finger to his mouth, silently motioning for everyone to keep quiet. They watched silently as the door shook. The knocking continued, and a voice said in Japanese, "Please, open the door. We prefer not to have to break it down."

There was no lock on the door. They could have simply pushed it open, but some innate sense of decorum held them back. Mother went to the door and saw four men outside, their faces covered with cloth as if they were ninjas, their hands behind their backs. The man who had been knocking bowed and said in polite Japanese, "We are sorry to disturb you, Oba-san, but our business is with your son. Our deepest apologies." Then the men rushed in and dragged Mickey outside.

"*Inu! Inu!*" they shouted. "*Kill the inu!*" One of the men held Mother while the others beat Mickey with their clubs. Mother bit down on the fingers of the man holding her, making him loosen his grip, and with a shriek, she threw herself on Mickey. "Enough! Enough!" the leader said. "Don't hurt the mother. Let's go."

Sammy, who had wheeled himself to the door, saw by the dim light that Mickey's head was bleeding, but his ramp had been pushed aside during the scuffle, leaving him helpless. Hiroshi and Sachi, awakened by the tumult, came running to his side and stood next to him, frozen in fear.

As soon as the attackers left, people began to come out of the barracks in twos and threes. Somebody found two hoes with which to make a stretcher, and they carried Mickey, unconscious and oozing blood, to the hospital. The doctor thought Mickey's skull might be fractured, so he was sent to a hospital in Phoenix.

It was nearly morning before Yukio returned, looking pale. "Mother, I just found out about Mikio. They said they were going after Sakai. If I had known they were coming here for Mikio, I would have stopped them."

A week later, soldiers in jeeps came to their block and arrested Yukio and Jack. In all, 27 men were arrested throughout the camp. Except for Jack, they were all members of the Seinen-kai. The soldiers knew exactly whom to arrest and where to find them. They had a list.

QUANDARY

1943 - 1945

When Hiroshi walked out of his barracks one morning and into the numbing winter cold of the Arizona desert, the first thing he saw was a hinomaru, the blazing sun emblem of the Japanese Empire. The huge, homemade flag—a big red ball on a white sheet—flapped grandly atop the Fuji-shaped butte that overlooked the camp.

For Hiroshi, the hinomaru had the feel of both nostalgia and danger. Before the war, it had often symbolized a harmless bit of fun, as when Mother would sometimes put a red pickled plum on bed of white rice for a "hinomaru lunchbox." Or it could be a frightening harbinger of war, and, after Pearl Harbor, a token of evil. Its sudden appearance above the camp was both funny and scary, and as Hiroshi joined his schoolmates on their way to school, he couldn't stop looking at it.

By the time the children got to school—essentially barracks that had been partitioned off into classrooms—the older kids on the high school side were bunched together and talking excitedly. Some were laughing; others were outraged and shouting at one another. No one could figure out if the flag was a sign of insurrection or simply a dangerous and foolish joke.

On the elementary school side, everything seemed normal, but when the bell clanged and Hiroshi and his classmates walked into their fourth-grade classroom to take their places, Miss Benson called him and Mitsuko to her desk.

Miss Benson was one of a handful of hakujin teachers at the school. Hiroshi had heard her described as a Quaker, but neither he nor his friends knew what that meant. She lived like the other hakujin in a separate compound outside the gates.

"I'm so sorry about what happened last night," Miss Benson said.

Mitsuko seemed to understand. She kept her head bowed and said in a voice that was barely audible, "That's all right, Miss Benson."

The teacher took Mitsuko in her arms and kept repeating, "I'm so sorry, Mitsuko. I'm so sorry about your father."

Hiroshi backed up a step, fearing he would be next. He had no idea what Miss Benson was talking about.

"Hiroshi," Miss Benson said, turning to him. "I'm so sorry about your brother."

"Mickey's okay," Hiroshi said. "He's coming home."

"I mean your brother Yukio."

"Yukio?"

"They arrested him last night. Didn't you know?"

When Hiroshi had gone to bed the night before, Yukio had not been with them. And when he awoke that morning, Yukio's bed had not been slept in. But that was not unusual. Yukio often spent the night with his bachelor friends on the other side of camp.

"I'm so sorry, " Miss Benson said once again and extended her arms to Hiroshi, who backed away, turned, and ran out of the classroom. He didn't trust Miss Benson. She rarely smiled and was cold toward the children. She would give the class arithmetic problems to work on, or have them write letters to President Roosevelt about how good America was, and while the children were working at their benches, she would stare out the window, looking as if she were about to cry. The children thought Miss Benson didn't like being with Japanese children and was thinking of home, of being with her own people. So it came as a shock when she hugged Mitsuko. Hiroshi was not about to let her do that to him.

When he reached his barracks, Mother was sitting on her bed and talking to Sammy in soft, furtive whispers. She held a small handkerchief in her hands that she kept folding and unfolding, using it to dab her eyes.

"Where's Yukio?" Hiroshi blurted out as he burst into the room. "The teacher said the police took him. Did he put up the flag, Sammy? Did Yukio put up the flag?"

"Such a foolish thing to do," Mother said under her breath, as if talking to herself.

"The flag has nothing to do with it, Mother," Sammy said. "That was just an act of defiance. They were going to be arrested anyway. The Seinen-kai was right. There was a list, and Yukio was on it."

But Mother was hardly listening. "So foolish," she kept saying. "Such a foolish thing to do."

Only then did it occur to Hiroshi to wonder how Miss Benson had known.

A year later, the startling sight of the hinomaru flying atop the butte was still clear in Hiroshi's memory. Sammy might have been right that its disturbing appearance by itself had no lasting importance, but in Hiroshi's mind, it marked the beginning of the family breaking apart. Yukio never came back. He was sent to Tule Lake, a camp for "disloyals." Mickey joined the Army to fight in Italy, and when summer came, Sachi left for a college in Minnesota.

By the time winter arrived once more, only Mother, Sammy, and Hiroshi remained.

With the departure of the political activists, the prison camp that been a hotbed of resentment, rage, and violence became a placid settlement in which the people had only the heat, cold, and boredom to contend with.

The soldiers who had initially guarded the camp had over time dwindled in number, and by end of the first winter, they were gone entirely. With no one to prevent it, the fences and guard towers came down, one piece here, another piece there. The barbed wire was dismantled and used to protect chicken coops against desert predators or as part of evocative sculptures representing camp life. The wood from the guard towers was turned into baseball backstops and basketball courts, and a stage was built for movies and kabuki performances. In Hiroshi's block, as elsewhere, men built private shower and toilet stalls in the women's latrine. A full-blown pavilion replaced the gazebo by the showers. Throughout the camp, barracks were adorned with trellises covered with morning glories and lush green castor plants. Fresh vegetables were grown for the mess halls, and poultry and pigs were raised for meat and eggs. Eventually, even a few fishponds dotted the grounds of the once desolate prison camp.

With the fences gone, the desert became a full-time playground for Hiroshi and his friends. They climbed the buttes, hunted Gila monsters, rousted brightly colored desert birds out of sagebrush, chased and scooped up horny toads that would go to sleep on the palms of their hands when their bellies were stroked.

But the peace and quiet that descended on the camp during this period was hard on Sammy. Yukio was gone. So was Jack, the hundred percent Jap who, in Sammy's mind, was more American than any Nisei he had ever met. Sammy missed even the political dissension that had split the camp; it had at least been relevant, keeping the camp in the real world.

That spring, the once dangerous and hostile wasteland became stunningly beautiful, with sagebrush sprinkled with white flowerets, the buttes ablaze with yellow and red blooms of cholla cacti. It was around that time that Father was released from the Army prison camp in Montana. He was thin and looked worn out, but encouraged by his wife and old neighbors, he soon recovered some of his old vigor. He had been a prominent figure in the Japanese communities in California, and his name was well known among the older people still left in the camp. They elected him block manger. After that, he would spend his time in a room in one of the barracks that served as his office, playing go and entertaining lovers of the Japanese theater with his narrative chanting. His favorite piece at the time was *Kanshusei*, the heroic tale of a loyal retainer who sacrifices his own son in service to his lord. Small audiences would gather to hear him, and the women who attended would wipe tears from their faces as the tragic tale reached its climax. From time to time, he and other block managers would even throw joint parties that featured home-brewed sake, which was said to be of prewar quality.

Father had long recognized Isamu as perhaps his most intellectually gifted son. It pained him to see him sitting alone next to the shower house day after day. As block manager, he arranged to have a bridge built over the drainage ditch so Sammy could wheel himself to the canal. From there, he could look out over the landscape. After that, Sammy would often sit under a willow tree, spending hours reading or looking out into the desert and into the flowing waters of the canal. For a time, Kaz sometimes kept him company there, but after a while, she too left—to Tule Lake to be with Yukio.

Surprisingly, once Kaz left, Mr. Nakashima became the closest thing that Sammy had to a companion. He would often come to sit with Sammy by the canal, and the two would talk and smoke Bull Durham tobacco, which Mr. Nakashima taught Sammy how to roll. The pair would get odd looks from people, who no doubt wondered what in the world the cripple and the old eccentric could have in common. What no one knew was that they had become acquainted in Hacienda before the war.

Yukio had been the first to see in Mr. Nakashima a kindred spirit, a man in a state of continuous warfare with himself, and Sammy had often accompanied his brother on his visits to Mr. Nakashima. In camp, Yukio had continued to be one of the few people who would visit now and then with the old man. With Yukio gone, Mr. Nakashima sought out Sammy to talk to.

Mr. Nakashima had come to Hacienda as an organizer for the Industrial Workers of the World. Farmers like Father had been alarmed at first, but soon saw that Mr. Nakashima posed no threat to them. Times were hard, and farm workers were not about to jeopardize their livelihood by joining a union. The IWW itself was strapped for funds, and Mr. Nakashima had to find fieldwork to support himself.

Yukio had struck up an acquaintance with Mr. Nakashima shortly after returning from Japan. He had come across Mr. Nakashima when the old man was staging a quixotic and unauthorized boycott against gambling in Nakano's Pool Hall. Yukio, who had read German philosophy while at Tokyo University, had a passing familiarity with Marx, so when he saw Mr. Nakashima passing out Marxist leaflets, he'd stopped to talk. That was the beginning of something like a friendship between the two. Mr. Nakashima was deeply grateful to have an interlocutor with whom he could expound upon his views with some chance of being understood. Yukio, though still in his early twenties, was intrigued by this old man who, like him, seemed to belong neither to Japan nor America.

Mr. Nakashima's protest lasted only two days. It ended after a committee of elders, Yukio's father among them, approached him to point out that Nakano's hana tables were a better alternative to the Chinese game of fantan; whereas fantan was often manipulated by clever Chinese croupiers who used slight of hand to cheat the stupid Japanese, hana was a game of skill. Furthermore, hana kept Japanese money within the Japanese community. Such arguments had little impact on Mr. Nakashima's way of thinking, but they did give him a face-saving way to end a demonstration he had begun impetuously, sparked by one of his fleeting, alcohol-induced inspirations. A grateful Mr. Nakano had subsequently delivered a bottle of Johnny Walker Red Label to the rooming house where Mr. Nakashima resided.

Yukio and Sammy were surprised to see the bottle of Scotch still standing unopened on the shelf above Mr. Nakashima's bed when they visited him for the first time several days later.

"Ah, Kono-kun," Mr. Nakashima said, addressing Yukio collegially. "You brought your brother. Good. Good."

Mr. Nakashima said he was fifty-eight, but he looked older. His face and body had been ravaged by alcohol and a hard life. He seemed as worn out as the threadbare and faded clothes he wore. His face was bony and lined and withered like driftwood, but his eyes were bright with vigor, intelligence, and humor.

Mr. Nakashima's room was small, eight by ten feet, and lit by a lone naked light bulb that hung from a low ceiling. Still, despite its fetid air, it was remarkably neat. Even the empty quart bottles of beer along the bottom of one wall were lined up in an orderly row. The only decoration in the room was a tattered and fading poster that showed two distinguished-looking hakujin men with full white beards. Below the two heads, a parade of apes and half-apes evolved progressively into a man who marched erect, waving the rising sun flag of Japan.

Mr. Nakashima noticed Sammy staring at the poster.

"Do you like it?" he asked. "It was never used. It was made

for the Social Revolutionary Party of San Francisco in 1907. I was a member—very young, very idealistic, wild. I even tended toward anarchism in those days. The white socialists didn't want us, so we formed our own party.

Yukio, who had also been studying the poster, said, "Nakashima-san, I think I know who those men are. Marx and Darwin."

"Yes, yes, Marx and Darwin," Mr. Nakashima said excitedly, "but you need to hear the whole story. You have to understand our frustration. In Japan, we were students at the best universities. You were at Todai. You know what it was like. We were intellectuals and free thinkers. We were socialists, anarchists."

"Not I," Yukio said. "I was there to study and to learn—to honor my family and my father."

"Ah yes, a very noble sentiment. I once felt that way myself. But at the university, my eyes were opened. Descartes, Kant, Schopenhauer. 'Dekansho,' we called them. 'Dekansho, Dekansho, half the year we live with them, the other half we sleep.' That was our drinking song. They were difficult, but we persevered because they taught us how to think. Surely you read them too, Kono-kun."

"Yes, of course, but I didn't really understand them. I was more interested in science and mathematics."

"And Marx and Engels?"

"A little. I only read them because it was forbidden. I read the Manifesto in secret," Yukio said with a shy grin. "It was like political pornography."

"Pornography! Shame on you, Kono-kun. But I know what you mean. Reading Marx for the first time is like having a woman for the first time. A whole new world opens up to you. Yes, that was how it was."

Mr. Nakashima went on tell the story of Japanese socialists in America at the turn of the century. "We couldn't get real jobs in America, so we worked as domestic servants for people with no real learning, without a grain of social conscience. But what we wanted was to organize the immigrant Japanese. No easy task. Most of them were peasants. The educated among them came from the petite bourgeoisie—no offense, Kono-kun, but people like your father."

"My father is a learned man," Yukio protested. "And a patriot."

"Exactly. Patriotism. Reverence for the Emperor. Those were our main obstacles. Are you a patriot, Kono-kun?"

Yukio did not reply immediately.

"I, I don't know," he said finally.

"Ah," Mr. Nakashima said, beaming at him. "You don't know. That's progress. If the Japanese in San Francisco had been intelligent and courageous enough to question kokutai, we might have had a chance. The Japanese constitution, the entire Japanese government, you must realize, Kono-kun, is founded on backwardness and superstition."

"Nakashima-san," Yukio said, looking shaken, "If you said such things in Japan, you would be beaten, maybe even killed. Even in Hacienda."

"I know, I know. I know how to be careful. This old fox has learned to see snares in tall grass. But there was a time when I was not so wary. You wanted to know about the poster. Some of us in the Social Revolutionary Party thought we needed to dramatize our cause. Revolutionaries can withstand persecution; we can stand up to physical and verbal attacks. What we cannot stand is being ignored. So we nailed a letter on the door of the Japanese Consulate. We said science shows that all humans are descended from monkeys. The Emperor, too! We are all, therefore, equal. The Emperor and all Japanese! All humans are descendants of monkeys! All the same, all equal, all brothers!"

Yukio and Sammy gasped in unison.

"Yes, calling the Emperor a monkey probably went too far," Mr. Nakashima said, then added with a wicked glint, "even if it is true. When word got out about our letter, the Japanese community was very angry. No—more than angry. We had spat in their faces. We had urinated on the graves of their ancestors. Some toughs, good-for-nothing hoodlums, raided our office soon after. They were gamblers, thieves, men with no moral or social conscience, but they claimed to be outraged by what we had done. I think they were hired by the Japanese Consulate. They beat up two of our comrades who happened to be in the office that day. They set fire to all our books, pamphlets, and leaflets. The only reason that poster on the wall wasn't destroyed in the raid was because it was in my room. It's probably the only one that survived."

After that first visit, Yukio and Sammy dropped by to see Mr. Nakashima several more times, always bringing beer or whisky with them, much to the old man's delight. Yukio in particular was interested in Mr. Nakashima's take on Japanese aggression in China and peace negotiations with the United States. Much to their surprise, the old Marxist defended Japan.

"Japan's imperialism is petty," he insisted. "The imperialism threatening world peace is that of the West—Europe and America."

Several days after the attack on Pearl Harbor, Yukio and Sammy visited Mr. Nakashima to see if he was all right. They were also curious to hear what he might have to say about the war. They found him drunk and slumped on his bed. Empty beer bottles were scattered on the floor, as were his books and papers. Even his beloved poster had been taken down and ripped to pieces. Alarmed, Yukio and Sammy asked him what was wrong. He took a long time to respond.

"The fools," Mr. Nakashima said finally in a soft voice. "A minor power like Japan attacking the United States. We don't have a chance. Japan will be destroyed, utterly and totally destroyed."

Then he put his face in his hands and began to sob. Yukio and Sammy, not knowing what to say, quietly let themselves out of the room.

The next time the brothers saw Mr. Nakashima was the day the Japanese were herded out of Hacienda under military guard. They were astonished but pleased to witness Mr. Nakashima's confrontation with the military policeman on the train. He seemed to have recovered some of his spunk.

In the camp, Mr. Nakashima's behavior turned even more bizarre. He began talking about how he'd heard on an imaginary short-wave radio that Japan was winning the war. When Yukio confronted him about this, he said he was only trying to keep up morale.

"People like your mother are never going to believe that Japan is losing," he said. "They need to have something to believe in."

It was the old labor organizer in him talking. He said he was genuinely worried about what would happen to them, not when Japan won, but when she lost and America had rescued and repatriated her nationals and prisoners of war.

"What will America do then with the Japanese prisoners in these concentration camps? We won't be needed anymore. That's what worries me."

After Yukio's arrest and removal to Tule Lake, Mr. Nakashima became deeply dispirited. He had no one to talk to but Sammy.

"My life has been devoted to bringing down the capitalist system," he mused, "and now I sit here in the middle of a desert, helpless and forgotten. When the war started, agents of American capitalism ignored me. Me! Who had devoted my life to bringing them down! Instead, they arrested Buddhist priests, Japanese-school teachers, shopkeepers, businessmen, rich farmers like your father. They arrested the bourgeoisie—pitifully harmless people. They arrested their own kind!"

The old man's only other activity seemed to be solitary walks in the desert. He would go out wearing a straw hat and carrying a walking stick, a canvas water bag slung over one thin and bony shoulder. It didn't seem to make much difference to him whether it was in the heat of summer or the cold of winter. He had nowhere else to be.

The one other person who provided relief from Sammy's solitude after Yukio, Jack, and Kaz left was Hiroshi. The boy was safe for the moment, apparently happy playing with his friends in his desert playground, but he also loved stories and had a natural and instinctive curiosity that Sammy enjoyed feeding. Hiroshi loved the rhymes and rhythms of poetry, but he also wanted to know what the poems meant, what the poet was trying to say. His latest favorite was Edgar Allen Poe. He liked "Annabel Lee," but Sammy said it was too depressing, so Hiroshi took to reciting "The Raven" instead.

"That's good, Hiro," Sammy said after an especially dramatic reading. "You gave it a lot of feeling."

"I don't get it," Hiroshi said. "Why does the raven keep saying 'Nevermore'?"

"It means the man's never going to be happy again. The raven is fate speaking to him. You know what fate is?"

"Yeah, maybe. What do you think it is?"

"Fate is the same as destiny. What's going to happen is going to happen. We all have our destiny, and we can't change it. We're just stuck with it. It sticks with us forever."

Hiroshi thought about that for a moment. Then he asked, "What's my destiny, Sammy?"

"I don't know. I think maybe you're too young to have a destiny. I think you can still make your own."

"Okay," Hiroshi said, brightening up. "I'm going to be a football star like Mickey."

In the early disorder that had accompanied their dislocation and internment, the children had run about like packs of wild dogs with very little oversight. School days were random, the hours irregular, the days almost indistinguishable. This state of affairs lasted only until the beginning of that first winter, when Mr. Steelmann, the principal, arrived. After that, classes began and ended precisely on time, and strict discipline was imposed—and enforced when needed by a two-foot paddle Mr. Steelmann kept hanging in plain sight on the wall of his office.

Hiroshi was among the first to feel its sting.

Kachi, who lived in Hiroshi's block, had started it. None of boys in the block liked Kachi, who was always picking fights. One day, before school, he said to Hiroshi, "Your brother was a troublemaker. That's why they arrested him. He's a Jap." "He's not," Hiroshi retorted lamely. He wanted to walk away, but Kachi wouldn't let up. "And your other brother's a Jap too. They just didn't arrest him because he's a cripple."

"You take that back," Hiroshi said. "You take that back," he repeated, clenching his fists.

"He is," Kachi said. "He's a hundred percent Jap, just like his crazy friend."

Hiroshi struck Kachi in the face, and soon both were wrestling on the ground. When Mr. Steelmann arrived on the scene, he grabbed Hiroshi under his arms and lifted him off Kachi. Inside the principal's office, Hiroshi refused to say what had caused the fight, as did Kachi. Unfortunately, what Mr. Steelmann had seen was Hiroshi punching Kachi in the face, so Hiroshi was the one who got the paddling. Leaning forward with his arms outstretched on Mr. Steelmann's desk, Hiroshi got six smarting whacks. Kachi smirked at the tears that Hiroshi couldn't stop from welling up. That, for Hiroshi, was a worse punishment than the paddling itself.

Mr. Steelmann was a strict disciplinarian, but he meant well by the children. He established a special mess hall where the elementary school children could eat their lunches. It served more fresh vegetables than the regular mess halls did, and the children were even allowed to go back for second helpings.

He also hired Horse Fukuda to be the physical education teacher for the kids. Horse had gotten his nickname while playing fullback at a junior college in California before the war. "I played against your brother in high school," he told Hiroshi once. "He was a great runner. Too bad he stopped playing."

For gym class, Horse divided the boys into four teams that played football or baseball according to the season: the Seals, the Lions, the Bears, and the Tigers. In memory of Mickey, he had Hiroshi play halfback for the Seals.

Under the prodding of Mr. Steelmann, Horse also started a Cub Scout troop. None of the boys could afford a full uniform, but all of them managed to get the official blue and yellow caps and scarves.

To earn merit badges, the boys would often go out into the desert with a compass and draw maps or identify birds, lizards, and plants. According to Horse, the merit badge awarded for learning how to cook was a particularly important one. So once a week, a team of three or four boys would join Horse at the school mess hall and cook him a breakfast of fried eggs, bacon, and toast. The school mess hall was especially well supplied thanks to Mr. Steelmann's influence, but even there no one ever got bacon and eggs for breakfast.

When it was Hiroshi's turn, he and two other boys served Horse his coffee with cream and sugar as he sat alone at one of the long tables in the mess hall. Horse sipped the coffee carefully, rolling his tongue in his mouth before saying, "Very good."

Coffee was followed by a plate of bacon and eggs fried sunny-side-up, as Horse had requested. The boys were exceedingly proud that they had not broken the yolks. The toast was buttered and served on a separate plate.

Horse lifted the edge of the eggs with his fork to see if it was browned but not burnt. He picked up a piece of bacon delicately with his fingers and bit off an end, chewing it carefully. "Just right," he said, as the boys beamed with pride.

Then, as they watched anxiously, Horse ate his breakfast, making appropriate sounds of approval and dabbing his mouth with the paper towel the boys had placed on the table. After draining the last bit of coffee from his cup, he made a circle with his thumb and index finger, indicating that the boys had passed the test.

"That was good work, boys," he said. "Now all you have to do is wash the dishes and clean up the kitchen."

With that, Horse left the mess with a soft smile on his face, patting his belly. When Hiroshi told Sammy about his new merit badge, Sammy laughed. "Only Horse Fukuda could think up a scam like that," he said.

Hiroshi and his friends remained attached to Horse. Unlike Mickey and his friends in the Loyalty League, Horse would have been happy to stay with the boys, waiting out the war in the camp. But soon he too was gone, drafted into the Army and sent to Italy.

With the arrival of summer, the second since coming to the camp, the tempo of camp life began to slow down as usual. Temperatures could rise to 120 degrees or higher by midday, so Hiroshi and his friends would often go to the canal to cool off. At first, signs had been posted explicitly forbidding any canal-related activities—a boy had drowned the first year they were there. But those signs had long since disappeared. No one wanted to enforce the ban on swimming in the heat of summer.

One day, while swimming and playing by the canal, the boys saw Mr. Nakashima cross the bridge and go to the desert side. As usual, he was carrying a canvas water bag and a gnarled walking stick made of ironwood, something many of the old men in camp were fond of making. He wore a stained and battered straw hat and had wrapped a bandanna around his neck.

The boys didn't think much of the sight. They had seen Mr. Nakashima go off into the desert many times before, and it wasn't unusual for old men to go foraging in the desert for petrified wood, rocks, and rare stones that they would then turn into sculptures, jewelry, and the like. It wasn't until the following morning, when it was discovered that Mr. Nakashima had not returned, that people became alarmed and started forming search parties.

As soon as he heard that Mr. Nakashima had gone missing, Sammy wheeled himself to the bridge over the canal and insisted that Hiroshi help him get across.

"But Sammy, you won't be able to get back by yourself," Hiroshi said.

"Never mind, never mind," Sammy said. "I just want to be on the other side where I can see better. I'm not going far."

People from the block went into the desert on foot, and the administration sent out jeeps, but after three days, they gave up the search. There was no chance that an old man could have survived more than two days alone in the blistering heat.

Sammy took Mr. Nakashima's disappearance especially hard. Hiroshi had taken him across the canal yet again, and the two were looking out at the desert, when Sammy said, as if to himself, that Mr. Nakashima had given him his bag of Bull Durham tobacco and two packs of cigarette paper.

"Why'd he do that?" Hiroshi asked.

"He said he wanted to quit smoking."

Then, after a long silence, Sammy said so softly that Hiroshi barely heard him, "He committed suicide. He never intended to come back."

"How do you know?" Hiroshi asked.

"Mr. Nakashima had nothing left to live for. He thought his life was finished. He knew Japan was losing the war. He didn't really want Japan to win, but he didn't want America to win either. He was in a quandary. Do you know what a quandary is?"

Sammy often said things that Hiroshi couldn't fully understand. It was almost as if he were talking to someone else—

or maybe to himself.

"A quandary, Hiro, is when there's no right answer, when there's no place to go, when there's no hope, no future."

It frightened Hiroshi to hear Sammy talk like that, so he said, "Sammy, you want me to roll a cigarette for you? I know how to do it."

"You shouldn't be smoking," Sammy said. "It's bad for you. But you can get me some matches. Ask Father for some. Tell him it's for me."

Okay," Hiroshi said. Relieved that he could do something for his brother, he ran to their barracks.

By the following winter, Mr. Nakashima had been forgotten by everyone except maybe Sammy, who kept the bag of Bull Durham his friend had given him in his pocket even after it was empty.

On Christmas Eve, Mother sent Hiroshi out to check on Sammy, who was sitting by the canal as he liked to do even in the cold of winter. There weren't many Christians in the camp. Like the Konos, most of the families were Buddhist, but the children liked to celebrate Christmas regardless.

Sammy assured Hiroshi that he was fine and declined Hiroshi's offer to push him to the mess hall for the holiday celebrations. Sammy wished Hiroshi a Merry Christmas and told him to go and have a good time.

When Hiroshi entered the mess hall, he immediately recognized Mr. Tanaka, the head cook, even though he was dressed as Santa Claus and wore cotton wool over his face. The children, who had been served hot cocoa and cookies, were in the midst of singing "Jingle Bells" when a bright flash of light illuminated the room, followed by a loud crack of thunder that sounded like a cannon shot. The storm was close by; lightening had struck a tall saguaro cactus just outside of camp. A massive downpour immediately followed, with water gushing down from the sky as if a huge dam had burst. The drainage ditches were already overflowing, and the street looked like a rushing river.

Dry and warm inside the mess hall, no one paid much attention to the tumult outside. After the storm subsided, the children were given presents of crayons, coloring books, dolls, toy cars, and trucks. The afternoon ended with a singing of "Silent Night."

When Hiroshi returned to his barracks, Mother asked him if Sammy had been at the mess hall.

"Isamu didn't want to go," Hiroshi said helplessly. "He wanted to stay by the canal."

Father and Hiroshi went to the canal, but could find no sign of Sammy. They checked the shower house, the laundry room, and the mess hall, knocking on doors everywhere. But no one had seen Sammy. The next day, Sammy's wheelchair was found washed up on the banks of the canal; Sammy was nowhere to be seen. When they heard the news, Father and Mother huddled together, weeping in a way Hiroshi had never before seen. Father seemed to think it was his fault that Sammy was gone. "I could have hired tutors," he said. "His body was broken, but his mind was strong and sharp. He was the brightest of my sons."

Five days later, an Indian goatherd discovered what they presumed to be Sammy's body in an arroyo several miles south of the camp. The remains were so decomposed, however, it was impossible to make a positive identification. The body was cremated, so what Hiroshi saw at the funeral was a black box hardly big enough to hold a cantaloupe. Father and Mother cried over the box, but Hiroshi refused to believe Sammy was inside. He thought that Sammy, in concert with Mr. Nakashima, had staged a clever escape. He imagined them laughing together somewhere and smoking Bull Durham cigarettes.

The following summer, the end of the war was declared and the camp started to empty out. Indian families began to move into barracks that had been abandoned by the Japanese, using the pigpens and the coops for their own livestock, which consisted mostly of chickens and goats.

At first only old people and very young children moved in. Later, young men appeared as well; they could be heard at night shouting what to Hiroshi sounded like war chants. But they were all friendly—well-disposed, it seemed, toward the Japanese.

One old man with long white flowing hair, a high, sharp nose, and withered brown skin seemed to enjoy talking to the Japanese children. It was a mutual fascination. The Japanese boys had never seen actual Indians before, and the old man, who wore jeans and a flannel shirt, looked nothing like what they'd seen in movies. The Indians, in their turn, had never seen Japanese before either. But they seemed to feel at ease with the Japanese, perhaps because they were also brown and sun burnt.

The old man, whom the Hiroshi and his friends took to be the chief, seemed to know that the Japanese in the camp were prisoners of the white man. When asked, he told the boys his young warriors were indeed practicing war chants. "The white man," he said, "has stolen our land. One day, there will be a great war, and we will have our land back."

As he listened to the chief talk, Hiroshi thought he understood the old man's feelings. Over the past three years, the desert had become Hiroshi's home. Hacienda seemed very far away to him, both in terms of time and distance, and he didn't want to go back. In his imagination, he could see himself as an Indian brave, fighting to establish once and for all his ownership of this vast territory.

But the desert was not where he belonged, and these were not his people. The ancient land was being reclaimed by its rightful inhabitants. After three years spent there, he would soon be set free, but he'd become a rootless stranger, like the bonsai his father was fond of, trees made portable by cutting their roots. There was nowhere for him to go—not to Japan, and certainly not to Hacienda, which had expelled him. It was more than a quandary with impossible choices—he had no choices at all.

That night, Hiroshi dreamt of Sammy and Mr. Nakashima lying together on the desert sand. He was there with them, looking up at the glistening night sky, which seemed like an enormous black-lacquered bowl thickly speckled with granules of gold and silver. The light from the stars was so bright it brought tears to his eyes, and he had to blink them away. The sand and gravel on which he lay was still warm from the sun, but the air was getting cold; he could feel the chill of the wind against his cheek. He looked to the sky once more. The stars that had glittered so brightly were beginning to fade as dark clouds rolled in. Along the periphery of his vision, he thought he could see shadows circling, so he snuggled closer to Sammy. The specters seemed to go away, but he didn't dare to look into the darkness again, so deep and impenetrable was the utter blackness that now surrounded them. He reached for the water bag, holding it close to his chest. Moisture was seeping out of its pores in an ever-growing stream. Soon the water was gushing out, becoming a raging torrent as he lay helpless with Sammy and Mr. Nakashima, melting into the desert floor.

RAMON

1945 - 1946

In August of 1945, Hiroshi and his parents returned to Hacienda and moved into a house behind an empty storefront. Their former home had been mysteriously destroyed by fire during their absence, and since the insurance on it had lapsed due to failure to pay premiums, it had been a total loss. Father's farms, all leased, were gone, as was the packinghouse, which had been a major source of his wealth. After Father's arrest and the expulsion of his family, the bank had foreclosed on the packinghouse, auctioning it off at a fraction of its worth. Less than seven hundred dollars remained in Father's account after the bank, his partners, and lawyers took their share of the proceeds, but it was enough for the family to survive on until they could find work.

Before the war, the house and storefront had been rented to Mr. Matsutaka, the grocer, but he and his family had chosen not to return to Hacienda. The house consisted of two small bedrooms with cracked and splintered pinewood floors. The kitchen, with its peeling linoleum, was barely big enough for a card table and three chairs; a fourth room, no bigger than the kitchen, served as a parlor. At night, rats stampeded across the ceiling on tiny clawed feet while the strong night winds made the house groan and sway on its wooden supports As they settled into their new home, Mother wondered aloud how the Matsutakas and their four children could have lived in such a small and miserable dwelling. But if Father felt any embarrassment or shame at their reduced circumstances, he didn't show it

Before the war, the Konos had been a family of seven; only Hiroshi and his parents had returned to Hacienda. Yukio, married to Kaz, was in Arizona with the Kubotas working as a gardner. Mickey, out of the Army and also married, was living in Los Angles and helping his father-in-law reopen his Little Tokyo restaurant. Sachi was still attending college in Minnesota.

Hiroshi knew that his siblings had their reasons for not returning home, but he felt abandoned and betrayed nonetheless. He spent his nights sulking, bearing as best he could the dark and bitter weight of loneliness.

In September, Hiroshi was once again enrolled in the Hacienda Elementary School. That first year, he was the only Japanese boy in school. Most Japanese families were not able to or chose not to return to Hacienda so soon after the war. One of the white boys whom Hiroshi had known before the war had a fondness for speaking loudly in his presence about how his brother, a Marine, had "killed a lot of Japs" in the Pacific. Once, on the playground, this same boy called out to their teacher Mr. Brady, also an ex-Marine: "Hey, Mr. Brady, how many Japs did you kill in the war?" The teacher didn't respond, but he turned his head toward Hiroshi with a look of cold indifference. A newcomer to Hacienda, Mr. Brady might not have been used to Japanese people; Hiroshi once overheard him talking to Mr. Nash, the principal, about "the

Jap kid" in his class. But he never hit or slapped Hiroshi as he sometimes did the other kids, especially the Mexicans. He just never called on him or looked at him. The students mostly ignored him as well.

With the first frost that came with winter, a Mexican boy named Ramon suddenly appeared on the scene. The white kids, who ordinarily paid no attention to Mexicans, seemed to know enough about Ramon to keep a wary distance from him. He had been in reform school, they said, and was the son of Pedro Diaz, an ax murderer doing time at the California State Prison in Soledad.

Ramon looked too old to be in the seventh grade. He had broad, muscular shoulders that gave him a squat appearance and a square, slightly awkward gait that Hiroshi associated with sumo wrestlers. His face, with its brownish yellow cast, was that of a full-blooded Indian: broad, protruding cheekbones, a sharp, angular nose, and dark unblinking eyes. His thick hair, which swooped down across his narrow forehead, shone like ebony. To Hiroshi, whose mind was filled with images from books and movies, Ramon looked like an Apache.

Hiroshi's first encounter with Ramon came in shop class. They met in the narrow aisle dividing the power tools. Ramon stood in Hiroshi's way, gave him a slight push with an open hand, and, looking directly into his eyes, said: "You dirty yellow Jap."

His words were steady and measured. Though he spoke softly, Hiroshi heard him clearly above the whine of the band saw and the crunching-whirring of the drill press. The other boys stopped their work, and the shop got very quiet. Hiroshi was almost as tall as Ramon, but he was skinny and, at twelve, still a boy. Ramon was as hard and dangerous as a hatchet. Hiroshi stepped aside and squeezed by him. The other boys resumed their work. No one had expected him to fight Ramon; that would have been madness.

After their encounter in the shop class, Ramon seemed to lose interest in Hiroshi and in everyone else. He wandered about alone during recess and lunch like a wolf on the prowl, usually walking the far edges of the school grounds. Sometimes he could be seen smoking a cigarette. He didn't bring a lunch to school like the other students, and he was never seen eating. No one, not even the Mexican kids, made any attempt to befriend him. They just nodded their heads at his solitary figure and made what sounded like derisive comments. Hiroshi didn't understand Spanish, but he could sense what sounded like scorn in their voices.

In class, Ramon sat at the rear of the room gazing out the windows or, when the teacher insisted, looking straight ahead, his unblinking black eyes directed at the blackboard without seeing anything. Once, as he took his usual place, he looked over to Hiroshi, who sat two seats away, also at the rear of the class. Hiroshi started to turn away, but he saw that Ramon was not being unfriendly and only wanted so say something. But just at that moment, the teacher called the class to order, so no words were spoken.

One day in May, when the school year was nearly over, Hiroshi was sitting alone as usual, eating his lunch in the eucalyptus grove, when Ramon strolled by. He stopped in front of Hiroshi and stood gazing into the distance at the hazy outlines of the Tehachapi Mountains.

Then, suddenly, as if noticing Hiroshi just at that moment, he said, "Hey, whattaya eatin'?"

"Egg sandwich."

"Yeh? You like that shit?"

Hiroshi didn't respond.

"Hey, hombre," Ramon said. "I didn't mean nothin' when I called you a Jap."

Ramon stood awkwardly in front of Hiroshi, his hands deep in his frayed pants pockets, shuffling his feet. He didn't seem like the dangerous, prowling bully he had tried to be before. Hiroshi, still cautious, only said, "That's okay," hoping the boy would go away. But Ramon continued to hover over him—not menacingly, more like a looming shadow. Mainly to break the awkward silence, Hiroshi said, "You want some of my sandwich?"

Ramon laughed happily, like a boy being offered candy, but he managed to get a hold of himself and, squaring his shoulders, said in his tough-guy voice, "Shit. I ain't goin' to eat your lunch."

"Maybe you want my orange," Hiroshi said.

"Naw," Ramon said. Then, suddenly, he turned and walked away.

After that, Ramon would often walk by during lunch and say, "Hey, man, howya doin'?" Sometimes he would sit next to Hiroshi, but he always refused Hiroshi's offer to share his lunch. All he wanted was for Hiroshi to listen to him expound on how much he hated the school and everybody in it, especially the principal, Mr. Nash.

"That gringo sonafabitch used to beat me with a fucking stick. Then he sent me to Lompoc. Shit, I wanted to stay there. I never wanted to come back to this fucking place."

Hiroshi didn't ask Ramon what he had done to deserve a beating, but he knew that Mr. Nash and the teachers were especially rough on the Mexican kids. The principal kept a two-foot long paddle hanging on his office wall just as Mr. Steelmann had done in the camp school.

Mr. Brady, the newcomer, was meaner than Mr. Nash ever was. He slapped Mexican boys if they swore in Spanish, just to let them know he understood. "You think I don't understand? Huh?" he would growl as he slapped their heads. "Huh?" Then, for good measure, he would slap them again with a full swing of his arm.

Other boys, even white kids, sometimes got slapped just for sneaking a comic book into class or for talking too much, so Hiroshi could well believe that Ramon had gotten his share of beatings.

"Why'd they send you to reform school?" Hiroshi asked.

"I kicked him. I kicked him in the balls."

"Mr. Brady? You kicked Mr. Brady?"

"Naw, man. Not Brady. Nash. I kicked the shit outta that gringo sonafabitch."

Hiroshi didn't believe him, but it became a private joke between them. Whenever Mr. Nash was seen at the school, Ramon would wink at Hiroshi and a make a kicking motion with his right foot. Sometimes, if no one else was looking, he would put his hands between his legs, tilt his head, and pout at the sky as if howling in pain. Hiroshi had to laugh in spite of himself.

The two outcasts seemed to be developing a guarded relationship that approached friendship, but when school let out for the summer, Ramon dropped out of sight. Hiroshi wondered whether his disappearance had anything to do with the newspaper reports that his father, Pedro Diaz, had escaped from prison. In his imagination, Hiroshi saw Diaz trudging toward Hacienda dragging a blood-stained ax. But as the weeks passed, nothing more was heard of either father or son.

Late one afternoon toward the end of August, as summer vacation was coming to a close, Hiroshi was on his back porch adjusting the chain on his bicycle when he heard someone shout, "Hey, whattaya doin'?"

He looked up to see Ramon leaning on the three-foot-high fence that separated their backyard from the road. Ramon leapt over the fence and came up to Hiroshi.

"That your bike?"

Hiroshi nodded.

"I know all about bikes," Ramon said. "I used to take them apart all the time. I can take any bike apart."

Ramon grabbed the pedal of the bike, which was turned upside down on the porch, and began spinning the rear wheel. He put his ear next to the sprocket. "Hear that?" he said. "It needs to be greased. They put me in the bike shop up there. There ain't nothin' I don't know about a bike."

Hiroshi assumed Ramon was talking about the reform school, but he didn't ask.

Ramon took up the wrench Hiroshi had laid aside and started loosening the bolt on the rear wheel.

"Hey, don't," Hiroshi said.

"You got some newspaper?" Ramon said. "Get some newspaper. You don't want to get your parts dirty."

Feeling uneasy, Hiroshi got up and went inside. The only newspaper in the house was the *Rafu Shimpo,* which Father had delivered from Los Angeles. When he returned, Ramon was disassembling the sprocket.

"What're ya doin'?" Hiroshi said.

"Give me the newspaper," Ramon said. "What's this? Japanese? Hey, hombre, can you read this? Caramba. That's pretty hard shit."

"Put it back together," Hiroshi said as Ramon spread the parts out on the newspaper: nuts, bolts, washers, gears, ball bearings, springs, rings, cylinders. Hiroshi had no idea a bicycle had so many parts.

"What's that say there?" Ramon said, pointing a greasy finger at one of the headlines.

"I don't know. I can't read it. It's my father's newspaper."

"Yeah? Your old man can read that?" Ramon shook his head slowly from side to side. Turning again to the bicycle, he said, "You got any gasoline? And grease. I need grease, too."

Hiroshi wanted to say, "Why would I have gasoline and grease in my house?" But he only scrunched his face.

Ignoring him, Ramon got to his feet and said, "I'll be back. Don't touch nothin'." Then he ran across the yard, leapt over the fence, and disappeared.

Hiroshi looked despondently at his bicycle, now spread out in pieces on the newspaper. Ramon had pulled a mean and nasty trick; he had no intention of coming back. His parents had always said you had to be careful with Mexicans. Even so, he waited for Ramon to return. After a while, he tried putting the parts together, but it was a hopelessly intricate piece of machinery. He was trying to fit a ring of ball bearings into a socket when he heard a noise and, looking up, saw Ramon put a tin can on the crossbeam of the fence before clambering awkwardly over holding what looked like a piece of paper in one hand. Ramon was smiling broadly as he came up to Hiroshi.

"Mira," he said. The tin can was half full of gasoline. On the ragged piece of brown paper he was carrying was a dab of axle grease.

"Where'd you get that?" Hiroshi said.

Ramon smiled and winked.

"Did you steal it?"

"Naw, I know the mechanic over at the Shell station. I help him all the time with the cars."

Hiroshi knew he was lying. "You stole it," he said. He looked toward the fence, expecting to see someone chasing after Ramon.

Unconcerned, Ramon picked up the half-assembled parts. "Hey, I told you not to touch. You have to know what you're doin'. You can't just mess around with this stuff. Why'd you try to put it back together without me?"

Hiroshi shrugged.

"You thought I wasn't coming back?" Ramon glared at him, looking hurt.

Hiroshi remained silent.

"Aaww," Ramon said and spat. "You have to wash off all the parts real good in gasoline. You got a rag? Get me a rag."

When Hiroshi returned with an old sock, Ramon was stirring the parts in the tin can with his finger. "You gotta clean the parts off real good," he said. After wiping the parts dry, he started greasing them and fitting them back together. As he worked, he kept saying over and over, "There ain't nothin' I don't know about a bike."

The sprocket was reassembled with amazing speed. After

putting the chain back in place, Ramon turned the pedal. It was tight, and the sprocket made a clicking sound. He loosened the bolt on the rear wheel to give the chain more slack, but the wheel remained tight, and the clicking seemed even louder.

"That's nothin'. I can fix that," Ramon said, "but you might have a bad part. I can't do nothin' 'bout a bad part."

Hiroshi cursed himself silently for allowing Ramon to touch his bike; he should have somehow stopped him.

The sun had sunk low behind the woods at the back of the town. It was starting to get dark, and Hiroshi knew that his mother and father would be coming home from work soon. He didn't want Ramon to be there when they did.

"You better hurry up," he said.

Ramon looked up at him from his squatting position; he had that impassive Cochise look on his face again. "Don't worry," he said.

Ramon had just finished reassembling the sprocket for the second time when Hiroshi's parents came home.

Mother, her delicate face smudged with dirt, wore a wide-brimmed straw hat tied at her chin with a dish-cloth. At 53, her figure remained slim and upright, but her work clothes hung loosely from shoulders, making her look like a scarecrow. She had always been graceful in her movements, but after a long day of stoop labor thinning lettuce or harvesting celery, she waddled painfully from side to side.

Father wore a flannel shirt and a baggy, patched-up pair of suit pants. He also wore an old fedora, now shapeless and stained, a remnant of former times when he had a closet full of fine hats and tailor-made suits from Los Angeles. He did his best to walk upright and tall, and he kept his mustache carefully trimmed, but at 62, his body was stiff and sore. Because he was unable to hoe a long row bent from the waist like the others, Mother had sewn padding inside his pants legs so he could shuffle along on his knees.

Before the war, Father had operated three farms totaling a thousand acres. He had called them "ranches," a hangover from the days when Mexicans had ruled the California landscape. In the early days, Father had gone around on horseback like a ranchero, instructing his Mexican work gangs. As he aged and prospered, he took to driving around in a big Chrysler and dressing in three-piece suits, his gold watch on a chain that looped from his vest pocket. He bought his shiny, pointed shoes from the best stores in Los Angeles. But the war had changed all that.

"What is the Meshikan doing here?" Father asked, speaking in Japanese.

"He's fixing my bicycle."

"Fixing the bicycle." Father repeated, twisting the words tightly in his mouth. It was not a question, but a command.

"Hai," Hiroshi said, meaning he would get rid of Ramon as soon as possible.

When Father and Mother had disappeared into the house, Hiroshi turned to Ramon and said, "I think you better go now."

Somehow, Ramon understood; he was preparing to leave even before Hiroshi spoke. "All you have to do is put the chain back on," he said. "Put a little grease on it. You can do that."

Then he left.

Hiroshi replaced the chain and cranked the pedal; the wheel was too tight and the clicking was still there. He adjusted the slack and greased the chain, but nothing helped.

Going inside, Hiroshi heard Father in the bath, a daily pre-dinner routine for him. He was drizzling stinging hot water over himself with a wash-cloth and chanting about Akechi Mistuhide, the tragic grand usurper. He had already reached the climactic scene in which Mitsuhide, blinded by the steam of a bathhouse, mistakes his mother for an assassin and kills her with his spear.

"*Aaaaaaah,*" he howled. Hiroshi recognized the anguished cry of Mitsuhide, who only now realizes his error.

For as long as he could remember, Hiroshi had heard his father practicing joruri, the narrative chanting of classical Japanese puppetry, but since their return, these grisly scenes of death and mayhem had become a nightly ritual: sons killing mothers, fathers killing sons, lovers stabbing one another, gory tales of internecine warfare.

After his bath, Father had a shot of whisky with his beer. Before the war, he had rarely drunk whisky and beer, but these days, he drank both regularly. They were cheaper than sake, and, in the case of whisky, more potent.

Mother had prepared beef stew for dinner. These days, they often ate American food. Mother would cook the meals the night before and heat them up when they came home from the fields.

Like Father, she also bathed before dinner and was fastidious about her appearance. She would change into the one silk dress she still owned, a black one with white lace around the neck and sleeves. She would wear a string of pearls that had survived the war, and sometimes even apply a faint touch of rouge to her cheeks and lips. She was still beautiful—delicate and fair—even if her movements now lacked the smooth grace she had once possessed.

Despite her weariness, she always managed to put flowers in the parlor; in winter, she would create an arrangement of branches, dried flowers, or cattails.

Father did not bother putting on a coat or tie for dinner, but he, too, remained the same in many ways.

"Who was the Meshikan?" he asked Hiroshi.

"His name is Diaz."

"Diaz?" Mother said. "He couldn't be Diaz's son, could he?"

"Diaz had two sons," Father said. "He could be the younger one."

"Who's Diaz?" Hiroshi asked.

"He worked for me before the war at the Oso Flaco ranch. For a Meshikan, he was a good worker, reliable when sober. That's why I made him foreman and let him live on the ranch. But when he had money, he drank. And when he drank, he lost control. He ended up killing a man in a fight. He stabbed him with a knife."

"At school, they say he killed a man with an ax," Hiroshi said.

"An ax?" Father laughed. "When the police came, he threatened them with an ax. I was there. There were two policemen, both with guns drawn. They would have killed him if his wife had not persuaded him to put the ax down."

"Wasn't it because of his wife that he killed the man?" Mother asked.

"Unh," Father said. "The dead man was her lover, a worthless drifter. After they sent Diaz to prison, I let her and her children stay at the ranch rent-free."

A few days later, when Hiroshi was polishing his shoes on his back porch, Ramon came by again. He avoided looking at the bicycle leaning against the house no more than six feet away. "Hey, whattaya doin'?" he asked.

Hiroshi was tempted to say, "What do you think I'm doing?" but he simply said, "Hey, Ramon. How you doing?"

"You going some place?" Ramon asked.

Hiroshi shook his head.

"I was in Pismo last night," Ramon said, "at a whorehouse. You ever been to a whorehouse? No? You never had a piece of ass? Hombre, I'm going to take you to Pismo sometime. I know all the whores up there. I could get you a piece for five bucks. You got five bucks?"

Hiroshi shook his head.

"That's okay," Ramon said. "When I get some money, I'll take you. Okay?"

"Okay," Hiroshi said.

They sat silently for some time. Ramon stared out toward the woods as Hiroshi busied himself with his shoes.

The woods extended for miles to the west of Hacienda. Before the war, Hiroshi and his friends had been forbidden by their parents to go there because it was marshy and possibly dangerous. They did so anyway, though they never ventured very far into it.

"You ever go out there in the woods?" Ramon asked.

"Before the war, I did."

"There are mountain lions out there," Ramon said. "They come down from the mountains."

"No there aren't."

"Yeah, I caught one. And there's quicksand. I got stuck in quicksand once and my brother had to pull me out. I was down to my chest when he threw me a rope. Then he couldn't pull me out, so he had to get his pickup. By then I was down to my neck. I was almost a goner."

"Where's your brother now?"

"Tony? He's around. You know, he knows your father. He worked for him before the war. Tony says your father was a cheap guy, made him and my mother work and didn't pay them nothin'. They had to shovel shit out of the stable every day and your old man never paid them one centavo."

"That why you wanted to fight?"

Ramon looked at him with a puzzled expression. Then he laughed.

"Naw. I just wanted to start a fight. I wanted to get out of that school. I thought maybe they'd send me back to Lompoc."

"Reform school? You liked it at the reform school?"

"It wasn't so bad. You just gotta show them right away that they can't push you around. I got a lotta amigos up there. But you didn't wanna fight. Shit, hombre, I wouldn't have hurt you. Not too bad anyway. Maybe just a little. You know."

He jabbed a fist at Hiroshi's eye and laughed.

Hiroshi was getting annoyed with Ramon, so he said, "There aren't any mountain lions in those woods. That's bullshit."

"You don't believe me? Hey, I'll take you out there. You got a rope? Get a rope. A long one. I'll show you how to catch a mountain lion. I did it once before. You want to? Tomorrow maybe?"

Hiroshi shrugged. He had finished polishing his shoes, and Father and Mother would be coming home soon. "I gotta go inside," he said.

"Okay," Ramon said. "I'll see you tomorrow morning." He trotted toward the fence, leapt over it, and was gone.

When Hiroshi's parents came home, Father, as usual, was the first to enter the bath. Soon, his chanting was resonating through the thin walls of the house. He was still stuck on the tale of the grand usurper. He would often work on a particular piece for weeks, even for months, before switching to another one—almost as if rehearsing for a performance.

"*Yaaaaah!*" Father shouted. Akechi Mitsuhide was looking down on his enemies from the balcony of his castle. The tortured cry contained the agony of Mitsuehide's defeat and his fury over the fickleness of his fate.

"*Shan-shan-rin, shan-shan-rin. Shan-shan-rin-sha. Shan-shan-rin...*" Father sang, simulating the furious strumming of the shamisen that was meant to bring the action to a fever pitch. Standing on a balcony, Mitsuhide bares his body. With a fierce cry of defiance, he rips open his belly with his sword, spilling his guts onto the heads of his enemies below...

Hiroshi was helping his mother set the table for dinner.

"Mother," he said, "did Father make Diaz's wife clean out the stable and not pay her?"

"Who told you that?"

"Diaz's boy."

"Saah," Mother said. It was her way of not answering a question. A glint in her eyes warned Hiroshi to let the matter drop.

Hiroshi kept setting the table in silence, but the words came bursting out of him, almost on their own: "I think it was wrong. Father should have paid her."

"Hiroshi," Mother said, looking directly into his eyes. "I don't know whether he paid her or not, but you must not trouble your father with such trivial matters."

"But Mother, it wasn't fair. Before the war, some people said that we were too rich, and that Father wasn't fair to his workers."

Mother turned her head and quickly wiped a tear from her cheek. Hiroshi was alarmed.

"Mother, what's the matter?"

"How can you say such a thing?" Mother said. "Your father did more for the people of Hacienda than anybody. Only a few ungrateful people whispered lies about him."

"I know, but Father should have paid Ramon's mother."

"Stop it!" she shouted. "How can you say such things? Can't you see what has happened? Why do you think I dress every evening, fix my hair? Why do you think I bother with flowers in this miserable place? I want your father to remember the man he once was, the wealthiest, the most important man in Hacienda. Have some pity, Hiroshi. Don't trouble your father with trivialities about a lowly Meshikan woman!"

Hiroshi had never heard Mother speak of others in such a way before. Nor had he ever heard her speak of his father with such passion. She had always treated Father with great respect, but now there was something more than respect in her voice— something more than pity as well.

"I'm sorry, Mother," he said. "I'm sure Father paid Diaz's wife. The Diaz boy lies." When his mother did not respond, he added: "I will not speak of it again, Mother."

His mother, daubing her eyes, only nodded.

The next day, Hiroshi was alone in the house once again when he heard a knock on the door. Opening it, he saw Ramon standing there with a rope coiled around his shoulder. "Come on," he said. "I'll show you how to catch a mountain lion."

"I can't. My mother wants me to stay home and clean the house."

"Clean the house? Hombre, that's for girls. Come on."

What Ramon said was true. Mother never asked Hiroshi to do housework. "I'm not feeling so good." Hiroshi said. "I think I'm getting sick."

Ramon laughed. "You're scared. Look, you don't have to be scared. I'll show you how to catch 'em."

"I'm not scared. And that's a lotta bullshit. There aren't any mountain lions out there. I used to go out there before the war."

"Yeah? You think it's bullshit? Come on then. I'll show you. Come on, if you're not scared."

They entered the woods where it bordered the road and made their way toward the west.

"Hey, keep your eyes on the top of the trees!" Ramon shouted. "Mountain lions climb on trees, and they'll jump on you if you don't watch out."

The woods were full of birches, and the sun off the white bark was dazzling. Hiroshi had to squint and shade his eyes as he peered into the branches. As they walked deeper into the woods, they saw oaks and maples with large, overhanging branches that could easily have supported a mountain lion.

"You gotta look real good," Ramon said. "Sometimes they're hard to see because they lie flat. They look like part of the tree. Hey, look! There's one."

"Where?"

"Up there!" Ramon said. He pointed to the top of a giant maple. The sun glinting through the leaves made wavering shadows. They looked intently, shading their eyes.

"Naw, I guess not," Ramon said finally. "Hey, but sure looks like it! A big fat mama lion."

Hiroshi had to agree that it did look as if a large animal,

partly obscured by the leaves, was crouching on a branch about two-thirds of the way up the tree.

"Just in case, we better not walk underneath," Ramon said, and they moved some distance from the trunk, keeping a sharp eye overhead.

Later in the day, when Hiroshi stepped into a marshy area, Ramon said it was quicksand and that he shouldn't move. The water came only to his ankles and he wasn't sinking any deeper, but by then Hiroshi was enjoying the game.

"The more you move, the faster it'll suck you in," Ramon said.

He threw one end of the rope and instructed Hiroshi to tie it under his arms. He tied the other end to a tree just to be safe. Then, planting his feet firmly on dry ground, he slowly pulled Hiroshi out of the marsh.

"It's a good thing I brought the rope," he said.

As they were making their way back out of the woods, they came to a barbed wire fence surrounding a pasture. Ramon immediately ducked through the strands of wire and looked back at Hiroshi, who remained standing on the other side.

"Come on," he said. "Whattaya waitin' for?"

"There used to be a bull in there. We should go around."

"A bull? Look, you see a bull anyplace? Come on, don't be scared."

Ramon held the strands of barbed wire apart with his foot and hands and cocked his head at Hiroshi, so Hiroshi reluctantly crawled into the pasture.

The part of the pasture they had to cross was more than two hundred yards wide. To the north, it extended to the woods, where it was shaded by large, overhanging trees.

As they walked, Ramon handed the coiled rope to Hiroshi and took off his t-shirt. He held it with both hands to the side of his body.

"Like this," he said. "That's how the bullfighters do it. You make the bull go for the cape. They're dumb. You can fool them easy."

They were more than halfway across the pasture, with Ramon swinging his t-shirt in both hands and shouting "Toro! Toro!" and prancing about like a matador, when Hiroshi saw the bull, a big black one, loping toward them from the far end of the pasture.

"The bull!" Hiroshi shouted.

"Holy shit!" Ramon said.

As they ran for the fence, the bull quickened its pace and began charging at a full gallop. They were still fifty yards from the fence when the bull began closing in on them.

"Split up!" Ramon shouted, and he started swinging his t-shirt to draw the bull in his direction. The boys ran in a V pattern toward the fence, with the bull following Ramon, who began to zigzag. This seemed to slow the animal. Then Ramon stumbled and fell. When Hiroshi saw his friend rolling in the grass to avoid the charging bull, he ran toward them, waving his arms and shouting, "Toro! Toro! Ha! Ha!" This confused the bull long enough to allow Ramon to get to his feet. He and Hiroshi both sprinted for the fence and dove through the strands of barbed wire. The bull, thwarted and infuriated, remained on the other side, snorting and stomping its feet, its mouth frothing, the whites of its eyes showing all around.

The boys lay on the grass, gasping for breath and laughing.

"Caramba!" Ramon said, "That was a close one, amigo. You saved my life."

"No, you saved my life."

"Amigo, you!"

"No, you!"

The bull stood only a few feet beyond the fence until his fury subsided. Then, with a parting snort, he turned and made his way back to his accustomed haunt.

It was mid-afternoon, and the sun blazed overhead as Hiroshi and Ramon lay side by side on the warm grass, laughing and slapping the ground as they recalled and embroidered the tale of their narrow escape.

"The bull was sticking his horn up my ass," Ramon said.

"Yeah, but I pulled his tail."

"I grabbed his horns. The bull didn't know which way to go."

As they talked, a breeze scented with the fragrances of the sun-warmed meadow wafted across their sweating bodies. Ramon chewed on a blade of grass as he gazed into the sky, shading his eyes with his hands. Meanwhile, Hiroshi lay with one arm flung across his eyes, a happy smile on his lips. His shirt was in shreds from the barbed wire, his pants were torn, and he had scrapes all over. He'd have to make up some kind of a story about it for his mother, but he'd worry about that later. Ramon had a long scratch on his chest, but it wasn't deep, and it hardly bled at all.

"Ramon," Hiroshi said after a while, "I dropped your rope. It's still in there."

"Go get it, then."

"You crazy? I told you there was a bull in there."

"Hombre, that's no bull. That's a pussy cat."

They both laughed, pounding the grass with their fists.

"Doesn't matter," Ramon said. "I swiped it anyway."

That was the last time Hiroshi saw Ramon. When school started again two weeks later, Ramon was not there. Hiroshi hoped he had not been sent back to the reform school in Lompoc. He never really believed that Ramon liked it there.

Later that week, a story appeared in the Santa Marguerita *Gazette.* Pedro Diaz, convicted murderer and escapee from Soledad, had killed his wife and her lover. The story said he had bludgeoned the two to death with a hammer. There was no mention of Ramon or his brother Tony.

There was a lot of talk at school about the murder trial, but no one ever knew for sure what happened to Ramon. One of the

Mexican boys said Ramon died after being mauled by a bear in the Oso Flaco region. Another said he was at Pismo Beach working as a pimp for a whorehouse. Hiroshi wasn't sure what a pimp was, but that was just the kind of story Ramon would make up. After a time, the kids stopped talking about Ramon, and everyone seemed to forget about him. But Hiroshi thought of him whenever he rode his bicycle, which was never quite the same after Ramon messed with it. The rear wheel loosened up after a while, and the bike seemed to ride more smoothly, but the clicking never stopped.

THE FOX

1947 - 1950

Even before the war, the 10-mile ride from Hacienda to Santa
Marguerita had been an ordeal. Father would often insist on
taking Hiroshi on this road when he went to inspect his farms; it
was his way of showing paternal affection. But Hiroshi had never
liked traveling in the big Chrysler. It stank of cigars. Now, gazing
out the windows of the school bus, the gray, flat monotony of
fallow autumn fields gave Hiroshi's eyes no place to rest. He could
smell the rot left over from the harvest even through the closed
windows.

Hiroshi imagined the passage from Hacienda to Santa
Marguerita as being like the crossing of the Rio Grande—the
muddy huts of Mexican peasants replaced by the clipped lawns
and grassy estates of the gringos. Santa Marguerita High School
was a cloistered adobe building covered by a red-tiled roof and
surrounded by tall, graceful elms, broad lawns, sculptured

boxwood bushes, and well-tended flower beds. Inside, the buildings boasted vaulted ceilings, terracotta floors, heavy oaken doors, and leaded casement windows. All the teachers and nearly all the students were hakujin.

For Hiroshi, Santa Marguerita had always seemed an alien land touched with enchantment and danger. But Hacienda was no longer a familiar haven, either. Its once bustling Japanese colony, with its Buddhist temple, language school, drugstore, fish market, and doctor and dentist offices, had disappeared. The few Japanese who had crept back to Hacienda after the war formed a shadowy half presence on the fringes of the community.

Like everything else, the ryoria restaurants were gone, so on his days off, Father would drink at home, chanting endless rounds of joruri—stories of fallen and hunted heroes, of murder and vengeance, of demons and foxes that took human form.

When Hiroshi commented on Father's whisky drinking to his mother, she shouted at him, "How dare you criticize your father! Don't you see what has happened to him?"

Hiroshi barely recognized the gentle woman who used to lie beside him and sing to him about hares and tortoises and mischievous monkeys in a soft, lilting voice. In the past, he and his mother had spent many long evenings alone together. Now Father was always home, and his parents seemed to have become closer. Alone in his room at night, Hiroshi could hear them talking through the thin wall that separated their bedrooms. Father's low rumble and Mother's clear, melodious voice seemed to carry an intimacy that was new to Hiroshi, further sealing his isolation.

Gradually, more Japanese families began drifting back to Hacienda, lured by the possibility of fieldwork. More Japanese kids were being bused to the high school as a result, but Hiroshi avoided hanging out with them. He would look away embarrassed when he saw them walking down the hallways in groups like mice creeping cautiously close to the wall.

The year before, Hiroshi had taken a Japanese girl, June Watanabe, to a movie, and the stupid girl had told her mother about it. Mrs. Watanabe had then spoken to Hiroshi's father. That evening, Father was sputtering he was so angry. "I have never been so ashamed," he said. "Mrs. Watanabe was laughing at me. Laughing! At me! Hiroshi, you are a high school student. How do you expect to support a wife? I've never been so ashamed!"

"The Watanabe girl is illegitimate," Mother said. "It was a scandal when she was born. To bring such a person into our family..."

"Intolerable!" Father said.

"Hai," Hiroshi said. It was simpler that way. There was no point in trying to explain that things were different in America—that taking a girl to the movies did not mean you were going to marry her. Father and Mother did not really live in America. They never had. Though Hiroshi cursed June's stupidity, his parents would have found out one way or another. The Japanese community was not what it used to be, but nothing went on within the group that everyone did not know about.

Hiroshi stayed away even more from other Japanese after that. The feeling was mutual. Hiroshi imagined himself to be like the fox Father chanted about, an elusive and daring creature capable of changing his form to go where other foxes dared not. Like the fox, he could be brave and resourceful, keeping his wits about him and taking risks to show he was not afraid. He insinuated himself into an elite group of college-bound boys, even though not all of them welcomed his presence. One of them, Steve Bowles, blocked Hiroshi's way once when he tried to join them for lunch, saying "We don't want you here." The boy's blunt and naked hostility embarrassed the others, who said, "Aw, he can come," and "Leave him alone, Steve." Hiroshi merely ignored him, asking the others with feigned insouciance: "What's his problem?"

In class, Hiroshi established a reputation for himself as a

wit, or perhaps just a smart aleck. When young Miss Taylor, the English teacher, gave out a lengthy reading assignment that made everybody groan, Hiroshi said in a stage whisper, "Just listen to her, she's drunk with power." Then, like a fox, he skipped nimbly out of the room before she could respond.

Once, during an open discussion session during a school assembly, Hiroshi went up to the microphone and argued that jazz performers should be brought to the school instead of classical pianists and violinists because jazz was an American art form. After that, some of the football players began calling him "Jazzbo," sneering at him in an Amos-and-Andy accent.

For all that, Hiroshi did well in his classes and was generally liked by his teachers despite his wisecracking. Miss Sherman, the vice principal, was an exception. She was an ungainly woman who was friendly enough with hakujin but who avoided even looking at the Mexican and Japanese students. She took an active dislike to Hiroshi early on because of his cheekiness. Once, during assembly, she made him stand up for having feigned a cough while she was making an announcement concerning a flu epidemic. "Stand up," she said. "Yes, you there. You know whom I mean. Do you wish to make this announcement?"

"No, ma'am," Hiroshi mumbled and tried to sit down.

"I didn't say you could sit yet. I will not have any more interruptions from you. Have I made myself understood?"

"Yes, ma'am," Hiroshi said softly. Only then was he allowed to take his seat.

It seemed to Hiroshi that Miss Sherman had been waiting for a chance to put him in his place, to expose him. It was common, after all, for students to make irreverent noises during assembly, and the teachers were usually good-natured about such things.

There was only one student whom Hiroshi could think of as a friend, a girl named Imogene McPhearson. At Hacienda Elementary School, Hiroshi had taken up the trombone, practicing on an instrument the school had on loan. When he started going to high school, his parents had, after much pleading on his part, bought him a used trombone for forty-two dollars. This meant he could play in the band. That was where he'd met Imogene.

Imogene played the glockenspiel in the band. She also played piano for a jazz combo that performed at school assemblies. Hiroshi was enchanted by the group—and in particular by their theme song, "Dream."

"I can't get that song out of my mind," he confessed to Imogene. "It's always in my head."

Imogene, round-faced and slightly chubby, was not one of the popular girls in school; if it had not been for her piano playing, nobody would ever have taken any notice of her. But to Hiroshi, she was the nicest girl he had ever met. She even invited him, along with Dave Linquist, to her house, where the three would listen to jazz records together. Dave led the jazz combo and played lead trumpet in the dance band. Hiroshi knew it was really Dave that Imogine wanted to spend time with, and that she'd only invited him because she felt awkward about asking Dave to come over alone. But he convinced himself that it didn't matter. He just liked being with her.

Imogene's favorite records were those by George Shearing. "Don't you just love his chords?" she would say. "They're so different." She gave Hiroshi her beginning piano books so he could practice on the piano in the school music room and maybe even learn to play some chords himself. Hiroshi bought every George Shearing record he could find and played them at home when he was alone. Imogene was right; Shearing's chords did have a different sound; they had an acid sweetness, a poignancy that made him tingle.

When Hiroshi turned 16, his parents allowed him to work summers in the fields, and he made enough money to buy a used upright piano. He began taking lessons with Mrs. McKenzie, a skinny, gray-haired woman with steel-rimmed spectacles who drilled him on scales, arpeggios, and tinkling children's pieces that didn't sound anything like George Shearing. But he persevered. With his piano and trombone, he was finding his own way, creating a world away from the wretchedness of his rat-infested house and Father's incessant tales of murder and mayhem.

In his sophomore year, Hiroshi began playing trombone in the band that played at school dances. During breaks, he would go with some of the others to Dave Linquist's car and drink vodka and orange soda and smoke cigarettes. Imogene played in the dance band, too, but she wouldn't join them when they were drinking. From time to time, Dave would talk about her, about how he had "made out" with her. Hiroshi hated him for talking like that about Imogene. Afterwards, he wouldn't be able to get the thought of them together out of his mind. The vodka helped. Under its influence, he was able to look nonchalant and even a little bored as he watched couples do slow dances, squeezing and rubbing their bodies against one another.

Hiroshi was careful to rinse his mouth out with water and chew several sticks of gum after these dances, just in case his parents were still up when he got home. He would creep into his house like a burglar so as not to wake them.

Once, coming home late, he went into the kitchen and switched on the light, catching a rat by surprise as it sat on the counter next to the sink. Instead of fleeing, it stared brazenly back at him. "At night, the house belongs to me," it seemed to say before slinking away contemptuously in a low, slithering crawl. Hiroshi picked up a knife that had been left on the table and hurled it at the rat's retreating form. He missed. If he had caught the slimy little rodent, he would have bit it in two.

Hiroshi often met Imogene in the school music room, where he went to practice piano during lunch and after school. There they could sit and chat in a way Hiroshi had never done before with a girl. They talked about movies, about how ugly Miss Sherman was, and about bebop, which Imogene was not sure about. "You like Charlie Parker, Hiro? And Dizzy Gillespie? Dave is just crazy about bebop, but it's too weird for me, too dissonant. You know what I mean? I think bebop is for men mostly."

Sitting on the piano bench one afternoon, Imogene played with the hem of her skirt, raising it above her knees to smooth it out.

"You were drunk Saturday night, weren't you," she said. "You and Dave."

"Oh, no," Hiroshi said.

"That's all right. I know what you boys do during the breaks."

Hiroshi didn't reply. He didn't know why Imogene was talking about such things. He had in fact been drinking vodka and orange soda Saturday night, but it wasn't something he wanted to talk to her about.

They were silent for a while. Then she continued, "You ever go out with girls, Hiro? I mean, American girls?"

Hiroshi shook his head. He wanted to get up and leave the room, but he couldn't think of a way to do it.

Again, there was silence. Finally Imogene smiled. It was an angelic smile, sweet and pure.

"I'm just teasing. Don't be mad. It doesn't matter to me that you're Japanese."

"I gotta go," Hiroshi said and left, leaving Imogene looking stunned on the piano bench.

Hiroshi couldn't get what Imogene had said out of his mind. He almost hated her for it. He would call her home just to see if she would answer the phone, then hang up before anybody could even answer. He would put his George Shearing records on the phonograph, turn off the lights, and imagine it was Imogene playing. He loved the music, but the sensation the music aroused in him was so intense he didn't know if it was pain or pleasure.

Evenings, when he was given use of the car, he would go to

Santa Marguerita and drive past Imogene's house, a modest frame bungalow across the street from a strawberry farm on the outskirts of town. One night, a green Chevy that Hiroshi recognized was parked outside. Through the rear window, he thought he saw two people inside. He drove to the end of the street and turned the car around, driving past the car again, this time illuminating the front end of the Chevy with his headlights. He recognized Imogene with Dave Linquist.

When he got home, he parked under the weeping willow at the edge of the yard. He recalled how Father often laughed at their neighbor, Mr. Katsutani, who had a fear of willows. In Japan, willow trees grew in graveyards and were thought to harbor the spirits of the dead. As Hiroshi drove under the tree, its drooping branches shut out the light of the moon and stars; it felt as if he were entering a cave. He got out of the car and headed for the house. He could hear frogs croaking and rustling noises coming from the ditch that carried the overflow from a marsh across the street.

The ditch was overgrown with moss and marsh grass and populated by minnows, frogs, and water snakes. Every once in a while, during the daytime, Hiroshi would hear a high rhythmic squawking coming from it; once, when he went to investigate, he saw a frog protruding from the unhinged jaws of a snake. It receded into the serpent's mouth in tiny, spasmodic jerks, finally turning silent as it disappeared into its host. Walking across the ditch now, he thought he could hear strange, unnerving noises coming from the dark waters. He shuddered and hurried into the house.

Father was in the bath, chanting of Tadanobu, the fox driven nearly mad by the call of a distant drum. Hiroshi slipped into his room and went immediately to bed. He fell asleep to the sound of a rat gnawing the baseboard and dreamt of being chased by an enormous snake that rose four feet off the ground hissing his name: *Hiroshiiii, Hiroshiiii.*

At the Homecoming Dance in Hiroshi's junior year, the gym was decorated as usual in the school colors, with red-and-white bunting and crepe paper that drooped tent-like from the ceiling to the basketball hoops along the walls. Miss Sherman, looking as always as if she had a bug up her nose, was there as chaperone. The football players were in high spirits because their team had won.

When Hiroshi stood up to play a solo, Jason Barnsby, one of the jocks, shouted, "Hey, look at Jazzbo!" Hiroshi had been drinking vodka and was feeling a little reckless, so after he finished his solo, he said, "Fuck you, asshole," carefully mouthing the words.

Barnsby wasn't paying any attention and couldn't hear him above the music, but Miss Sherman, who had been staring directly at Hiroshi, seemed to have understood.

During the break, she stopped him as he tried to go outside with the others.

"I want to have a word with you," she said.

"I didn't do anything," Hiroshi said.

"I think you have a big mouth, young man. I'm warning you. You better watch yourself. This is a decent school."

Hiroshi was nearly in tears as he walked away. He wished he had had the courage to tell Miss Sherman to fuck off. She had heard Jason Barnsby call him "Jazzbo"—Barnsby had said it loud enough for everyone to hear—but she hadn't said a word to him.

Outside in the parking lot, he went to Dave's car. Two of the band members were drinking vodka and orange soda and smoking.

"Where's Dave?" Hiroshi asked.

"He's in Jimmy's car with Imogene."

"What's he doing in Jimmy's car?"

The boys laughed. "What do you think, Hiro?"

It was easy to find the car, a stripped down '37 Ford with skirts over the rear wheels and chrome-plated dual exhausts.

It was at the far end of the parking lot, screened from the gym by a hedge of boxwood. If he hadn't had that run-in with Miss Sherman, Hiroshi would probably never have gone to investigate. But he felt humiliated—first by Miss Sherman's unfair and mean-spirited rebuke, and now by the innuendos about Imogene, which made him feel dirty and ashamed. He had hoped to find Jimmy's car empty, giving lie to those dirty little thoughts.

When their break was over, Hiroshi didn't go back inside with the rest of the band. Instead, he sat in Dave Linquist's car drinking vodka and smoking. He didn't bother with the orange soda; he liked the burning sensation of the alcohol making its way to his belly. He could hear the band playing a Les Brown arrangement they shouldn't even have tried. It was too difficult for them. He was listening with his eyes closed, hoping Dave would miss the high C, when the door to the car suddenly opened. It was Miss Sherman, with Mr. Farnsworth right behind her.

"Drinking!" she said. There was note of triumph in her voice. "Step out of the car. And give me that bottle."

Hiroshi got out of the car.

"Here," he said, and let the bottle drop to the asphalt where it shattered, splattering vodka on Miss Sherman's shoes.

"You did that on purpose," Miss Sherman said. "You are in serious trouble."

"You shouldn't have done that, Hiro," Mr. Farnsworth said. He had always liked Hiroshi and seemed genuinely concerned.

"I'm sorry," Hiroshi said.

"You're going to be even sorrier, young man," Miss Sherman said. "I don't want you back in the dance. We'll see you Monday morning in Mr. Baxter's office. You'll be there, too, won't you Mr. Farnsworth?"

Mr. Farnsworth nodded. After Miss Sherman left, he stayed behind. "You better go home now," he said. "Are you okay? Can you drive?"

"I'm okay. I have to get my trombone."

"Never mind that. I'll take care of it."

Mr. Farnsworth started to say something more, but seemed to think better of it. He turned and walked back to the gym.

It was past midnight when Hiroshi got home. He couldn't get himself to go into the house. It was cold, but he took off his coat and tie and unbuttoned his shirt. The night air chilled his body as he shed the rest of his clothes piece by piece.

Imogene had been on top. Her skirt had been lifted over her head and the milk white skin of her buttocks had shone in the dim light filtering through the boxwood hedge.

Hiroshi lay naked on the ground, staring up at the night sky, listening to the croaking of the frogs. When he finally got up and started looking for his clothes, he was so dizzy and disoriented that he slipped in the mud and fell with a splash into the ditch. "Fuck!" he said. "Fuck! Fuck! Fuck!"

Hiroshi lay there, too dispirited to move. He felt squirming bodies under his back and legs, though it might only have been the effect of the current flowing through the marsh grass. The water wasn't very deep, but it was freezing cold. He could have gotten up easily, but what was the use. He stayed—frozen, motionless, listening—listening for the sound of the drum.

CIRCLE

1950 - 1954

In the summer before his senior year in high school, Hiroshi
and his parents moved to San Pedro on the southern edge of Los
Angeles Harbor. Mickey and his wife, Amy, had opened a small
chop suey café there that catered mostly to dockworkers and
"wharf rats," denizens of the seedy bars and raunchy strip joints
in the area. It wasn't fancy, but for Mickey, eager to set up his
own business, it was the most he could afford.

All five of them—Hiroshi, his parents, Mickey, and Amy—
lived together, crammed in a small, creaky house behind the
café. It was not much bigger than the place they'd left behind
in Hacienda, but Father and Mother were pleased to no longer
be doing fieldwork. They now helped out at the café, chopping
vegetables and meats and doing other chores, while Hiroshi
washed dishes, pots, and pans and mopped the floor.

Mickey paid him for his work, so Hiroshi, eager to continue

his piano lessons, asked Mr. Watkins, the band director at San Pedro High, to recommend a teacher. He said Samantha Chatham was the best in town.

From the San Pedro waterfront to Mrs. Chatham's hillside home was a drive of only fifteen minutes, but from her doorstep, Hiroshi could see the entire sweep of Los Angeles Harbor laid out before him. It was a world apart from the rat-infested, garbage-strewn alleys of Beacon Street, where he and his family now lived.

Mrs. Chatham's house was built in the Old California style, with adobe walls, recessed casement windows, a red terracotta roof, and a sturdy oak door whose over-sized wrought-iron hinges looked as if they had been built to withstand a battering ram.

A Mexican woman in a plain brown dress and white linen apron answered the bell.

"I'm Hiroshi Kono," he announced. "I have an appointment with Mrs. Chatham."

Five years had passed since the war, but the woman still seemed unsettled to see a Japanese standing at the door.

"Come in," she said finally.

A large black-and-white photo portrait, two feet in height, caught Hiroshi's eye as he entered the vestibule. It was of a distinguished-looking man, dressed in black and wearing the collar of a clergyman. He had a stern, unsmiling face.

Glancing behind the maid and down a hallway, Hiroshi glimpsed an elderly, white-haired woman as she walked quickly into one of the rooms carrying what looked like a bedpan.

The Mexican woman led Hiroshi into a cool and spacious living room with a dark hardwood floor covered with Navajo rugs. Paintings of brightly colored geometrical shapes hung on the walls, and a Steinway concert grand occupied one corner of the room. Several open books of music layered one against the other covered the piano rack, and more books and sheet music were stacked high on either side. A metronome teetered precariously on one of the piles.

"Mrs. Chatham is waiting for you outside," the maid said. She opened the French doors to a stone terrace.

It was an unusually warm day for late September. Samantha Chatham was lying on a chaise lounge wearing a strapless sundress. She set aside the book she had been holding and pushed her horn-rimmed glasses to the top of her dark brown hair in a way that was both casual and appealing.

"Such a lovely day," she said to Hiroshi. "I thought we could talk out here." She turned to dismiss the maid, saying, "Thank you, Maria," then motioned with an extended hand toward one of the cushioned, wrought-iron chairs that stood near a glass-topped table. As Hiroshi took a seat, his eyes couldn't help traveling along her bare, roundly tapered legs. She was a woman in her early forties and showed signs of bulging that her brief, form-fitting dress couldn't quite conceal, but Hiroshi—still in his late adolescence and an ardent moviegoer—found her attractive in a theatrical sort of way. She had big, brown, slightly protruding eyes and hair set in a pageboy cut. A half-drunk glass of what looked like iced tea stood on the terrace beside a butt-filled ashtray, a pack of filtered cigarettes, and a slim, gold lighter.

"Your name again?" she asked, picking up the pack and shaking out a cigarette.

"Hiroshi. Hiroshi Kono. Everyone calls me Hiro."

"Hiroshi. That's Japanese? Oh, sorry. Would you like a cigarette?"

Hiroshi had been smoking on the sly whenever he could since he was a child, but no adult had ever offered him a cigarette before.

"Oh, no thank you," he said. Then, mischievously, he added, "I'm trying to cut down."

Mrs. Chatham guffawed. She had obviously been toying with him.

"I think we're going to get along just fine," she said.

For Hiroshi, Mrs. Chatham seemed like a character he had

previously only experienced in movies and novels—urbane and sophisticated. Back in Hacienda, Hiroshi's piano teacher had been Mrs. McKenzie, a humorless old crone who would smack his fingers with a pencil whenever he played a wrong note or used incorrect fingering. If Mrs. McKenzie was a rice ball, Samantha Chatham was sushi.

When Mrs. Chatham questioned him about his previous piano training, he said, hoping to impress her, that he had memorized Mozart's C-major sonata. She smiled and said softly, almost to herself, "Yes, that old chestnut."

"I can also play the slow part of the other one, the hard one," Hiroshi said, but Mrs. Chatham remained unimpressed.

Undeterred, Hiroshi offered to play it for her. But she said that wouldn't be necessary.

"Jim Watkins and I go back a long way," she said. "His recommendation is good enough for me."

Someone stepped onto the patio—a blond, youngish looking man whom Hiroshi recognized as his high-school harmony teacher.

"I'm off, Sam," he said, ignoring Hiroshi. "Don't wait up for me."

He left without waiting for a response, and Mrs. Chatham crushed her cigarette with some force into the ashtray.

"That was Mr. James," Hiroshi said.

"Timmy's my husband," Mrs. Chatham said. "I know it confuses people, but I kept the name from my first marriage."

By the time Hiroshi left Mrs. Chatham's house, his head was swimming. He had been accepted as a student by a twice-married woman who looked like Bette Davis and lived like a movie queen.

Classical music wasn't his first love, nor was the piano. He'd been in the thrall of swing and jazz since he'd started playing the trombone in the seventh grade, but he made good progress on the piano nonetheless. It was like a game for him—something with which to occupy his lonely hours.

Under the guidance of Mrs. McKenzie, even Mozart became a technical exercise. He attacked every piece as if it were a feat of digital dexterity. The metronome marking for the first movement of the Mozart sonata was 132 beats per minute, but he could play it at 144.

Mrs. Chatham was horrified. She said he was killing the music. He didn't understand what she meant at first, but gradually, as Samantha Chatham performed for him music he had previously thought to be hopelessly old fashioned and square, he began to understand that it could be truly moving. Mrs. Chatham was an accomplished pianist who played with great feeling. Hiroshi thought he could detect her passion for the music from the scent of her breath and body as he sat next to her on the piano bench.

Under Mrs. Chatham's tutelage, Hiroshi went through a book of sonatinas that included works by Kuhlau, Clementi, Mozart, Beethoven, and Dussek in record time. Mrs. Chatham said he progressed faster than any student she'd ever had, with the possible exception of one. She never said who that other student was, and Hiroshi never asked.

Though she had Hiroshi doing scales and other technical exercises, the bulk of their work together was on the music itself. She even threw in some Bartók and Prokofiev—pieces that the stick-in-the-mud sourpuss Mrs. McKenzie would probably not have even recognized as music. Hiroshi was captivated. He practiced long and hard, motivated by his wish to impress his glamorous and sophisticated teacher.

His fascination lasted throughout his senior year in high school, but as he grew into his new surroundings, Hiroshi's world began to widen. Compared to Santa Marguerita, San Pedro, with its wider mix of races, was positively cosmopolitan. This was especially true of the school band. Though Hiroshi was the only Japanese member, Armando, a Filipino boy, played tenor sax, and Oscar, a colored boy, played the trumpet.

Oscar's first question to Hiroshi when they met was, "Hey, man. You dig bop?"

Hiroshi answered in the affirmative, establishing himself as one of the "cats" in the band. Over time, Oscar, Hiro, and Armando became inseparable, visiting each other's homes to listen to records by the leading lights of bebop, which, being the cool cats they were, they referred to simply as bop.

After graduating from high school, the three formed a group that performed weekends in waterfront bars, playing mostly honky-tonk blues to please the crowd and switching to their best efforts at bop during the quiet hours.

These late nights gradually began to take a toll on Hiroshi's piano playing. Until then, he had been a model piano student—Mrs. Chatham even called him a prodigy. But by the end of Hiroshi's second year of instruction, his progress was beginning to flag.

"You're not working at all on your scales and arpeggios are you," Mrs. Chatham said. "You need to work on them every day, at least fifteen minutes a day, though a half hour would be better."

"I know, but they make me feel like a squirrel trapped in one of those wheels, going around and around, getting nowhere."

"Repetition," she said. "That's the key. Do the exercises over and over until you can do them automatically. Your hands should just glide over the keyboard—smoothly, evenly. Like this. Here, move closer and put your hands on top of mine. I want you to feel how my hands move."

As their hands traveled across the keyboard like coupling spiders, Hiroshi's chin brushed against Mrs. Chatham's shoulder. Under the neckline of her blouse, he glimpsed the top of her breasts. The movement of her arms was making tiny wrinkles on them.

The following week, Mrs. Chatham was even less pleased with Hiroshi's progress. When the lesson was over, she looked into Hiroshi's bloodshot eyes, frowning.

"You don't look well, Hiro. Are you all right?"

"I'm okay. I was up late last night playing a gig. I think I drank too much."

"Well, you certainly look a little under the weather. Have you eaten?"

"No, but I'm not hungry."

"Silly. Come to the kitchen. I'll fix you a sandwich."

"No, please, I'm really not hungry," he said, but he followed her into the kitchen.

She made him a tuna sandwich and brewed herself a cup of tea. As they sat at the kitchen table, a sharp, sickly sweet odor penetrated the room. Hiroshi looked over Mrs. Chatham's shoulder and saw an old man in a rumpled, soiled bathrobe. The man's eyes were rheumy and vacant, and spittle was running down the corner of his mouth.

Mrs. Chatham got up and began shouting. "Mother! He's in the kitchen! Come and get him out of here!"

A white-haired woman in a plain cotton dress and slippers came into the kitchen. Hiroshi recognized her as the woman he'd seen on his first visit. He hadn't seen her again during the two years he'd been coming to the house for lessons.

"Get him out of here! Just get him out!" Mrs. Chatham shouted.

"Come on, Father," the old woman said softly while leading the man away.

"Was that your father? And your mother?" Hiroshi asked dumbfounded. "I didn't know. I'm sorry."

"There's nothing to be sorry about." Mrs. Chatham whisked away a fly that had settled on the bowl of tuna on the table. "It's just impossible to keep flies out of this house," she said angrily. "Would you like another sandwich, Hiro? If not, I'll put this away."

"No, thank you. This is plenty." Hiroshi ate his sandwich

and didn't speak for some time. It occurred to him that the photo in the vestibule could be a portrait of her father. He said, "Was he a minister? Your father, I mean."

"Yes, a very imposing man, highly respected. But I don't want to talk about that now. Do you mind?"

"No, that's all right. I know how you feel."

Mrs. Chatham stiffened and looked sternly at Hiroshi. "Now, what is that supposed to mean?"

"Nothing. It's just that sometimes I want to shout at my parents, too."

She looked inquiringly at him, then softened. "It was awful of me, I know. But it's hard to see my father this way, especially when I remember how he used to be. But tell me about your parents. What are they like?"

"Well, you know, they're just parents. They were born in Japan."

Hiroshi was uncomfortable, so he asked if it would be all right for him to smoke.

"Of course," she said.

Hiroshi took out his cigarettes and offered her one. She hesitated for a moment, perhaps sensing she was crossing some line, then accepted. When he struck a match to light it, she cupped his hand softly with both of hers as if protecting the fire from a wind. The gesture seemed intimate, even erotic, and it added to Hiroshi's confusion and uneasiness.

"And what does your father do?" she asked, tilting her head and pursing her lips to blow a stream of smoke toward the ceiling like a movie star.

"Not much any more. He putters around my brother's café, he and my mother. I work there, too, making deliveries, washing dishes, mopping up."

"Oh, yes. You told me about your brother's restaurant. Are you close to your mother and father?"

"No, I don't talk to them much. My Japanese isn't very good

anymore. Besides, we don't have much in common. They don't like my friends. They don't like my music. I can't talk to them about the books I read. I can't tell them about the things I do."

Mrs. Chatham raised an eyebrow and looked archly at Hiroshi.

"Such as?"

"You know, girls and stuff."

"Do you have girlfriends?"

Hiroshi took a deep drag on his cigarette. "Naw. I was lying about the girls."

"No girlfriends? You're an attractive young man, tall for a Japanese boy."

She looked intently at Hiroshi, who remained impassive. "And your eyes, Hiro. I think they're beautiful. You are a bit skinny—you really need to fill out—but your cheekbones and hollow cheeks give your face a sculptured look, like an Asiatic prince. Oh, but I'm embarrassing you!"

Hiroshi did not respond.

"Hiro?" she said, lowering her head to look into his eyes.

"There aren't many Japanese girls around here, you know," he said finally. "And the ones I meet think I'm strange."

"Do you ever date American girls?"

"White girls won't go out with Japanese guys. And besides, my parents would go nuts if they found out I was dating one. My mother keeps reminding me of what happened to the Nakano boy."

"What was that?"

Hiroshi regretted having brought up the subject, but he couldn't think of a way to change the subject gracefully or to leave. So he told the story, a major scandal in Hacienda before the war. Ichi Nakano, whose father owned the local pool hall, ran off with a hakujin woman when he was twenty years old. Two weeks later, he was found in a flophouse in Los Angeles—broke, near starving, and too ashamed to go home.

"She was a whore," Hiroshi said. "Sorry, a prostitute."

Mrs. Chatham chortled, her big, brown eyes rolling toward the ceiling.

"You're such a prude, Hiro! 'Whore' is a perfectly good Anglo-Saxon word. You don't have to be afraid of words like that, at least not with me."

Hiroshi understood that this was urbane sophistication talking, but he was beginning to feel uncomfortable.

"I think I better go now," he said. "Thanks for the sandwich." He nearly toppled his chair as he got up. "I'll try to work more on my scales, thirds, and octaves," he said as he left the kitchen and found his way out of the house.

The following week, Hiroshi arrived twenty minutes late. As he walked up the steps, he could hear Mrs. Chatham playing "Greensleeves" through an open window.

Maria was gone for the day, so Mrs. Chatham answered the door herself.

"I'm sorry I'm late," Hiroshi said with a grin.

"You don't look very sorry, Hiro."

Instead of going to the piano, Hiroshi sat himself on an Ottoman next to the coffee table. Mrs. Chatham, looking puzzled, perched herself in her usual spot on the edge of the piano bench and looked expectantly at him.

Being with Mrs. Chatham had become difficult for Hiroshi; he had begun having fantasies that troubled him. He was thinking about quitting, and before the lesson, had gone to fortify himself at a bar near Fort MacArthur that was frequented by young GIs. The bartender there was relaxed, and Hiroshi had been there before without being questioned about his age. This time, as before, he ordered a beer. When that came, he asked for a shot of rye to go with it. That was what the dockworkers drank at the Lido Bar where he and his friends worked on weekends.

"Well, Hiro," Mrs. Chatham said in the familiar tone that

she had begun using with him. "Are you going to just sit there all night, or are you going to tell me what's going on?"

The alcohol had not steeled his nerves sufficiently, so to stall for time he said, "I just had some beers with my friends, Mrs. Chatham. I lost track of time. I'm sorry."

"Feeling no pain?"

Hiroshi did not understand.

"It's just an expression."

"Oh, yeah, feeling no pain. Sure, that's the way I feel."

He laughed, and Mrs. Chatham laughed, too. She seemed to have gotten over her pique.

"Well, you're late, but we still have time for a lesson."

Hiroshi chose to play Chopin's dirge-like "Prelude in C Minor." It was one of his favorites because of its bold and extended harmonies. As he played the chromatically descending base line, he was glad he hadn't mentioned wanting to quit, for by the time he got to the end of the piece, a crashing C-minor chord played fortissimo with the pedal pushed to the floor, he had changed his mind. "Wonderful," Mrs. Chatham said softly. "You played that beautifully, Hiro. Bravo."

It seemed to Hiroshi that there was nobody else with whom he could share such moments of ecstasy and sadness, not his mother, not his bebop-loving friends, no one. After playing another Chopin prelude, the "Raindrop" in B minor, he excused himself, saying he wasn't feeling well. "I'm sorry I was so late tonight," he said as he left the house. "I love coming here."

"And I love your being here, Hiro," Mrs. Chatham said in a lilting voice that remained in Hiroshi's memory for days.

Piano lessons quickly became the high point of Hiroshi's week—to the extent that his parents worried he was becoming obsessed with the instrument and neglecting his work at the café. But Hiroshi was driven, practicing long hours.

Then, inexplicably, Mrs. Chatham began to lose interest.

There were times when she seemed surprised to see him at the door. "Oh, you have a lesson today?" she would say. Things got worse with every passing week. Mrs. Chatham would sit through his lessons looking distracted and slightly disheveled. Already a heavy smoker, she now smoked even while he was playing. At times, Hiroshi detected liquor on her breath.

On a particularly dreary evening in February, when rain and hale were battering the window panes like buckshot, Hiroshi began his lesson with the playfully wistful "Doctor Gradus ad Parnassum," a piece from Debussy's *Children's Corner*. When he finished, Mrs. Chatham didn't say a word. She merely remained sitting on the edge of the piano bench, her legs crossed, one elbow cupped on her lap, a lit cigarette in her mouth. Unnerved, Hiroshi proceeded to play the lively and playful "Golliwogg's Cakewalk." Even after he concluded the piece, bringing his arms down full force on the E-flat octaves, she remained silent. So Hiroshi simply waited. Finally, she said, "My divorce came through today; I don't know how I feel about it."

Hiroshi, caught completely by surprised, didn't know what to say. "Your divorce?" he repeated. When he was finally able to process what she'd said, he was speechless. He couldn't understand why she would tell him about such a private matter. "I'm so sorry, Mrs. Chatham," he said gamely. Not getting a response, he continued, "Maybe we can finish the lesson some other time."

She remained seated for some time, smoking her cigarette. Finally, straightening herself, she said, "You're right. I'm really not up to giving a lesson tonight. But I don't want to be alone. We can talk about Debussy if you like—those modal harmonies that you like so much." She looked at him appealingly. "You find them in English folk songs, too."

She pushed him aside on the bench with her hips and played "Greensleeves," a melody in the Dorian mode. Hiroshi recalled that he had heard her playing the song once before, but he couldn't remember when.

When she finished, she invited Hiroshi into an adjoining book-lined room that, she said, had been her father's study. After gong to her record collection for an album of English folk songs, she seated herself next to Hiroshi on a plush, Victorian sofa. They sat side by side, quietly listening to sad and haunting love songs sung to the accompaniment of a lute. One of them had the words, "as I lay in my bed with you in my arms."

"Rather risqué," Hiroshi said, trying to sound worldly.

"Yes, they can be. That one was Jonathan's favorite."

"Jonathan?"

"Oh, sorry. My first husband. We spent a lot of evenings listening to music back when we were first married. We had a little place off of Gaffey, on Twenty-Fifth Street. That was before Jonathan's father died and left him all that money. I always missed our little apartment; it had a gorgeous view of the harbor. We'd sit on the balcony, listening to music and drinking wine."

"Did he die? Your husband, I mean."

Mrs. Chatham smiled ruefully.

"In a manner of speaking," she said. "But I don't want to talk about that. Would you care to take a glass of sherry with me, Hiro?"

"I guess. Sure."

She went to the dining room and brought back a decanter and two aperitif glasses gilded and etched with a grape design. She sat on the sofa next to Hiroshi and carefully filled both glasses. "Cheers, Hiro," she said, lifting her glass.

Hiroshi took a small, cautious sip. "It's pretty good," he said as he took another sip, staring intently into the wine. "Mrs. Chatham, I really like being with you. The thing is, I've never had anybody I could talk to before, and I don't know if it's right to talk about certain things."

"Don't you talk to your friends?"

"They're music friends. All we talk about is music, about

jazz. You know, bebop."

"Yes, I've heard of bebop. What is that exactly?"

"Some people call it modern jazz. Everything about it is different—the chords, the riffs—but it's not just the music. We talk different, too. Like, 'You dig, man? You hip?' We get high on grass, listen to records, jam. . ."

"You mean marijuana, Hiro? Do you smoke marijuana? That's so dangerous. Why, you could be arrested."

"Naw. At the Lido where I work, everybody's getting stoned. The cops don't care."

"That's shocking, Hiro. Somebody should report it."

"Don't do that, Mrs. Chatham," Hiroshi said, genuinely alarmed. "You could get me in a lot of trouble. Not just me. Everybody. Besides, I don't do it much anymore."

"Good for you," Mrs. Chatham said. "But truly, something should be done about Beacon Street. It's an absolute disgrace."

Hiroshi wondered if Mrs. Chatham might be a rice ball, after all. To appease her, or perhaps to test her, he said, "There must be something wrong with me—maybe I'm morally defective. But I kinda like Beacon Street."

Mrs. Chatham arched her left eyebrow and squinted her eyes, signifying that she was onto Hiroshi's impudence.

"Are you being smart with me, Hiro? You're being a little cheeky, aren't you?"

Hiroshi didn't respond; he wasn't sure if she was really angry. After a few tense moments, she relented. "All right. Maybe I was being a little stuffy," she said, reaching out and putting her hand on his.

Hiroshi was startled, but tried not to show it. He smiled and said, "Oh, that's okay," and drew his hand away. "I read a lot of poetry," he said, straining to change the subject. "I really like the romantics. Like Coleridge—'Kublai Khan,' 'Rime of the Ancient Mariner,' stuff like that. And Oscar Wilde. Is he a romantic?"

"Maybe post-romantic."

"Yeah, whatever. I really like him, especially the 'Ballad of Reading Gaol.' Wilde says everybody kills the thing he loves. Is that true? Maybe it's just yourself you kill, a part of yourself."

Mrs. Chatham looked at Hiroshi and didn't respond. Instead, she refilled their glasses.

"Yes," she said at length. "Perhaps you're right. Oscar Wilde is a favorite of mine as well. I used to read his poems to Timmy when he studied piano with me."

"Mr. James was your student?"

"That was many years ago; that was how we met."

"Oh," Hiroshi said. He wasn't sure what to make of that information. "It's getting kind of late," he said, looking at his watch. "I'm sorry. I didn't mean to keep you up so late. I just sort of lost track of time." He picked up his glass of wine and drained it in single gulp. "I better be going now," he said, standing up.

Mrs. Chatham also stood. "I'm not sure I can stand much more of this either," she said.

Hiroshi looked at her, trying to understand what she meant. When they reached the front door, he asked, "What did you mean by that? Did I do something wrong?"

She patted his cheek and said in a low voice, "I was just joking, Hiro. I love you being here." She kept her face close to his, and Hiroshi, suddenly unsteady on his feet, closed his eyes for a moment. Then he lurched forward and kissed her flush on the lips. It was a wet, awkward, clumsy kiss. He had never kissed a girl before, much less a woman twice his age, and he had no idea what to expect. Frightened by his own boldness, he backed away. "I'm sorry," he said.

Mrs. Chatham remained still and smiled. "There's no reason to be," she said.

"Oh," Hiroshi said. "I have to go. Thanks for the drinks. That's really good stuff." He paused. "Better than grass almost," he said with a broad grin and bolted out the door.

Not long afterwards, Hiroshi's lessons were changed to Thursday evenings, when Mrs. Chatham's mother went to church for her weekly board meeting and canasta game. Though they kept up the pretense of piano lessons, they mostly just played for fun, sitting together on the bench and playing duets. He and Mrs. Chatham would read poems to one another, listen to records, drink wine, and talk. Sometimes they held hands. She insisted on his calling her Samantha, which was difficult for Hiroshi at first, but became easier after a while. Before he left, they would kiss, sending Hiroshi into a dreamy state of mind he had never before experienced.

Hiroshi had never been happier in his life. His mother noticed the change in him and asked him what he was smiling about all the time, so he struggled to keep a straight face when he was home. His father would sometimes return to the house to tell Hiroshi he was needed at the café, only to find him lying on his bed, staring at the ceiling with dreamy look on his face, his hands clasped behind his head.

Hiroshi's intimacy with Samantha had begun in the dead of winter, and by summer, the relationship had reached a fever pitch. On the days they were supposed to meet, he would count the hours until it was time to go.

One evening in August, when Hiroshi arrived at Samantha's door, he was surprised to find her in a state of dishabille. Her hair was windblown and mussed, giving her a boyish look Hiroshi found appealing. The rest of her attire, however, was purely feminine: white satin slippers, a black kimono decorated with large white and orange orchids, and a red sheer silk scarf tied around her waist. Hiroshi noted a scent of jasmine coming from her.

"I lost all track of time," she said. "I'm not quite ready."

"I can come back later."

"Don't be silly. I just have to finish my hair. Come into the bedroom, and we can talk there."

She went to the far end of her bedroom, sat at her dressing table, and began brushing her hair. Hiroshi walked in cautiously and sat on the edge of the bed between her and the door. There was perfume in the air, the same jasmine scent he had detected at the door.

"It's all right," she said with a low-pitched, lilting laugh, "I'm not going to attack you." She turned, and as she crossed her legs, the folds of her kimono opened, exposing her thighs. She did not have anything on underneath. She delicately pulled her kimono close again with the tips of her fingers.

Hiroshi saw that she was wearing more makeup and a darker shade of lipstick than usual. He thought of the women who came to the Lido. He swallowed hard and said, "That's not what I'm worried about."

"What then?"

"Nothing."

"All right, Hiro. Out with it."

"I guess it's just that I've never had a girl before—a woman, I mean. I don't know how."

"Oh, Hiro," she said. She came to the bed and sat beside him, putting her cheek against his. He wanted to stand, but she took his hand and guided it inside her kimono. She undid the scarf around her waist, and her kimono fell open.

"I don't..." Hiroshi said, but she put her finger on his lips.

"Hush," she said. She kissed him softly, her mouth open, then fell back on the bed, pulling him over her. At that moment, a shadow caught his eye, and he bolted upright on the bed. "Oh, my God," he said.

There, standing at the open door was her father—silent, drooling, eyes vacant.

"Oh, damn," she said, getting up quickly and tying her kimono shut. "I'm sorry, Hiro." Halfway to the door, she turned and said, "You don't have to worry. He doesn't understand a thing. I just need to change him. That's when he wanders from his room."

Hiroshi walked to the door and paused. There was another odor in the air now, a sickly sweet smell. A fly buzzed around his head, trying to land on his ear. He swatted at it. Then he walked out of bedroom, down the hall, and into the living room. He hesitated for some moments before leaving the house.

He drove around aimlessly for a while before going at last to the bar near Fort MacArthur. It had been nearly a year since Hiroshi had last visited the place, but the bartender seemed to recognize him.

"What'll it be?" he said.

Hiroshi looked around to assure himself that there was still a telephone booth next to the restrooms as he'd remembered. When he looked back, the bartender was leaning toward him with both hands on the bar.

"So?" he said.

"A Schlitz and a shot," Hiroshi said. "Rye."

He didn't know why he'd asked for a boilermaker any more than he knew what he would say to Samantha when he called her.

The bartender brought him his beer and poured whisky into a shot glass.

"Buck-fifty," he said.

He would call her in the morning, Hiroshi decided, absently putting two dollar bills on the bar. Or maybe early next week. After draining his beer, Hiroshi got up abruptly and left, leaving two quarters and the shot glass full of whisky on the bar, untouched.

JONAH

1954 - 1957

Juanita Sanchez, owner of the Lido, refused to allow Hiroshi to have even a single beer at her bar because he was underage. It seemed to Hiroshi that if he could play in a band for her—also underage and illegally—he ought to be able to sneak a beer. But Juanita was quirky about how she observed the law and enforced morality. So he was surprised when, after he enlisted in the Army, she threw him a party with all the free booze he could drink. Then again, Hiroshi was only a month away from his twenty-first birthday by then, which Juanita might have thought was close enough.

Open bottles of tequila and a tub full of iced beer stood on the bar counter. Laid out next to them, in bowls and chafers, were tacos, enchiladas, chile rellanos, rice, refried beans, tortillas, and salads—all made in-house under Juanita's personal supervision. Mariachi tunes, exotic and out of place in the Lido's honky-tonk atmosphere, put the mostly Mexican staff and the few regulars who'd been invited to the party in a festive mood. Armando and Oscar rolled their eyes over what they called "bull-fighter music" and went out to the alley to smoke a joint, but Hiroshi took full advantage of the open bar.

Hiroshi had never drunk tequila before, and was just returning from vomiting in the restroom when Juanita took him by the arm and pulled him toward the end of the bar.

Juanita was a woman who, having grown stout in her fifties, wore heavy makeup and a black, low-cut, lacy dress befitting her status as the proprietress of an established waterfront saloon. Flanked by a rent-by-the-hour-hotel and a heavily caged-in bail bond agency, the Lido sat on San Pedro's Beacon Street, a gaudy, neon-lit stretch along the south side of the Los Angeles Harbor. Once reputed to consist of the toughest two blocks in the world, Beacon Street was neither as wild nor as dangerous as it had once been. Juanita, a hard-bitten boss lady who could let fly a torrent of curses in both English and Spanish if anyone gave her any sass, made sure that things never got out of hand in her establishment. But she could also be sentimental and warm—even motherly— with her staff and her regulars, mostly old and lonely drunks who came during the day and left when business began to pick up in the evenings. On slow nights, she could be seen alone in her office, smoking cigarettes and drinking tequila while staring at photographs on the wall. Taken in the early days of the Lido, the yellowing prints showed a trim and jaunty Juanita in a Mexican peasant costume, arm in arm with her husband Roberto, both smiling back at the camera.

Juanita was unsteady on her feet as she backed Hiroshi against the bar and grabbed him by his lapels as if he were an unruly drunk. "You crazy! Just like my Roberto," she said. "Why you doing this?"

Hiroshi started to say he had joined the Army because he couldn't avoid the draft forever, and playing in an Army band was better than lying in a foxhole. But in a mood of boozy bravado, he said, "I want to see the world, Mrs. Sanchez. You know. Get the hell out of San Pedro."

Letting go of his coat, she put her fists on her hips.

"Men, boys. You all the same."

She glared at him. Then, softening her gaze, she took his hand and put something in it—a silver medal the size of a 50-cent piece. On it was a bearded man carrying a child on his shoulders. Engraved around the man's head were the words, "Protect Us."

"I wanted to give it to my Roberto," she said. "But he didn't want it. 'For fools!' he said." She shook her head. "He was killed in France."

"I know," Hiroshi said, still feeling the tequila in his gut. "You told us. A lotta times."

Juanita took no notice of his rudeness, so intent was she on driving home her point. "It would have protected him. I know it would have protected him." She was in one of her morose moods and getting teary. "I should have made him take it. I should have made him." Her mascara was starting to make black streaks down her cheeks. "You take it!" she said. She appeared to be angry with herself as she squeezed Hiroshi's hand. "It's a St. Christopher medal blessed by Father Antonio. It will protect you, Hiro. Promise me you carry it."

A ceasefire in Korea had been announced months earlier. Hiroshi would never have enlisted, even for the band, had there been a war going on. "Mrs. Sanchez," he said, "the war is over. There's no danger now."

"Call me Juanita," she said. "You're a good boy, but you must be a man now. St. Christopher. Promise me you carry him."

"Okay, Juanita," he said.

Before he could say anything more, she held him close against her overflowing bosom and planted wet kisses on his cheeks. Then she turned and walked away.

Hiroshi found himself thinking of his mother. He'd told

his parents he was enlisting in the kitchen of their small house behind Mickey's café. Mother, sitting on a rusting chrome and vinyl kitchen chair, had said nothing at first. She seemed almost to have expected the news. Her eyes grew heavy and her gaze fell to the chipped and curling linoleum, then drifted up to the small window that looked out onto the brick wall of a second-hand furniture store. She had long ago given up on worrying about Hiroshi—about his late nights, his clothes smelling of liquor and cigarettes and other strange and curious scents. She looked down at her hands in her lap. "Perhaps it is for the best," she said.

Father, once a Japanese patriot, no longer had anything good to say about any army, Japanese or American. Hiroshi had prepared himself to hear a lecture about how the military was an instrument for murder and mayhem, anarchy and chaos. Instead, there was only silence. At last, his father asked: "How do you know you won't be sent to Korea?"

"Father, the war is over in Korea. The fighting has ended. I will be playing in a band."

"You must be absolutely sure, Hiroshi," he said. "I will not have another son foolishly risking his life."

Those words came from the heart. Mickey had survived the war with only a minor wound—just bad enough to win a Purple Heart—but his fighting in the American Army had been a torment to his parents, especially for Father. Mickey dying while fighting for the enemy would have been a tragic irony Father could scarcely have endured.

Leaning against the bar at the Lido, Hiroshi was troubled that he could still be thinking of his parents, even in a boozy, smoke-filled, bawdy waterfront saloon. What he had told Juanita was true—he wanted to escape. He wanted to get the hell out of San Pedro, and he wanted to see the world, all of it, whatever there was to see.

As Hiroshi watched Juanita's ample hips swing unsteadily back to the party, the bartender Chico approached him. Chico was hip and knowledgeable about jazz, a true connoisseur. Beyond that, unbeknownst to Juanita, he hustled dope at the Lido.

Chico flashed his gold teeth at Hiroshi. "Come outside with me," he said.

Out in the alley, he handed Hiroshi a reddish-brown bottle, the kind used by pharmacists for cough syrup.

Hiroshi held it up to the light above the door and saw it contained what looked like over-sized aspirins. "Bennies?" he asked.

"Going away present," Chico said.

"Wow. Thanks, man."

"Hey, man, don't sweat it. They'll help your playing. And sometimes, man, you could use a little help," he said with the evil grin he always wore when pushing dope.

Chico had tried to push bennies on him before, but Hiroshi never used anything stronger than grass. Marijuana was a plant, like tobacco, but the other stuff—heroin, coke, even bennies—was made in laboratories or cooked up in somebody's basement.

Hiroshi put the bottle of pills in his pocket with the St. Christopher medal, and, inebriated, thanked Chico again with great warmth and affection.

The bottle of pills— unopened and undetected, tucked in either his duffle bag or in a canvas case that the GIs called an AWOL bag—traveled with him through basic training and several Army posts.

During basic training, he put the St. Christopher medal on his dog-tag chain, but when a drill sergeant commanded him to remove it, he took to carrying it in his pocket. He used it like a worry bead, rubbing it when nervous or bored.

In the middle of the winter of 1955, after a year in the Army, Hiroshi found himself on a rusting troop ship that, following a stomach-churning passage through the North Sea, finally docked at Bremerhaven, Germany. There, he and some others were placed on a train to Verdun, France. They arrived at noon the following day and waited another hour before being loaded onto an Army bus. Through the bus window, Hiroshi saw a bleak city, its streets slushy with dirty snow, its buildings black with soot and grime. The air was thick with the acrid smell of burning coal. Snaking through the town was the Meuse River. It looked cold and inhospitable, its waters a light, murky green.

The US Army units in Verdun were housed in the Maginot Caserne, a former French Army post that had been built in the previous century. Upon arrival, Hiroshi and the others were herded into a barracks that served as a reception center. A bespectacled staff sergeant in an immaculately pressed Class A uniform conducted the orientation session.

France, the sergeant said, was not yet fully recovered from World War II, but Verdun still had problems that dated back to World War I. A vast network of tunnels, a labyrinth whose plan had long been lost or destroyed, surrounded the town. Walking around a World War I battlefield was dangerous; the ground could suddenly give way and swallow you up. Every year, the sergeant said, some poor sightseeing fool was lost that way and never heard from again.

After orientation, the bus took Hiroshi to a four-story structure that housed the 118th Regimental Band. With its arched doorways, tall casement windows, and decorative floor tiles edged with floral patterns, the building gave off a sense of decayed elegance. Hiroshi entered with his duffle bag over his left shoulder and his AWOL bag hanging from his right hand. Inside, the plaster on the walls was cracked and the paint faded or peeling; a sweet-and-sour odor of rot, overlaid with the sharp, alkaline scent of GI soap, permeated the building. The smell got stronger and heavier as Hiroshi descended into the basement where the 118th Regimental band was quartered.

The company clerk, a young corporal with blond hair and a southern accent, led him to one of the squad rooms, which held a dozen bunks. Two of the beds were occupied, but the men in them barely glanced in Hiroshi's direction. One was reading a book; the other lay on his back, his hands behind his head. Neither bothered to get up.

"This one's yours," the corporal said, pointing to an empty bunk with a rolled up mattress. "Come on back when you're squared away. There's beer."

The room was not totally shut off from the outside world; narrow windows close to the ceiling let in the pale grey afternoon light despite the brown snow banked up against them. Now and then, people, visible only from the knees down, could be seen walking by.

Hiroshi had just started unpacking his duffle bag when a soldier with dark hair and a neatly trimmed mustache walked into the room. His appearance was striking; tall and slender, with big, dark eyes and a strong jaw, he could have been a movie star, a Rudolph Valentino, a Tyrone Power. This made his first words all the more startling.

"Hey, Wop!" he shouted. "Let's go suck some pussy!"

"Aw shit, Dooley," said the soldier who'd been reading quietly on his bunk.

"Come on, man. We'll tear up the joint!"

The "Wop," a small, dark-haired man with a big nose who seemed inured to the vulgar epithet by which he was called, got up, put on his shoes and jacket, and followed his friend out the door, mumbling repeatedly, "Aw shit, Dooley. Shit, man. Aw shit..."

Deep-throated laughter erupted from the far end of the room. "Every motherfucking day, same fucking thing." The speaker got up and ambled toward Hiroshi. "That was Antoine Dooley. He's our drum major, biggest fuck-up in this motherfucking Army. Had the clap six times. One more time, and they'll Section Eight his pale ass right out of here. Sharp motherfucker, though. I'll give him that. Man, you should see him out there on the parade ground. Hmmm uh! Kiss my ass! A sharp motherfucker!" He laughed the same deep-throated laugh again as he walked up to Hiroshi with his hand extended.

"Name's Munsey."

Munsey was a short, small-boned man. His small round eyes were yellow and set wide apart. His mouth was full of crooked, tobacco-stained teeth, and a thin, scraggly mustache looked lost on his horsey upper lip.

Hiroshi took Munsey's hand. It felt a little clammy. "Hiro Kono," he said. "First name, Hiro. Last name, Kono."

"What, you Hawaiian or what? Man, you sound like a volcano! You know?" Munsey laughed good-naturedly. "I'm sorry, man. What you play? Trombone? Another boneman? Hey, that's cool. That's what I play. I hope you're not one of them square dudes, playing Wagner and shit."

As the weeks passed and Hiroshi got to know Munsey, he found that his new friend was not always as chatty as he had seemed to be at first; Munsey's loquaciousness came out in bursts. He might suddenly go into a lengthy monologue, addressing an individual or a room full of bunkmates, but he could just as easily retreat into a moody silence that would last for days. During these down times, Munsey could be seen off hours in a black trench coat with a black beret slung low over one eye and a scowl on his face, walking purposefully with one shoulder cocked. Munsey was from Harlem, and even when he was not being communicative, he was hip.

This was Munsey's second hitch in the Army, and he was about halfway through. He was one of those malcontents who could never make it past corporal because they would inevitably get busted for brawling or some other mindless infraction of military regulations. But he was from the Big Apple; he had a missionary's zeal for expanding the horizons of the provincials and farm boys with whom he was forced to share his quarters. He often talked about baseball—in particular, the Giants. He liked Willie Mays, but being a true aficionado, a purist who just liked the game, he was also an admirer of Joe DiMaggio, despite his racial handicap.

"Man, you ain't seen nothin' til you've seen DiMaggio play centerfield," Munsey said one day. "Yankee Stadium. A man could get lost out there in centerfield. You need a fucking compass to find your position. You could be wandering around for days, miss the whole fucking game. Sheeit! DiMaggio? He's running to the wall even before you hear the crack of the bat." He got up and started jogging across the room, looking over his left shoulder. At the far end, he leapt. Bracing himself with his right foot planted on the wall about two feet off the floor, he stretched out his left hand, landed lightly on his left foot, then threw in elegant slow motion to the cutoff man. Lest the audience miss the point, he repeated the performance. "Just like that, man. Kiss my ass! That fucking DiMaggio."

At other times, sitting on his footlocker, he would tell stories about Harlem.

"There was this chick at this party once—big droopy hat, earrings down to here, her legs crossed like this, smoking a cigarette, long, thin, custom-made. Shit, her fingernails were an inch long, man, bright red, matched her lipstick and her shoes. I mean, she got necklaces, bracelets, rings, she's a fucking jewelry store, and she talks like her shit smells like Chanel Number One. 'Oh deah me,' she says. 'Isn't that adorable, so precious,' shit like that. Well, this big dude can't take more of that shit, so he stands in front of her, unzips his fly, and lets it stick out, all fourteen inches. That was some terrible tool, man. Just terrible! The chick's eyes bug out, like this. Then she gets on her knees and starts sucking the dude's joint, like she wanted to swallow it, get it all in her belly. Man, the place went wild after that. There was bare ass and titty all over the place. That was some party. Kiss my ass!" Munsey got dreamy eyed as he recalled the scene.

Hiroshi wanted to think of himself as mature and worldly, but when Munsey told stories like that, he'd remember what his father used to say about anarchy and chaos, and he'd find himself rubbing his St. Christopher medal. It had become a talisman, a rabbit's foot, even if it was a piece of foolishness he carried only because of a drunken promise he'd made to Juanita Sanchez. It felt like an anchor, or maybe a spiritual buoy—something to preserve him from the dark undertow of Munsey's lurid imagination.

But there was more to Munsey than his seductively outlandish tales. There was art in the way he told his stories and how he carried himself, in the bluesy licks he played while warming up, in the easy way he moved while listening to music. Munsey had a collection of records—Dizzy, Bird, Powell, Miles, all the leading lights of bebop—and he talked about them with knowledge and understanding. Hiroshi knew these records, too; he had listened to them with his friends in San Pedro. Now he listened to them with Munsey, drinking beer and chewing the shit in the band room after hours. They competed with one another on their trombones, improvising alternating four-bar licks, using the blues progressions they heard in their heads. Sometimes Hiroshi would play chord changes on the piano—either the blues or standards like "I Got Rhythm," and "Perdido"—while Munsey let loose with fragmented but recognizable imitations of J.J. Johnson, whose virtuosity he had no chance of even approaching. Munsey had a real gift for jazz, but as a trombonist, he was mediocre at best. He just barely got away with playing in the 118th Regimental Band because he could fake his way through a Sousa march by playing every other note.

Munsey's talent for ellipsis was best displayed at the Blues Grotto, the enlisted men's club in town where he made extra money by playing in the band on weekends. The Grote, as it was called, was housed in a converted underground armory that had once been part of the Maginot Line. Its stone walls were painted black and swirled with bubbles of multicolored lights that bounced off a glass ball revolving above the dance floor. The air was close and had a humid, tropical warmth even in the dead of winter.

The Grote was a black club in every way. Its atmosphere had an air of racial intimacy and unspoken exclusivity that white soldiers immediately sensed. They would come in from time to time, but they felt out of place and out of step with the Grote's easy beat and funky rhythms, and they never stayed very long.

The house band, led by Bags Bagley, a trumpet player and career Special Services sergeant, played mostly up-tempo blues. "Follow the riff," Bags would say before going into one of his standard blues numbers. Munsey would stand with his eyes closed, weaving slowly from side to side or leaning on a pillar for support, playing every third or fourth note. When he soloed, he left blank spots that the listeners filled in with their imagination. Somehow, he swung. It was magic.

At first, Hiroshi came to the Grote mainly to hear Munsey, whose playing fascinated him. Somehow Munsey's technical mediocrity enhanced his innate musicality. Hiroshi played first trombone in the 118th and Munsey played third, but Munsey had something Hiroshi knew he would never have, an intuitive feel for the blues that flowed naturally and unbidden. Hiroshi was not shy about showing his appreciation: "Go, man!" he would shout. Munsey, for his part, called Hiroshi "My man. My volcano man."

The black patrons didn't know what to make of Hiroshi. He was thin and, at five ten, tall for an Asian. He was always dressed in what was pretty much standard garb for young West Coast jazz musicians: a navy blue blazer, gray flannel slacks, and blue suede shoes. His hair was longer than Army regulations allowed—the 118th band was more relaxed about such matters than the line units—and it usually drooped over his eyes. He also sported a mustache and wore sunglasses, even at night. Though the shades rendered him nearly blind in the dim lighting of the Grote, they provided him additional cover in what could sometimes be hostile territory. Munsey approved of Hiroshi's appearance. "You're cool, my man," he would say.

Munsey's friendship might have given Hiroshi entrée to the Grote, but he never tried to push things too far. He rarely mingled, except with other black members of the 118th who would drop in from time to time. He mostly sat alone at the bar, sipping a beer and listening to the band.

The best looking whores in Verdun hung out at the Blues Grotto, where money and quality booze flowed more freely than anywhere else in town. American cigarettes, worth more than cash when traded on the black market, were readily available in exchange for sexual favors. One could do well at the Grote, but the women were made to understand that it was a black club; consorting with white soldiers would be duly noted and could wear out their welcome. Munsey casually mentioned this unspoken rule to Hiroshi one day without making clear how it might apply to his volcano man.

The most eye-catching of the whores who worked out of the Grote was Suzanne. She wore her blond hair in an upsweep like a movie star; her slender nose had a slight tilt, and her thin, drawn lips gave her a classy Lana Turner look. She wasn't tall, and were it not for the spike heels she wore, she could have been called petite. She had a slim waist that she kept cinched with wide, shiny-colored plastic belts that accentuated her pointy breasts and the soft flow of her thighs. In short, she was the most gorgeous woman Hiroshi had ever seen. If ever he were tempted to test the Grote's rule on interracial fraternization, it would be because of Suzanne. But the matter was academic; Munsey called Suzanne "my woman," and hinted that he was "shacking up" with her.

In the hierarchy of possible intimacies with women, shacking up was at the very pinnacle. Such a thing was possible even for an enlisted man—provided he could supplement his income in some way. Antoine Dooley sold cigarettes on the black market and used the proceeds to rent a room in town where he kept a succession of women. This inspired both envy and awe among his fellow bandsmen, even though the women were mostly sad and desperate refugees from Eastern Europe. In the squad room, Dooley came on like a raunchy sex maniac, but those who hung out with him said it was beyond belief how smooth he could be with women. His latest conquest had been a handsome, dark-haired widow from Silesia, but that relationship seemed to have soured fairly quickly, because Dooley was soon back to spending his nights with the rest of the band.

Munsey made money playing at the Grote, but it was unclear whether or not he had actually attained the exalted status of shacking up with Suzanne. Nevertheless, shacked or unshacked, she was his woman. During one of his storytelling sessions in the squad room, he told his fellow bandsmen how it had all begun.

Munsey had met Suzanne in Paris, in a bar near the Étoile. "I saw right away she was different. I mean, she had fucking class, man, nothing common about her. I parlez-vooed up a storm with that chick. Then we went to a hotel where I just sat her on my face. Why mess around? Just like that. Whomp! Right on my face. After a while, I get hungry, so I say, 'Let's go get something to eat.' 'Mangez,' I say. 'You compris?' She gets up. Wouldn't let me put on my pants. Takes the fucking key and locks me in the room. 'Toute suite. Toute suite,' she says and locks me in the fucking room. Can you beat that? She comes back with a loaf of good French bread, jambon, I mean beaucoup jambon, man, some of that French fromage, that soft shit that smells like ripe pussy, and two bottles of vin rouge. Man, we scarfed up a storm. Two days we kept that shit up. Every time she goes out for food, she locks me in the room. 'No go, cheri,' she says. I tell her, 'Cheri, baby, I ain't goin' no place.' Two days in that hotel room." Munsey leaned back, looking off into the distance as if reliving the experience. Then, after a dramatic pause, he lowered his head and said in a tone of resignation, "Next thing you know, she's here. Followed my black ass all the way to Verdun."

It was because of Suzanne that Hiroshi began sitting in with Bagley's band at the Grote. It was hard for Munsey to be on the bandstand all night watching Suzanne go in and out of the club with other men, but she was only plying her trade, and she always went out with black men. Then one night Antoine Dooley came in. When he spotted Suzanne, he went straight for her, turning a lot of heads. They sat together at a corner table, with Dooley pawing at her and Suzanne smiling and offering little resistance. She took his cigarettes, cupping his hand in hers as he lit them for her, and when they danced, they danced real close, with Dooley's hand on Suzanne's ass. Suzanne knew the rules, but it seemed that even a whore was not immune to Dooley's wicked good looks and easy, self-assured ways. Stares and murmurs of disapproval floated from table to table, and Munsey couldn't help but notice.

Munsey called Hiroshi to the bandstand and introduced him to Bags. "This is my man, Hiro Kono, the volcano. Boneman. He's cool," Munsey said. He handed Hiroshi his trombone, saying, "Here, take my ax," then walked across the dance floor to Suzanne and Dooley.

Hiroshi couldn't hear what was being said, but Dooley got to his feet, squaring his shoulders and pushing out his chest. He and Munsey shoved and grabbed each other, knocking over chairs and spilling drinks. The club manager, a burly, no-nonsense career sergeant, came over to separate them. Dooley wisely chose not to argue with the manager, and instead sauntered out of the club with a superior smirk on his face. A table-pounding, glass-breaking, shouting match between Munsey and Suzanne followed. It ended with Suzanne forcefully shoving Munsey away and leaving the Grote. Humiliated, Munsey retired to the bar where he drank hundred-proof Old Grand Dad for the rest of the night.

From then on, Hiroshi began sitting in at the Grote on the weekends for a couple of sets, and sometimes for the whole night. Bags was always asking, "Hey, man, where's your ax?" So Hiroshi began bringing his own horn to the club. Munsey persisted in calling Hiroshi "my volcano man," but at the Grote, this got shortened to "Cane." Hiroshi's playing was vastly superior to Munsey's, but the ease with which the notes flew out of his horn made him suspect to some of the denizens of the club. At the Lido, no one had ever paid much attention to the band, but at the Grote, the patrons actually listened. A black soldier came up to Hiroshi one night and said to his face, "You a phony, Cane. You don't fool me, you just faking it." Hiroshi shrugged and tried to ignore the remark, but he couldn't get it out of his mind. He started writing out "improvisations" and practicing them like musical exercises. That helped some, but there was a limit to how many improvisational riffs he could memorize and string together without getting repetitious, mechanical, and monotonous. He was beginning to think that he really was a phony. So finally one night, he decided to open Chico's bottle of pills.

He didn't feel any different at first, but he noticed the effect his playing had on the other members of the band. "Hey, Cane, you swingin'," they said. Bags peered back at him, looking a little startled. "Yeah, man," he said softly.

Hiroshi hardly drank beer or anything alcoholic anymore; he drank Coke and coffee, lots of it. He had an unquenchable thirst. Beads of perspiration would streak down his face as he played, and his shirt would be soaked through. It was always the blues, but beboppy; the piano's altered chords, pushing hard against the beat, came through clear as a bell. He felt the pulsating line of the bass vibrating against the soles of his feet. The driving rhythms of the hi-hat and snare, the thumping accents of the bass drum, the crashing cymbals, all propelled him forward into bluesy growls and big leaps to flatted fifths and ninths that he was scarcely aware of making. They came from within, and Hiroshi swung as he had never swung before. He played funkier somehow; he had soul. The patrons shouted, "Go man! Go Cane!"

It was not long before Hiroshi had become a regular at the club; Munsey hardly played at all anymore except for those times he filled in when Hiroshi was in Paris or elsewhere in Europe for the weekend. Hiroshi felt high during those months—not so much on the pills as on his own playing. One evening, during a break,

Big Bennie Broujeau, a career master sergeant and the grand arbiter of taste at the club, called him to his table.

"Hey, man," Big Ben said, "you blowin' up a storm up there. What'ya drinkin'? Coke? Hey, whatever works."

His invitation to sit at Big Ben's table was duly noted, and Hiroshi became a fixture at the club. When he sauntered in, he no longer got the stares he once did. "Hey, Cane, what's happenin' man," people would call out. He relaxed, or, as they said at the Grote, he got real loose. Sometimes, before heading out to the club, he would stroll over to his wall locker, singing softly, "Every time it rains, it rains bennies from heaven." Then he'd open Chico's bottle and drop a couple of pills into his palm. Once he turned to see Munsey looking quizzically at him from his bunk. He would remember this later when he came back from the shower to find his wall locker open and the bennies gone. He'd forgotten to lock them up. He swore under his breath and banged his head hard against the thin metal door, leaving a shallow indentation.

In the weeks that followed, Munsey's behavior became increasingly bizarre. He'd always been unpredictable, but he'd also always managed to keep his Harlem cool, his Big Apple sophistication. Now he was excitable and belligerent. He got into a fight with Bags over money he claimed was owed to him. "Cane was playing that night," Bags said. "You were out on your ass at the bar. Shit, man, if you can't hold your liquor any better than that, you don't belong up here." Munsey took a swing at Bags—a big mistake. Early in his Army career, Bags had been a Division welterweight champ. The fight ended quickly, with Munsey sliding on his back across the dance floor.

It didn't seem to Hiroshi that his playing was any worse for the loss of the bennies, but when he soloed, the reaction from the crowd and his fellow musicians was tempered. With Munsey out, Hiroshi's place on the band was secure, but he began to feel uneasy. He took to drinking whisky between sets to help him relax. At times, he had to lean against a pillar in the same way

Munsey used to, and his playing became a bit sloppy as he blurred and skipped notes. "It's cool, more soulful," he thought, even as Bags glanced back at him with fishy looks.

As for Munsey, his mood changes seemed to get even more volatile and unpredictable after his fight with Bags. Suzanne stopped talking to him, but he still saw her as his woman and would get into fistfights with anyone who consorted with her. Finally, the manager banned him from the club entirely. Shortly after that, Dooley began showing up again.

One Saturday night, Munsey managed to enter the club unnoticed while a crowd was milling about in front. Hiroshi was on a break and sitting at the bar when he saw Munsey make a beeline to the table where Dooley was sitting with Suzanne.

"Moonsey," Suzanne pleaded. "Please go. I don't want to talk to you."

"It's not you I want to talk to, cheri baby," he said. "It's your friend Antoine here."

Dooley gave his usual I-don't-give-a-shit grin. "Have a seat, man," he said.

There was a hush in the Grote. Everyone had been alerted to Munsey's presence by then. The crowd watched—some nervously, others with smiles of anticipation—as Munsey and Dooley sat facing each other. They grinned tightly at one another and talked through their teeth.

The bartender picked up the phone and made a call. Hiroshi reached into his pocket and grasped St. Christopher. But it seemed as though nothing was going to happen. Munsey merely sat there, looking relaxed. Dooley, with his devil-may-care grin, slouched in his chair and casually raised his glass to his mouth. When he dropped his eyes to drink his whisky, Munsey struck. With the heel of his hand, he smashed the glass into Dooley's face, shattering the tumbler and showering the floor with glass splinters, ice, whisky, and flecks of blood. Dooley went down, broken glass embedded in his face, blood frothing from his mouth. He was still on the floor, on his hands and knees, spitting out blood and pieces of glass, when two MPs came rushing in. Munsey was standing over Dooley, shouting, "Get up and fight, motherfucker. Get the fuck up and fight."

Munsey got sent back to the States; word on the street was that he'd been discharged from the Army on a Section Eight. They said the MPs found drugs on him, and he was lucky he hadn't been sent to Leavenworth.

Dooley stopped showing up at the club, and Suzanne's regular patrons stopped going to her. Even the other whores avoided her, so she sat alone. It was excommunication.

During breaks and on weeknights, when the band wasn't playing, Hiroshi took to sitting with Suzanne and buying her drinks. He had never spent time with a woman like Suzanne before, and he was liking it. She was older than she appeared at first to be. Close up and with his shades off, Hiroshi saw the lines at the corners of her eyes and mouth, the slight sagging of the skin below her chin. She wore more facial powder than had been apparent from a distance, reminding him of Samantha Chatham the night she'd tried to seduce him. He hadn't been prepared for Mrs. Chatham's advances and had run off like a frightened schoolboy. Afterwards, he'd been too confused, even a little frightened, to call her. The following month, after joining the Army, he'd written to her, apologizing for leaving without a word. She never responded—not even to a Christmas card he sent a year later.

Two years had passed since then, and Hiroshi wanted to think of himself as a man of the world. That Suzanne was a woman for sale gave him a measure of self-confidence—he was the one in control. But he pretended they were simply friends. Suzanne seemed to appreciate his restraint, taking it as a token of respect. "You are different, Cane," she said. "You are not like the others."

Hiroshi was not sure when the change began, but over time,

what could be called the politesse between them gradually began to fray. It might have started when Suzanne casually placed her hand on his for no discernable reason, or the time she brushed up against him and he caught the scent of her body coming through the false sweetness of her perfume. It was probably just Suzanne's way with men, habits acquired over the long course of pursuing her profession, but when he was with her now, she no longer seemed the iconic Hollywood figure he had once imagined. She was a woman, and an extremely voluptuous one at that—one who could be made available to him if he wanted. One night, with Nat Cole singing "Darling, Je Vous Aime Beaucoup" on the jukebox, he asked her to dance with him. As he felt the softly yielding points of her breasts pressing against his body, he knew he wanted her.

The following weekend, after fortifying himself with two shots of whisky, Hiroshi at last found the courage to say what was on his mind. First, he took out his St. Christopher medal and spun it on the table.

"Suzanne," he began, "what're you going to do now that Munsey's gone?"

Suzanne looked puzzled.

"Do? What I always do. Always the same."

Hiroshi took another gulp of whisky and resumed toying with St. Christopher. For all his carefully cultivated sophistication, he was a remarkably inexperienced twenty-two.

"You don't have to come here to the Grote," he said. "I could rent a room—your room maybe."

"What is that you play with?" Suzanne wanted to know.

"Just something I carry," he said and handed her the medal.

Suzanne stared intently at the object in her hand.

"You *catholique*, Cane?"

Hiroshi shrugged, not sure of what was on Suzanne's mind.

"You carry *Saint Christophe*," she said.

"It doesn't really mean anything. A friend gave it to me."

"A friend?"

"Yeah, a friend. A woman I know. Just a friend," he said. Then, in desperation, he reached into his bag of GI French. "Suzanne, *voulez vous couchez avec moi?*"

Suzanne twisted a corner of her mouth and raised an eyebrow in a look of mild, maybe tired, amusement.

"You are a sweet boy," she said, "*mais non.*" She reached over, gave him back his medal, and patted the back of his hand.

They sat for a while in silence. Then Suzanne seemed to arrive at some resolution. Or perhaps she wanted to temper her rejection. "Cane," she said, "you are, what we say, *très très gentil,* but I decide to leave Verdun."

"You going back to Paris?"

"*Paris? Non.* I'm from *Nancy.* I might go back there. I don't know."

Afterwards, he offered to walk her home, but she declined. She smiled at him in an almost agonizingly tender way and took his hand in both of hers. She turned her head and offered Hiroshi one cheek to kiss and then the other, the way he had seen other French women do. "*Au revoir,* Cane," she said and walked away.

A heavy fog had settled on the city. The glow of the street lamps and the blinking lights of the Blues Grotto sign barely made it to the pavement. Hiroshi stood in the dappled darkness and watched Suzanne's smoothly gliding figure until it faded into the distance. He reached into his pocket and took out his St. Christopher medal. He remembered his farewell party and the tears streaming down Juanita Sanchez's face as she gave it to him. At the time, he had no idea what the medal meant, but it seemed to mean a lot to Juanita, so he'd kept it with him in his pocket through all these many months. "It will protect you," Juanita had said. But Hiroshi was thinking of throwing it in the Meuse.

URASHIMA

1957 - 1958

Hiroshi had been at UC Berkeley for almost a year when Mich's letter reached him.

"You said you loved me," she wrote, "and you probably thought you did, but you didn't respect me. I don't think you're capable of respecting a woman."

Hiroshi was stunned. He had to read the letter several times before it became clear to him that Mich was dumping him.

It was late afternoon, and he was alone in the three-bedroom apartment he shared with four other students above a taxi dispatch office near school. He didn't know what to do, so he went out and began walking—down Shattuck Avenue, then through the Berkeley campus and into Strawberry Canyon, where he sat on a rock until dark, smoking cigarettes.

While Hiroshi was away in the Army, Mickey had sold his San

Pedro café for a substantial profit, using the proceeds to open a seafood restaurant on Wilshire Boulevard in Los Angeles. Mickey, his wife Amy, and their new baby boy now lived with Mother and Father in a spacious, hedged-in bungalow in North Hollywood. Their neighbors in the predominantly white neighborhood hadn't made any friendly overtures toward them since they'd moved in, but neither had they protested or shown any open hostility. They'd simply ignored their new Asian neighbors, who took pains to keep their sidewalk, lawn, bushes, and driveway clean and tidy. Father, looking like a Japanese gardener, took care of the yard work, while Mother spent most of her time in the house looking after the baby so that Amy, a skilled chef who'd been trained by her father, could work at the restaurant.

Mickey's new restaurant was called Urashima. Its entrance was graced by a huge tank filled with fish that would swim in slow circles past a porcelain pagoda, a Chinese palace, and figurines of an Oriental princess and her entourage. Lobsters, their claws clamped shut with green rubber bands that had been disguised as seaweed, hunkered down, beady-eyed and sullen, on beds of multi-colored sand and gravel. Smaller tanks with tropical fish were set into the aqua green walls of the dimly lit dining area. The undersea motif helped to blur the lines between Japanese and Chinese culture, giving the place a vague, Pan-Asian feel. All this struck Hiroshi as claustrophobic, but the white patrons for whom the restaurant was designed seemed to find the décor exotic and appealing.

Mickey always took pains to explain to his customers that the restaurant was named after Urashima Taro, a mythical Oriental fisherman who lived with a beautiful princess in a kingdom at the bottom of the sea. An abbreviated version of the tale was even printed on the back of the menus, complete with a picture of a happy fisherman eating delicacies served by gracefully swirling water nymphs.

The actual tale was much darker than Mickey cared to

acknowledge. In it, Urashima Taro, a young fisherman, saves a sea turtle that is being tormented by a gang of boys. The turtle turns out to be a princess from an undersea kingdom. As a reward for his kindness, Urashima Taro is transported to a magical world at the bottom of the sea where he is greeted warmly by the lovely princess. After three days of what seems like unending pleasures, he is overcome by a yearning to see his mother. The princess reluctantly allows him to leave, but gives him a mysterious box, which she warns him never to open. When he returns to shore, he finds that not only his mother, but everyone he has ever known had vanished. Three hundred years have passed since his departure. In his despair, he opens the box. White smoke billows forth, turning Urashima Taro into an old man who crumbles into dust. The box had contained his 300 lost years.

After his stint in the military was over, Hiroshi moved in with Mickey and his parents while waiting to find out what schools had accepted him. He once again began working for his brother, this time waiting tables. He was glad of the chance once he realized how much waiters made in tips.

It was through his job at Urashima that Hiroshi met Michiko, a young elementary school teacher who worked there part-time as a hostess. She'd been an English major at UCLA, but once she'd graduated, she couldn't get a full-time teaching job, so she was working as an underpaid substitute teacher at an inner-city elementary school. Because the teaching stints were erratic, she'd been forced to find other work to supplement her income.

Hiroshi found Michiko stunning in her uniform, a silky red, form-fitting dress. As she swished her way between tables, the slit of her dress would reveal her slim and shapely thighs. With her mandarin collar and her hair piled high on her head, she looked like a Chinese princess.

At first, Michiko's glamorous appearance made Hiroshi shy of approaching her, but one day, when he found her picking out a then-popular tune on the piano that had been left at the restaurant by its previous owner, he sat down and played it for her. His simple improvisations seemed to impress her. In Hiroshi's experience, the piano player was usually the one who got the girl, and sure enough, he and Mich were soon dating

Father and Mother were delighted. Their biggest worry had always been that Hiroshi would marry a hakujin; if Hiroshi were to marry Michiko, a nice girl from a good Japanese family, they could die happy. They encouraged the couple to get married right away. When Hiroshi protested that he didn't have a college degree or a job, they said, "Don't worry about money. We will help." It was only after enlisting Mickey's support that Hiroshi was able to discourage them from engaging a baishakunin or marriage broker to begin negotiations with Michiko's parents.

The prospect of marrying Mich appealed to Hiroshi as well. She was attractive, bright, modest, and respectable—in short, everything one could hope for in a wife and the future mother of one's children. She was someone he could imagine himself happily settling down with. Within a month, even though there had been no formal engagement, the two began talking about what they would do when they were married.

Gradually, however, without being conscious of it, Hiroshi's demeanor toward Mich began to change. Anticipating his role as her future husband, he began to resemble his father— domineering and imperious, brooking no contradictions. Hiroshi no longer consulted Mich about the movies they would go see or where they would eat on their days off. He even dictated the kind of clothes she could wear when they went out together. There was nothing he could do about the sexy split dress she wore at the restaurant, but God help her if she wore anything like that on a date.

"I'm not really me when I'm with you," Mich once told him.

"So how are you when you're not with me?"

"I'm much wilder. I do crazy things."

"Like what?"

"You know, horse around. Break rules. Wave panties out of dorm windows."

"You did that?"

"Yes," Mich said. Then, noticing Hiroshi's shocked expression, she laughed. "Just kidding."

Despite her claims of wildness, Hiroshi and Mich never engaged in anything more risqué than heavy petting. "Look, Mich," Hiroshi once said, "I'm really not very experienced about sex. I had women in France—you know the kind I'm talking about. But I've never had a girl—I mean somebody like you."

"Well, I'm not one of those French women," Mich had said. Hiroshi was never quite sure what she was trying to convey by that comment.

On Valentine's Day, Hiroshi took Mich to a high-end restaurant on La Cienega Boulevard and introduced her to martinis. She took to them immediately. After her second one, she picked up his hand and kissed it slowly with an open mouth. It was not like her to do something like that, not in public. When he jokingly suggested they go to a motel, Mich laughed. Then, as if thinking the matter over, she picked up her martini, stared into it, and twirled the olive with the tip of her index finger. "All right," she said.

Mich had called Hiroshi's bluff and he found himself resenting it. He ignored her remark, and, after dinner, took her directly home. Hiroshi liked to think of himself as someone who'd been around. He was no longer the nice Japanese boy his mother thought she knew, and hadn't been for a very long time. But he didn't know what to make of Mich's response. It had frightened him, and like a scared little boy, he ran away.

Sitting on a rock in Strawberry Canyon, Hiroshi took Mich's letter out of his pocket once more. As he read it again, he began to understand what he should have figured out long ago: Mich was not a nice Japanese girl whose goal was to become the docile and obedient stay-at-home wife that his mother had been. But somehow, God help him, that was what he'd wanted.

He realized with bitterness that what Mich accused him of was true: he'd taken her for granted. After moving to Berkeley to attend the university, he'd expected—demanded—frequent letters from her, at least three a week, but he'd felt no obligation to answer them. When he did write to her, his letters had often been cold and petulant and filled with complaints about some slight or insensitivity on her part.

As soon as he returned to his apartment, he picked up the phone and called Mich's number in Los Angeles.

Her roommate Fumi answered.

"She's in New York," Fumi said. "She left last night."

"What's she doing in New York?"

"She's looking for a job there. Didn't you know?"

"She already has a job."

"Where've you been, Hiro? She quit her teaching job three months ago."

"Where can I reach her? Does she have an address? A phone number?"

"No, not yet," Fumi said. "She'll write to me when she's settled, but don't call me to ask for it. She told me not to give you her address."

"Please, Fumi," Hiroshi pleaded, but all he heard was a soft click on the other end of the line.

Only then did he remember that Mich had always talked about going to New York. She'd always wanted to be a writer. Hiroshi had never taken these ambitions seriously. In fact, her poems had annoyed him; he felt as though they took her away from him.

Until Mich, Hiroshi had never had what he could call a girlfriend. Because of her, for the first time in his life, he'd been free from his preoccupation with girls—with having them or not having them, with nagging feelings of inadequacy and want. With Mich anchoring his life, he'd felt secure, making it possible for him to focus on his studies and his future. Thinking about her had been a comfort, even when they were 300 miles apart. Now he was once again cast adrift.

Hiroshi was majoring in political science and thinking of applying to law school. He was already twenty-four and had to seriously consider what he was going to do to earn a living. Now, with his dream of domestic respectability gone, his motivation to do well in school faded as well.

It took a while for Hiroshi's roommates to notice the change in him. He took to sleeping in. He missed classes and would walk around the apartment barefoot and in his underwear, two or three days of stubble on his face.

Rolf, a Norwegian exchange student, was the first to notice that Mich's photo was missing.

"What happened?" he asked, pointing to the empty space on Hiroshi's desk.

"Nothing," Hiroshi said. "Nothing happened."

"Okay," Rolf said. Tall, blond, and blue-eyed, Rolf was primarily responsible for the parade of eager girls who passed through their shabby, unkempt apartment littered with empty beer bottles and discarded pizza cartons.

The following weekend, Rolf decided, they would throw a party.

Five girls showed up. One of them, whom Rolf steered not too subtly in Hiroshi's direction, was a woman in her late twenties, a graduate student in musicology. She was dressed entirely in black—black leotards, black skirt, black turtleneck, black horn-rimmed glasses. She wore no makeup.

Her name was Viola, and she was unlike any girl Hiroshi had ever known before—sophisticated, easy, soft, and warm. As the party drifted into a misty, boozy nonchalance, and couples faded into bedrooms and dark corners, Hiroshi left with Viola for a midnight stroll. They ended up at her apartment.

While in the Army, Hiroshi had lost his virginity more than once. At least that was how he saw it. Each time—he could count them on the fingers of one hand—it had been something new: a discovery, a revelation, a celebratory, born-again experience. Because all these encounters had taken place in Paris—on the fast and glittery Rue Pigalle—Viola was, so to speak, his first civilian. She was also his first instant conquest, even if he wasn't quite sure who had conquered whom. Once again, Hiroshi found himself in a strange and unfamiliar world.

The Beat Generation, though aging, still set the cultural tone in the Bay Area. Hiroshi had taken little notice of this while still focused on his studies and looking forward to a future with Mich. But everything changed after their breakup.

Viola moved in a totally unfamiliar milieu. Her friends were aspiring poets and writers. Hiroshi affected to be one of them, growing a beard and wearing black turtleneck sweaters, dungarees, and sandals. He took to sporting a beret he had acquired in France and began attending poetry readings in San Francisco's North Beach with Viola. Together, they went to Cimino's, a bar frequented by the fine arts crowd. Hiroshi wrote poems, enrolled in a fiction-writing course, and changed his major from political science to French.

Viola lived on a side street off Telegraph Avenue in a frame Victorian house that had been cut up into small units. She had a one-room, ground-floor apartment with a large bay window, a high ceiling, and a decorative, boarded-up fireplace. Nearly a quarter of the room was taken up by a baby grand, which she played daily with more energy than competence. Hiroshi winced inwardly as he listened to her fistfuls of wrong notes and botched runs, but he managed to keep an appreciative smile on his face.

Viola shared a kitchen and bathroom with a German art

student named Hilde, who lived in the next apartment. Hilde would often come over through the connecting kitchen when Viola was playing the piano. She would enter without knocking and sit on Viola's bed, listening intently with a solemn expression on her face. "You have a real gift, Feeola," she would say. "You should really study the piano."

Hilde was a blonde, bony, humorless woman in her mid-twenties with blue eyes, a narrow, straight nose, and a strong chin. Her accent, together with her Teutonic appearance, struck Hiroshi as a put-on. "How zoo you zoo," she said coldly when they first met, one eyebrow raised. Hiroshi took an instant dislike to her and complained to Viola about Hilde always being around.

"You don't understand her, Hiro," Viola said. "She's really a very warm person, and besides, she's a friend. I never ask you to give up your friends."

Without thinking, Hiroshi replied, "Yeah, but none of my friends are Nazis." As soon as the words were out of his mouth, he regretted them. But it was too late. He and Viola had their first fight as a result. They made up again after a week, but Hiroshi couldn't explain why he had said such a stupid thing. The memory of it made him cringe.

Just before she'd met Hiroshi, Viola had broken up with another lover, a lecturer in the French Department. She often talked about him, even comparing Hiroshi's love-making with his.

"You don't even know I'm around when you make love," she would say. "It's all right to talk and kiss, but you should look at me and say 'I love you.' Well, maybe you don't have to go quite that far, but you could say something sweet. And don't be in such a hurry!"

The women in France had never been so demanding.

Viola's former lover called once when Hiroshi was there. Viola had been curt with him. "David, it's no use. Everything that needs to be said has been said. It's time we moved on." Then she'd hung up. When the phone rang again, she put a pillow over it. The muffled ringing could be heard even through the pillow, and it seemed to go on forever.

"We were together for nearly a year," Viola said. "That's a long time for me." Then she took Hiroshi's face in her hands and said, "Oh, but things are different with you, sweet. You're the love of my life."

Hiroshi knew she wasn't serious, but later that week, when she missed her period, he considered the possibility that he might have to marry her. A month later, when it appeared certain that she was indeed pregnant, Hiroshi proposed to her, spurred along by a sense of virtue, righteousness, and old-world morality.

"Oh, Hiro!" Viola said. "That's so sweet of you. Do you really mean it?"

When he assured her that he did, she wrapped her arms around him and gave him a big, wet kiss.

Though it felt a little as if they were playacting, Hiroshi brushed away his doubts and suggested that they go out to dinner to celebrate the engagement.

"I'm going to make myself beautiful for you," Viola said. "Go to your place and don't come back until eight o'clock."

Hiroshi returned promptly at eight with a dozen red roses. He could have eaten for three days on what he'd paid for the flowers. He knocked on the door like a young man on a courting call. It took some time for Viola to appear. She opened the door slowly at first, then quickly for dramatic effect. She curtsied and looked at Hiroshi with an expectant smile. She was dressed in a satiny green dress cut so low that half her breasts were exposed. Her hair had been sprayed into stiff iron spikes and her face was powdered white like a geisha's. Her lips had been stained crimson, her lashes dripped with mascara, and green shadows darkened her eyes; in her sea-green gown, she seemed a watery enchantress. It took Hiroshi a moment to compose himself, but he knew what was expected of him. "Viola, you're beautiful," he said. "Wow, you're gorgeous. I didn't know you could look like that."

They went to Jack London Square for dinner. While waiting on a traffic island for the light to change, Viola clutched Hiroshi by the waist and pressed her body against his, tilting her head back. "Kiss me, Hiro," she said. Hiroshi didn't like kissing Viola in public. This wasn't the Deep South, where lynching was still a threat, but a Japanese man kissing a white woman in the middle of the street was unnecessarily provocative. As it was, the two of them would often get funny looks from people, even when they were just walking together. But he kissed her anyway. They held onto each other like a man and a woman hopelessly in love, oblivious to the passing cars that lashed them with the beams of their headlights.

After they made love that night, Viola said, "Hiro, you don't love me. You don't really love me."

"How can you say such a thing? Of course I love you. I love you very much."

"No, you don't. You don't love me, and you never will," Viola insisted. Then she rolled over and fell into a sound sleep.

Viola was right—he didn't love her. Mich had told him essentially the same thing, but he had loved Mich, more than he knew at the time. With Viola, it was a matter of commitment. He would stick by his word.

In December, just before Christmas break, Hiroshi was called home. Father had suffered a near-fatal stroke, and the whole family had been summoned to his hospital bed. Sachi, who lived nearby in Gardena, came with her husband, and Yukio and Kaz drove in from Arizona with their two-year-old son. Hiroshi was surprised to find that Yukio had named his child Seiji. There had been an estrangement between Yukio and Father after Yukio had been adopted into Kaz's family. He wondered what had motivated Yukio to choose his true father's name for his firstborn son.

It was the first time in a quite a while that the family had gathered together. When Hiroshi was a child, his father had been a huge and powerful man who ruled over his family like a god. Now he was lying barely conscious with tubes pumping oxygen into his lungs and dripping fluids into his body. Seeing his father ravaged by age and disease, Hiroshi felt as though he himself had somehow been diminished.

Sachi, who was in the early months of her first pregnancy, came into the room and stood next to Hiroshi. They remained silent for some time until, without a word, Sachi reached out and held his hand. This came as a shock. The two had never been close, but Hiroshi was moved by the gesture and found himself hugging his sister for the first time in his life.

Later, when Sachi asked him how things were going, he decided to tell her about Viola. He was engaged to be married, he told her. It was a secret. He hadn't told anyone else yet. But when he started to give more details about his future bride, Sachi said with look of alarm, "A hakujin girl? You need to tell Mom!"

Hiroshi remained silent. Sachi squinched her eyes and looked directly into his face. "You have to tell her, Hiro. Not Father, don't tell him. He's in no condition to hear something like that. But you have to tell Mom. And Mickey. Tell Mickey."

"Why?"

Sachi gave an exasperated sigh.

Hiroshi should have known better. Sachi was Sachi. She would never change. But she was not entirely wrong. He knew she would tell Mickey, but Mother needed to hear it from him, not from Sachi and not from Mickey.

When he finally spoke to his mother, she remained composed and quiet. She appeared resigned, much as she had when he'd told her he was enlisting in the Army.

She asked if the girl was pregnant.

Hiroshi was shocked that she could have guessed such a thing. How could she have known? But he didn't hesitate. He lied.

"No, Mother. We just like each other very much."

When he told her that Viola's family name was Novo, she asked if Viola was Portuguese. There had been many Portuguese families in Hacienda. One of Father's foremen, and another of his tractor drivers, had both been Portuguese. When Hiroshi confirmed that Viola's family was indeed Portuguese, Mother said, "They get fat when they get old. All those Portuguese women in Hacienda, all fat."

Hiroshi said he didn't care if Viola got fat because he loved her, but his mother said, "Don't be too sure." She herself had remained slim throughout her life. Now she extended her arms in front of her, as if holding a barrel. "Really fat. Like this," she said.

Things between Hiroshi and Viola had begun to unravel well before he told his mother about the engagement. He was determined to go through with the marriage regardless, but Viola's bohemian ways, which Hiroshi had found appealing at first, had begun to trouble him. Hiroshi was more Japanese than he liked to admit. Despite himself, he'd begun to question—there was no other way to put it—her morals. Though he claimed to believe in free love, it was for him a purely intellectual proposition. Viola lived it.

One day, she told Hiroshi about Edgar, her 70-year-old piano tuner. "An incredible man—so alive, so virile. You wouldn't believe the vitality of the man, Hiro. The first time he came to tune my piano, something seemed to happen between us—a certain electricity. I've never experienced anything like it before. After the tuning, he played Chopin's 'Military Polonaise' for me. I'd never heard it played with such power! It made me feel quivery all over. Then do you know what he played next? You'll never guess. 'Honeysuckle Rose'! Stride style, like Fats Waller! What a wonderful man!"

"Yeah, but seventy years old?"

"Oh, that doesn't mean a thing. I've never met a man with such vitality. And strong. All wiry, with skin like leather."

Being a man of the world, Hiroshi accepted Edgar. But when he came back after Christmas break, Viola told him about Nathan.

"A wonderful man. He plays the sax. He's a jazz musician, so he's on the road a lot. He was in town over the holidays."

"You saw him while I was away?"

"Sorry, love, but Nathan and I go back a ways, to when I lived in San Francisco. He's a wonderful lover. It's true what they say about colored men."

"I can't believe what you're saying! You're pregnant! You're carrying our child!"

"Oh, Hiro, you can be so sweet," she said. She paused for a moment, then took a deep breath and continued: "I'm not pregnant. I had my tubes tied while I was living in San Francisco."

Hiroshi could only stare at her. He'd thought he was prepared for anything, but this went beyond anything he could have imagined. "Why?" he asked. "Why did you say you were pregnant?"

"I didn't really say I was pregnant, Hiro. You just assumed it. I thought you'd run out the door, but you wanted to marry me. That was so sweet."

Hiroshi stood before her, stunned. It took a long moment for the pieces to fall into place. "You bitch," he said. He turned and walked out, slamming the door behind him.

A week later, he called her, but she hung up as soon as she recognized his voice. Without knowing why, he redialed. He let the phone ring and ring, knowing there was a pillow over it. It was a rite of exorcism.

Weeks later, he came across Viola at Cimino's. She was in a soft white angora turtleneck instead of her usual black, and she wore earrings. Even in the dim light, Hiroshi could see her heavy eye shadow and mascara. She was with Hilde, who looked stunning in toreador pants and a creamy silk blouse. Hiroshi had never noticed Hilde's figure before.

"You're really decked out," Hiroshi said. "You two double

dating?"

Hilde raised one eyebrow, the way she always did, but this time it struck Hiroshi as extremely sexy. "Just dating," she said as she took hold of Viola's hand.

The following weekend, Hiroshi got an urgent call from Mickey, who said Mother was sick and in the hospital.

"What's wrong with her? She was fine at Christmas."

"She's been sick for a long time. Didn't you know? They're removing one of her kidneys."

The operation was successful, but Mother looked weak and tired when Hiroshi went to see her. The nurse told him he shouldn't exhaust her, so he kept his visit short. Before he left, he told her he wasn't engaged anymore. "I'm not going to marry the Portuguese girl," he said.

"It's good you didn't tell Father," she said. "He was spared all the worry." She closed her eyes and appeared to fall asleep.

Outside the hospital, the air was cold and crisp and the sky was clear. Despite the lights of the city, he could see stars overhead. He thought of his mother asleep in her bed. Her face had been smooth and calm, distant but at peace. It seemed that the world he knew was still there for him, after all. He thought about Mich in New York and wondered what she was doing.

HOMECOMING

1960

At Tokyo's Haneda Airport, Father tugged Hiroshi's arm and whispered "pickpocket," nodding his head toward a gaunt, hollow-cheeked man who was standing alone next to a turnstile. The man had a day's growth of stubble on his face and wore an ill-fitting brown suit that was soiled and shiny with wear.

Japan had not yet fully recovered from the war, and the man's shabby appearance wasn't in any way unusual. Hiroshi didn't think he looked at all suspicious. Still, they'd been warned about thieves; apparently, American tourists were a favorite target. Even before the war, Father said, pickpockets in Japan had been noted for their skill. Sometimes they would work in pairs: one thief would distract victims by bumping into them, while another would slice through their pockets with lightening speed. They were said to be so quick and agile that you never even felt your pocket being cut open with a razor.

"Mother, Hiroshi," Father said. "Be careful of that one. He's been watching us." He looked around to see if he could spot a likely accomplice.

"Father," Hiroshi said, "he's just here to meet somebody."

Hiroshi knew he shouldn't have contradicted his father, and regretted the words as soon as he said them, but he was 27 and had outgrown the deference a good Japanese son pays his father.

As they left the terminal, Hiroshi saw the man in the brown suit walking out with a woman who looked to be his wife. He was carrying a small child. Determined to be a good son, Hiroshi refrained from pointing them out to his father.

Hiroshi's parents had asked him to accompany them on a group tour to Japan because they didn't feel secure traveling by themselves. Hiroshi, armed now with a degree in French, had been planning a trip to Paris, where he hoped to stay for a year or as long as his money held out. But when his parents offered to pay his way to Japan, he couldn't resist the opportunity.

Father, now 76, was still partially paralyzed along the left side of his body from his stroke. He walked at a slow shuffle, and when he stumbled, he could only watch helplessly as the ground came up to meet him. The others in their group were old as well— some even older than Father. Their expressions of concern, though meant kindly, clearly annoyed him. "Not so fast," the others would tell the tour guides. "We must be considerate of Kono-san. He has difficulty walking, you know."

Throughout the trip, the group was booked primarily in Japanese-style inns, which, according to the travel agent, were more comfortable and commodious than western-style hotels. In addition to offering better food and Japanese baths, they were also cheaper.

After having lived so long in America, however, it was difficult for Father to sleep on tatami mats on the floor. Beyond that, the traditional-style rooms had no doors or locks; a thief could slide open a shoji panel, enter their room while they were sleeping, and steal everything they had. All guests were encouraged to entrust their valuables to the hotel safe, but Father preferred to put his important items—his cash, traveler's checks, return airline tickets, and passport—under his futon, where the resulting bundle would make a reassuring if slightly uncomfortable lump under his body. In any case, Father insisted that he had no intention of sleeping too soundly. Unlike thieves in America, who simply used force to break into houses or robbed people at gunpoint, Japanese thieves had a reputation for being resourceful and crafty.

The group Hiroshi and his parents were traveling with was made up of former natives of Kumamoto Prefecture, so after a week of touring the usual tourist attractions—Tokyo, the hot springs of Hakone, the ancient shogunate capital of Kamakura, and the historic imperial city of Kyoto—they arrived at their final destination, Kumamoto City. Prefectural and city officials were there at the train station to welcome them when they arrived. Girls in brightly colored kimono presented flowers to each of the women, while reporters and photographers recorded the event.

In the evening, a banquet, attended by the prefectural governor himself, was held in honor of the visitors.

Father, who was widely known before the war for his oratorical skills, had been chosen to speak on behalf of the group. His voice was weak and shaky as he began.

"We left our native land more than half a century ago," he said with sadness in his voice. "We raised our children in a foreign land. Our flesh and blood became like strangers. But we persevered. We made great fortunes in America, and much was taken from us. We enjoyed great happiness and suffered deep and abiding sorrow."

Father turned away and wiped his cheeks. A murmur of concern went around the room. Was Seiji Kono going to let them down? Recovering quickly, he continued. "What kept us striving during these times of tribulation and loss was the thought that one day we would again see Nippon, our native land. In the morning, when we got up to work the fields, we would look toward the glow of the morning sun. 'There, in that direction is the sun,' we would say. 'There in that direction lies Nippon.' This gave us the strength to face the day. Nippon! Nippon was always in our hearts, in our dreams, and in our prayers. The land was our mother; she nourished and sustained us. She gave us hope, courage, and pride. Nippon. It was always Nippon."

Listening to his father speak, Hiroshi was glad that he'd agreed to come on the trip. Even though Father was only a shadow of what he'd once been, he still had a flair for drama. By the end of his speech, even the men were wiping tears from their eyes and cheeks. "That Kono," he overheard one of them say. "He has a gift."

Hiroshi didn't doubt that his father had been sincere in everything he'd said, and there was no denying that the speech was deeply moving. But he wondered what his father was referring to when he spoke of standing in the fields gazing at the sun. He'd presented himself as a man laboring alone in his field like a peasant in a Jean-François Millet painting. But that image, if accurate in any way, had become true for his father only after the war, after he'd lost everything. True, after arriving in America, Father had worked his way south from San Francisco picking fruit for 65 cents a day—but that period of his life had only lasted a few months. As soon as he'd reached Hacienda, everything had changed for him. Hiroshi had heard the story countless times at the dinner table.

Making his way south with a gang of fruit pickers, Seiji Kono found himself in Hacienda in late August 1903. There, broke and workless, he joined a group of Japanese immigrants who were squatting in a labor camp owned by the Sugar Company. When Harold Mahoney, the boss of the Sugar Company, came riding into camp on his buckboard, everyone was sure he was coming to evict them. Seiji, who'd attended a business college in Japan, was the only person in the group who knew any English. He'd long since realized that the English he'd been taught in Japan had little to do with the language spoken in America, but he agreed to speak to Mahoney on behalf of his campmates nevertheless.

Mahoney was a big man with broad shoulders. He looked strong enough to lift the horse pulling his wagon. Still, swallowing hard, Seiji squared his shoulders and said, perhaps louder than he intended to, "I Kono. You want talk?"

"You the spokesman for these people?"

"Spokesman?"

"Yeah, the leader. The contractor."

"Ah, contractor." Seiji knew about contractors. He had worked for one picking fruit on his way to Hacienda. "No," he said. "I no contractor."

"That makes no difference," Mahoney replied impatiently. "Look, I need boys. You understand? All the boys you have. Harvest sugar beets. Sugar beets." Mahoney went through the motions of pulling beets out the ground and topping them with a knife. "Savvy? Comprende?"

"You want us work?"

"That's right."

Seiji turned to the others. "He has work for us. He doesn't want to turn us out. He wants us to harvest his beets."

"The Chinese do that work," a man named Sato said.

"I hear the Chinese are asking for more money," someone else chimed in.

"Ahhh," several men said, now understanding why Mahoney had come.

"Ask him how many men he wants."

"How many boy?" Seiji asked Mahoney.

"Thirty, forty—as many as you have."

Seiji turned to the others. "He needs forty men."

The men started counting. There were only twenty-six of

them.

"That's not enough," Seiji said.

"Tell him we can do the work of forty Chinese," Sato said.

Seiji thought the matter over. Finally, he said, "We got sahty-soo-ree boy."

"How many?"

"Sahty-soo-ree," Seiji repeated, drawing two 3s on the ground.

"Oh, thirty-three. That's great. That's good," Mahoney said, nodding his head up and down.

The men began shouting at Seiji about the pay.

"Men say, how much pay?"

"Ten dollars an acre. Maybe more. Depends on the yield."

Seiji turned to the others. "I don't understand. I think he said ten dollars. Ten dollars for each acre. I don't understand."

"Never mind," another man said. "Tell him we'll take it."

"That's how they do it," the others chimed in. "Take it, take it."

Seiji was uneasy. This white man wanted to hire them because he thought they would be cheaper than the Chinese. But how much cheaper? Back home, he'd seen his father compete for fish against the big trading houses from Kumamoto City. He took a deep breath and smiled gently at Mahoney. He tried to look relaxed and calm, the way his father did when trying to strike a bargain.

"You explain," he said. "You explain me ten dollar acre."

"Ten dollars each acre," Mahoney said, holding up ten fingers. "But lots of beets, say fifteen tons per acre. Many, many beets, then maybe twelve dollars an acre."

Seiji pondered what Mahoney had said. He understood now that the price could be higher. He tried to imagine what his father would do.

"Fourteen dollar," he said finally.

Mahoney smiled and said, "Twelve."

"Sahteen," Seiji said, showing Mahoney ten fingers, then

three.

"Okay, okay," Mahoney said. "I bring contract tonight. You sign contract. Work begins tomorrow."

"I was nineteen, only three months in America, when I got my first contract," he would tell his family many years later. "It was a good contract. Not what the Chinese wanted, but it was good. Mahoney wanted me to supervise the work, so he gave me a horse to ride. I never did a day of physical labor after that."

Sitting at Seiji Kono's table at the banquet in Kumamoto City were Seiji's younger brother Kenjiro and his wife Okane. Both had come from the Kono family home in Nagasu, an hour's train ride away.

After Seiji finished his speech, he saw photographers and reporters converging at his table. He'd already begun mentally preparing some words for them, but instead of going to him, they went to Kenjiro and a man sitting next to him, whom Kenjiro had introduced as a friend and business acquaintance. The stranger's name was Kumagai, and from the conversation they'd had over dinner, Seiji concluded he was man with political connections. As photographers snapped pictures of Kenjiro and his friend, Kenjiro waved his hands in front of the cameras and said, "We have no comment. No comment. Everything will be in the prospectus." The reporters then turned to Kumagai. "When are you releasing the geologic survey report?" they asked. "Soon, soon," Kumagai said. "I have no further comment. No further comment."

After the reporters and photographers left, Seiji asked his brother what the fuss had been about.

"A new project I'm involved in near Nagasu," Kenjiro said vaguely.

"The reporters mentioned a resort."

"Yes, hot springs."

"Hot springs? They've been talking about hot springs in Nagasu for years. The old man once invested in a resort. Remember? He lost a small fortune that way. It nearly ruined him." Seiji didn't need to say that the money he'd sent from America at that time had saved their father.

"Yes, but there's been a new geologic study," Kenjiro said. "They were looking in the wrong places before."

As they left the banquet hall, Seiji's mind was still swimming in the afterglow of his speech. His thoughts were so filled with memories of the day when, fifty-seven years earlier, he'd left his native land that he scarcely noticed being jostled in the crowd.

Kenjiro and Kumagai wanted to take Seiji and Hiroshi drinking, so after dropping Mother off at the hotel, the four men took a taxi to the outskirts of the city where they stopped at a fashionable restaurant overlooking a lake. "If you're still hungry, this restaurant is famous for its fresh water fish," Kenjiro said.

"Ah, Kono-san, Kumagai-san," the proprietress said as they went in. "We have your usual room reserved. A clear night with a good view of the moon." Then she pouted and poked Kenjiro in the ribs with her elbow. "Where have you been, you naughty man! Have you found a pretty new face?"

"My older brother," Kenjiro said, clearing his throat, "just arrived from America. With his son. The West Room is fine. And your best sake."

"Hai!" the proprietress said, all efficiency now. "Right away, Kono-san. Hisako, Reiko," she said to waitresses, "show the gentlemen to their room."

The room, which had been built on stilts, extended into the lake, so they were surrounded on three sides by water. The night was indeed clear, the water a sheet of black glass that perfectly reflected the silhouettes of pine trees and a sharply etched crescent moon. The two waitresses who were serving the party flirted with both Kenjiro and Kumagai, blushing coyly at their remarks. In his old age, such games no longer appealed to Seiji. His taste for alcohol had also diminished. But rotund and rosy-cheeked Kenjiro, only three years younger than Seiji, drank heartily.

Though frequently short of breath because of his heavy smoking, Kenjiro was otherwise the very picture of prosperous good living. Encouraged by the waitresses, he and Kumagai, a man in his fifties, sang and danced in turn. Hiroshi, too, got into the spirit of things. To Seiji's surprise, Hiroshi did a dance while singing a popular drinking song.

"Where did you learn that?" he asked.

"In Tokyo," Hiroshi said. "The night the geisha came to the hotel. You went to bed early that night."

Seiji understood his son was an adult who'd been in the Army and traveled in Europe. But he felt he was seeing Hiroshi for the first time.

It was only after they had already left the restaurant that Seiji discovered his travel wallet was missing along with his passport, their return airline tickets, and 50,000 yen—nearly 150 dollars.

Kenjiro told him not to worry. He said that he would take care of the matter.

"The police are very efficient," he said, "There's a good chance they'll recover the passport and airline tickets—unless the thief destroys them, which isn't likely. The money, of course, you won't see again. But don't let that spoil your visit. Things will work out one way or another."

"You're an American," he added with a laugh. "The police still go out of their way for Americans."

Seiji resented his younger brother's patronizing tone. In 1923, after Seiji had established himself as a successful farmer, Kenjiro had joined his brother in America for a brief while. Staked by Seiji, Kenjiro had been able to lease land in Oso Flaco, where he'd had a remarkable string of luck growing lettuce. After only six years in the US, he'd returned to Japan with a substantial nest egg. He was one of those rare individuals who'd managed to do exactly what he'd intended, spending no more than a few years in America and returning to Japan with what most Japanese would call a fortune.

He'd subsequently squandered the money he'd made in a series
of ill-advised investment schemes just prior to the Depression,
but in the absence of Seiji, the eldest son, Kenjiro had eventually
inherited the family business and had as a result not just survived,
but thrived.

Kenjiro was a village elder now, living in the best house in
Nagasu. He was obviously well-connected politically, and the
family fish business appeared to be doing well. Its main office,
now in Kumamoto City, was run by his oldest son; Kenjiro himself
lived in semi-retirement.

Visiting his hometown of Nagasu again for the first time in many
decades, Seiji was struck by how the old fishing village, with its
unpaved roads and shanty-like homes, seemed hardly to have
changed. Even his old home looked much the same—from the
outside at least. The inside was a different matter altogether; it
now boasted a western-style sitting room, a modern kitchen, and
a tiled bathroom—luxuries one would generally expect to see in
the wealthier suburbs of major cities.

Before leaving for Japan, Seiji had sent ahead food items for
his brother's family—coffee, sugar, canned hams, cooking oil,
and lard. But Kenjiro had seemed amused by the gifts. "Coffee is
still very expensive here, a true luxury," he said. "And people will
be appreciative of the other stuff as well. But, of course, things
have improved much since the war." At this, Seiji couldn't help
recalling some unsavory rumors he'd heard even in the US about
Kenjiro being in trouble with the law for dealing in black market
items. But he couldn't deny that Kenjiro didn't seem worse off for
all that.

Otsui was glad of the western chairs in the sitting room.
After her years in America, she could no longer sit for long on her
knees in proper Japanese fashion. Seiji, a man, was permitted
to sit cross-legged, but not she. Otsui enjoyed resting in the
sitting room and chatting with Kenjiro's wife. Okane, a farmer's

daughter, was an easy-going woman with few pretensions, but Kenjiro felt he had married below his station and treated her rudely. He provided her with no household help, something a man of his wealth could easily have afforded. Back when the marriage between Kenjiro and Okane had been arranged, however, the family business had still been in a perilous state. So much so that it was Seiji's view that his brother should count himself fortunate in having married Okane. One could in fact argue that it was Okane who had married below her station, for in the hierarchy of old Japan, a farmer ranked above the merchant class. This was especially true of Okane's family, which farmed their own land.

Behind the house, the garden, his father's personal creation, was just as Seiji remembered it, with its gnarled pines, stone lanterns, and graveled paths. The old woodshed still stood at the far end of the garden behind a bank of camellias. Kenjiro, who could be extravagant one moment and parsimonious the next, had never bothered to replace it because it couldn't be seen from the house.

Looking closely at the shed's old door, which was nearly falling off its hinges, Seiji saw that it still bore traces of the scars he'd made on it with an ax more than sixty years before. As a child, Seiji had always looked forward to the annual village bazaar. One year, he'd spent weeks building a kite for the village festival, when Kenjiro, little devil that he was, stomped on it out of spite during one of his tantrums. Knowing he was in trouble, Kenjiro then dashed into the shed and barred the door from within. Enraged, Seiji had hacked at the door with an ax until their father had come to snatch it away from him. "You ruffian!" their father had shouted before boxing his ears. "Why kind of a brute are you to take an ax to your brother?"

Kenjiro had rushed out of the shed and into the arms of his mother, who'd cooed over him, saying, "Kenjiro, Kenjiro. Everything is fine now. Mother is here." As Kenjiro walked back to the house that day holding his mother's hand, he'd looked over his shoulder at Seiji with a smirk. Seiji's own mother had died shortly after he was born, so he'd never known her. Kenjiro was the son of his father's second wife.

As Seiji looked at the woodshed's scarred door, all the bitterness of the past came flooding back. Why hadn't Kenjiro repaired the door? Or simply torn the whole shed down? It seemed as if he'd kept the shed intact as a memorial to Seiji's long ago humiliation. As the first born, Seiji should have inherited his father's business. But his father had foolishly invested in a risky venture involving a new kind of fishing net that had never been tried before. When that investment had failed, Seiji had quit his studies and left for America in the hopes of making enough money to save the business and the family honor. Seiji had sent money regularly back to Japan, living in rickety barracks instead of a decent house in order to do so. Those remittances had been the only reason his father had been able to avoid utter ruin. Even after that first debt had been paid off, other failed ventures and requests for money had conspired to keep Seiji in America permanently.

In 1939, when Seiji was firmly settled in America, his father had written to him saying that his health was failing, and that before he died, he wanted to see the business on solid ground. "Seiji, you have prospered in America. You can be generous. Kenjiro has put in much effort in rebuilding the business. He has worked hard and learned the business from the ground up."

Seiji knew that his stepmother had put his father up to the request. She was a full twenty years younger than her husband, and he doted on her. But business was good for Seiji at the time; his investment in the packinghouse was doing well. So he did what his father asked of him and signed away his rights to the business that should have been his inheritance. Little did he know that catastrophe was just around the corner for all of them.

As Seiji stood in his father's garden, he was fully aware that the land beneath him was still legally his; he had not signed that away. But that was a mere legality. A piece of property in a failing, rundown fishing village was worth nothing. All he had left was the lingering bitterness represented by a broken-down woodshed with a scarred door.

Seiji always remembered the local village festival with great fondness, so he was pleased to find out that their trip would coincide with the annual fair. Every year, merchants from miles around would come and set up stalls along Nagasu's main street. Puppeteers, jugglers, and mimes would put on shows while vendors hawked noodles, baked yams, and sweet dumplings on a skewer. But the goods on sale were nothing like Seiji remembered—they were shoddy, probably made in Taiwan or Hong Kong, and the food carts swarmed with flies. Where were the big-city merchants and traders of the past? Behind the stalls, peddlers—unshaven, ragged, and dirty—and their unkempt wives tended to squalling, snot-nosed broods. Seiji was appalled by the squalor, but Kenjiro didn't seem to notice.

"It's the same as it's always been," Kenjiro said.

"No, no," Seiji said. "It was never like this. And the riff-raff. Look at that man over there. He's been eyeing me now for the past ten minutes."

The village was full of strangers, some looking decidedly too smooth, some in rags with their hands out. Others, shifty eyed, hugged the walls like rats. Nagasu was alive with con artists, beggars, and thieves.

Kumagai came to Nagasu during the bazaar to confer with Kenjiro. He brought good news. "The police," he told Seiji, "have arrested the thief. They caught him trying to cash in your airline tickets, the poor fool. The police need to hold onto them for a bit as evidence, but you'll have them back in plenty of time for your flight back. Your passport as well. As you know, the police in Japan are quite efficient."

After leaving the festival, everyone went back to the family home. Kumagai spent the rest of his visit in close consultation with Kenjiro. They walked in the garden, talking in hushed voices with their heads together. Kenjiro walked with his fists clenched at his sides, his shoulders hunched and rigid. From time to time, he and Kumagai could be heard shouting at one another. Kumagai did not stay for dinner; he returned to Kumamoto City on the late afternoon train.

After Kumagai's visit, Kenjiro was out of sorts. Something was clearly bothering him, but he declined to say what it was. "Just a business matter," he said, "nothing of any consequence. I may have to go to Kumamoto City next week for a few days. Nothing serious."

Hiroshi accompanied his parents to Tokyo and saw them off at Haneda Airport, but after a few days in Tokyo, he returned to Kumamoto City. He wanted to become better acquainted with his Japanese relatives, in particular his cousin Akira, Uncle Kenjiro's second son.

Akira and his older brother had both been born in the US. Because Seiji, who was already doing quite well, had sponsored Kenjiro's trip, Kenjiro had been able to take his wife with him to America. Akira, who was born in 1927, had been only two years old when his family had returned to Japan, so he had no memory of the place. Nevertheless, he and Hiroshi pondered what their lives might have been like had their individual destinies been reversed—if Akira's father had chosen to remain in America and Hiroshi's family had returned to Japan.

In 1944, when he was only 17, Akira had been conscripted into the Army and sent to Manchuria to guard against the Russians.

"We were ill-trained, ill-equipped raw recruits," Akira said, "placed there like scarecrows to the give the impression that a Japanese military presence still existed in Manchuria. We were replacements for the Kumamoto First Division, which had been sent to Saipan to fight the Americans. The Russians, of course, just rolled over us when they came. All we did was run and hide. Those of us who couldn't run fast enough were killed. I'll never forgive the Russians. They were barbarians."

"When that was happening to you," Hiroshi said, "I was in an American concentration camp."

"You were lucky," Akira said.

He said the only reason he was alive was that a Chinese rice merchant took him in and hid him from the Russians. "I was just a kid with fuzz on my face, so he felt sorry for me. When I met him, I didn't speak Chinese, but I wrote in kanji: 'Japanese,' 'Soldier,' 'Please Help.' There was no point in lying; he could see what I was. But he took me in. He told me later that he'd been impressed by my penmanship."

Now Akira was an executive in an insurance firm owned by his father-in-law. "He had daughters, but no son, so he adopted me," Akira explained. "Because I was the second son, Father had no objections. Plus, there were advantages to being connected in that way with the owner of Nishimoto Insurance."

As a result, Akira's name was not Kono but Nishimoto. He was married to Yuriko, Mr. Nishmoto's oldest daughter.

Oddly enough, these conversations took place at what Akira called his "real home," which he kept with his mistress Toshiko, a plain young woman, pleasant enough, who served tea and various treats during Hiroshi's visits but otherwise was kept smilingly in the background. Akira said his wife Yuriko was like a sister to him. He'd married her out of a sense of obligation to his adoptive father, but she'd never been his true love.

Hiroshi couldn't understand Akira's preference for Toshiko. Yuriko was by far the more attractive woman, and not only in appearance. She was well-educated, graceful, refined, and very much in love with her erring husband.

Yuriko told Hiroshi her side of the story when they met one day for lunch at Tsuruya, a downtown department store.

"It's true," she said. "We are like brother and sister, but

there never was any man but Akira for me. I know about Toshiko. We even met once. We have an understanding."

When Hiroshi expressed dismay at this, she said, "You are an American. You would not understand."

Hiroshi thought about Father cavorting with the young women in sexy kimono at the Nikoniko in the days before the war. Mother had known about them, but Yuriko's situation was different. For Father, the women at Nikoniko had been merely casual flirtations, but Toshiko was Akira's true love.

During the few months he was in Japan, Hiroshi's Japanese became fluent enough for him to consider finding a job there, perhaps with an American company in Tokyo. But as much as he felt at home in Japan, it became clear to him that Yuriko was right. He was an American, and thus a foreigner.

Shortly after Hiroshi returned to Los Angeles, Father got a letter from Kenjiro's wife Okane. She said there'd been a terrible scandal, and Mr. Kumagai and several of his associates had been arrested. She didn't say exactly how her husband might have been involved, but he'd suffered a fatal heart attack as a result.

It would be many more years before Hiroshi heard the rest of the story about his uncle's family. After the trip to Japan, Hiroshi settled for a time in France, as planned. When he visited Los Angeles again several years later, he brought with him his new French wife, Simone. His parents, who had long ago resigned themselves to the probability that Hiroshi would never marry a nice Japanese girl, were on the whole pleased with Simone. She was modest, well-educated, had excellent manners, and liked miso soup.

During their visit, Hiroshi learned that several months after Kenjiro's death, Okane had sent a packet of papers for Father's signature. "Our business," she had written, "has suffered severe losses. It will be years before it can be restored, if that is even possible. It would be such a comfort to me if the house and land could be settled on our son Masayuki. I know it is a lot to ask, but I hope you will be generous and kind."

Father said he took the papers the following day to the Japanese Consulate, where he'd signed them before the proper witnesses. He hadn't even thought twice about it. Mickey's restaurant was doing well, and he had plans to open another.

Still, Hiroshi could sense that there was more to the decision than Father was letting on. For Father, the ancestral home had become a burden on his heart and mind. "It was a relief to be rid of it," Father admitted at last. "We had no need for foreign holdings."

REWRITE

1964 - 1972

When Hiroshi got out of his car behind Baltimore's Eastern District Police Station he saw a pitiful looking dog chained to a dumpster with two handcuffs wound around its neck. He couldn't be sure if it was the vodkas he'd had over lunch, or the doleful look the wretched creature gave him, but Hiroshi couldn't let it go.

Once inside, he went to the desk sergeant. The nameplate on the massive oak counter identified the burly hulk of a man as Sgt. Edwin T. Gallagher. He was leaning sideways on his swivel chair reading the paper when Hiroshi walked up to him.

"Who're you?" Sgt. Gallagher said without looking up from the paper.

"Hiroshi Kono. I'm with the *Herald.*"

"Reporter?"

"Yeah."

Sgt. Gallagher turned slowly toward him. "Chinese?"

"Japanese. Sergeant, I'd like to ask about that dog outside."

"What dog?"

"The one you've got handcuffed to the dumpster."

Sgt. Gallagher put down his paper, placed an elbow on his desk, and stared down his thick nose at Hiroshi. He twisted his mouth halfway across his beefy face and squeezed his eyes so that Hiroshi could barely see his pupils. Hiroshi wasn't sure whether he was annoyed or simply bemused.

"You're pretty big for a Jap, ain'tcha?"

Hiroshi couldn't tell from the sergeant's tone of voice whether he was engaging in idle chatter or putting him in his place for being a smartass. But there was no point in taking offense. As Father might have said, sometimes in America, you survive by playing the fool.

"My parents were both big," Hiroshi said with his most winning smile. "Big Daddy and Big Mama. That's what everybody called them."

Sgt. Gallagher guffawed. "Big Daddy and Big Mama, eh? That's good."

"About the dog," Hiroshi persisted.

"Ya want it?"

"What?"

"Do you want the dog?" the officer repeated, making it clear this time that the question was a serious one.

"No, Sergeant. I was just asking about it."

"Look, if you want it, you can have it. It'll save me a lotta paperwork. I'm about to call the pound, so make up your mind."

Hiroshi had asked about the dog because he thought there might be a story in it, but instead he'd been ensnared by this wily Irishman. Now he was responsible for whether or not the miserable creature lived or died.

Against his better judgment, he decided to rescue it. The mutt, he discovered, was a bitch. On his way to the vet, as his car filled with the moldy burlap stench of an unwashed dog, he decided to name her Vodka.

The starting pay for a police reporter at the *Baltimore Herald* was just enough to get by on, provided he didn't indulge in extravagances such as restoring a mangy, half-starved and diseased animal to health. It took several trips to the veterinarian and heavy doses of vitamins and antibiotics to save Vodka. Had it not been for Simone's earnings as a graduate teaching assistant at the university, they would never have been able to afford the cost.

Hiroshi had met Simone three years earlier in Paris, where he'd landed after bumming around Europe for a while. At the time, American jazz musicians were the rage in Paris, and Bud Powell, a leading innovator in bebop, was playing regularly at a cellar bar in the Latin Quarter. That's where Hiroshi had met Simone. Though she was studying at the Sorbonne, she was far from the stereotype of the French intellectual snob. She had spent much of her childhood and adolescence in New York, where her father, a scholar in medieval French literature, had managed to get a position at Columbia University in time to escape the German invasion.

Simone was fluent in English, but she spoke to Hiroshi in French, sensing that it made him feel safer. He was hiding out in France, in much the same way she and her family had taken refuge in America. Like her father, she was a non-observant Jew in academia. She recognized in Hiroshi a fellow chameleon. It did not take the two of them long to sense that they had found a kindred spirit in each other. "Soul mates," they had said joyously, as if inventing the venerable cliché.

While in Paris, Hiroshi, who was by then running seriously short of money, found a way to use his college-level knowledge of French to land a job as an editorial assistant and stringer for the *Herald*'s Paris bureau. After three years, he had impressed the Paris bureau chief enough to get a recommendation from him for a job at the paper's home office in Baltimore.

Back in the US once more, Hiroshi and Simone rented a converted carriage house in Mount Washington, a neighborhood with towering shade trees and Victorian houses in the northwest corner of Baltimore. Mount Washington had once been a summer retreat for the wealthy, but by the 1960s, the summer sojourners had all but abandoned the place, and the area's permanent residents, folks of more modest means, were aging. Mount Washington was now attracting young professionals, mostly Jews.

Hiroshi and Simone had been worried about moving to Baltimore at first because anti-miscegenation laws were still on the books in Maryland, but no one ever made mention of them. Even so, Simone felt more comfortable moving into what was becoming a Jewish enclave. There were covenants excluding Jews from the better neighborhoods in Baltimore, and if there had been enough of them, Asians would probably have been barred as well. As it was, the Asian population consisted of a small Chinese community in the inner city and a few scattered doctors and researchers associated with Johns Hopkins Medical School.

As a police reporter, Hiroshi didn't rate the byline that gave more senior members of the staff minor celebrity status in their respective communities, so the presumption seemed to be that he, too, worked in the medical profession. When one of their neighbors persisted in addressing him as "Doctor Kono," Hiroshi didn't see the point in disabusing her. Still, something about the presumption rankled. Simone, on the other hand, was perfectly comfortable in Mount Washington and had no trouble making friends, most of whom were academics like her.

The vet couldn't determine Vodka's exact age, but he said she was fully matured and had been spayed. Restored to health and with some meat on her bones, she turned out to be a stunningly beautiful dog. Her long hair suggested that she was part husky; her coloration and pointed nose betrayed a collie bloodline; and her powerful chest and the downward slope of her body indicated German shepherd. When Hiroshi took her for walks, people would ask, "What kind of dog is that?"

"Siberian deerhound," he would say.

"Beautiful dog," was the invariable reply.

Thus imbued with pride of ownership, Hiroshi bought a tag engraved with his name, address, and phone number to put on Vodka's collar.

From what little Hiroshi knew of dogs, it seemed to him that Vodka was not far removed from a wolf. She would twirl three times before lying down, and when police or fire sirens sounded, she would lift her head to the sky and howl in chorus with the phantom pack. Many of his neighbors let their dogs run free, but those other dogs generally stayed close to home. Not Vodka. If she had any territorial instincts, they encompassed the whole of Mount Washington. It was not long before Simone and Hiroshi started getting angry calls about Vodka digging up flower-beds, overturning garbage cans, and barking and howling outside windows. One woman, who never identified herself, but whose voice Hiroshi learned to recognize, warned him that Mr. Weathersbee, who lived at the end of their street, was in the habit of putting out poisoned meat. Hiroshi doubted that the call was in good faith, but he didn't doubt that Mr. Weathersbee was capable of such a thing. An aging leftover from the old days, before the neighborhood changed, Mr. Weathersbee was a reclusive misanthrope who sat on his back porch with a loaded shotgun that he used to shoot marauding raccoons.

One morning, shortly after the woman's call, someone wrote "Jap House" with chalk on the street and an arrow pointing at their cottage.

Simone was unnerved. "We need to do something," she said. Although the slur might not have had anything do with Vodka, her disturbing the neighborhood was clearly directing unwanted attention toward them.

Hiroshi put up a dog run behind their cottage. He also studied books on dog training, bought a choke collar, a 20-foot lunge line, and a bag of dog biscuits.

It was clear from the beginning that Vodka was highly intelligent and, as it turned out, also highly discriminating. The dog biscuits didn't seem to be enough of an incentive for her to obey commands. When Hiroshi tried one, he found it dry and tasteless, like something one might give to feedlot cattle. So he switched to baloney. When she still wouldn't obey his commands, he ate the meat himself, making a big show of chewing and smacking his lips as he did so.

Hiroshi persisted in the training regimen for months, experimenting with various tactics gleaned from dog-training manuals. Eventually, he managed to teach Vodka to sit, stay, come, and even heel on command. But he came to believe that she was fundamentally untrainable. She would obey only if it seemed like the smart thing to do.

The *Herald* maintained a large Washington bureau and had correspondents stationed in all the major capitals of the world. This attracted ambitious young men from Ivy League schools whose singular focus was to get out of grimy working-class Baltimore and into the Washington bureau or some other prestigious foreign posting.

After their shifts, they would gather at Bellini's, a red-and-white checkered bistro where they could drink and wallow in their discontent. Most had never known a day of deprivation in their entire lives, but they felt exploited by the low pay, long hours, and the indignity of covering the inner city with its squalor, petty crimes, and utter desolation. Hiroshi was content to drink with the gang, but he had difficulty connecting with them. He, too, would have loved to go overseas—to Paris if possible, Simone would love that—but he felt lucky to have the job that he did and could scarcely believe his good fortune. Yes, he wanted to go to Washington or abroad, but he was also ambivalent about the prospect. The people of the inner city were the ones who really needed the coverage. To leave would feel like a betrayal.

One night, after indulging in too much of Bellini's cheap booze, he stopped the conversation cold by saying, "All we cover are petty crimes and fires. We don't cover what's really going on in the city. When you get down to it, the *Herald* is a fucking racist paper!"

Though the *Herald* had recently stopped mentioning the race of criminal suspects, the rewrite men still insisted on having that information. It was easy enough to provide because police reports routinely identified individuals as "c/m" for colored male and "c/f" for colored female.

At home, Hiroshi complained to Simone. "What difference does it make?" he said, "I'm a c/m too."

"No, you're not," she said. "You're a j/m."

They'd laughed at that, but Hiroshi sensed that it wasn't entirely a joke. Simone had always been fond of Asian art. A print of one of Hiroshige's Tokaido woodcuts hung in their living room, and the shelves were filled with Chinese objets d'art. Those invited to their cottage tended to assume that the Hiroshige, at least, belonged to Hiroshi.

When Hiroshi and Simone had met in Paris, they'd both been habitués of the Left Bank; Hiroshi had presented himself as an American expatriate in the tradition of Hemingway, Gertrude Stein, Ezra Pound, and the like. Simone might not have been completely convinced, but she was charmed by his anti-establishment views and amused by his rebellious and outré posturing when he had a bit too much wine. Like him, she distrusted the bourgeoisie and was mindful of its hypocrisies. She delighted in the so-called decadent poetry of 19th century French literature, especially the works of Rimbaud and Verlaine, great poets but seriously bad boys. In Hiroshi, she had an enfant terrible of her own.

But there was another side to Simone, one that had attracted Hiroshi more than he'd realized at first. Simone was a devoted daughter who kept in constant touch with her parents in Paris, writing them weekly and remembering their birthdays and anniversaries. When they first met, Hiroshi had told Simone that he had no family, that he was alone in the world. He had meant this figuratively—he was a little drunk at the time—but she had taken it literally and was immensely surprised to learn later that Hiroshi not only had a mother and a father, but also two brothers, a sister, and assorted nephews and nieces.

After they were married, Simone kept in touch with Hiroshi's family, especially Sachi, with whom she'd grown close on their first visit to Los Angeles. She always remembered the birthdays of Sachi and her children, as well as those of Hiroshi's parents, and never forgot to buy small gifts for Hiroshi to send them. Increasingly, Simone began talking about having children of their own, to which Hiroshi always replied evasively. He said he wanted to wait until they had a real home.

Heavy drinking was part of the newspaper culture at the time, and the *Herald* was no exception. In this regard, Hiroshi had no problem fitting in. Drinking came naturally to him; he'd started when he was a teenager and had kept it up in the Army, at Berkeley, and in France. He never let it affect his work, however. Within a year, he was taken out of the districts—a quick promotion. After another year as a general assignment reporter, he was put on the desk as a rewrite man.

Hiroshi's nightly routine soon involved going to Bellini's for "lunch" after the early edition had been put to bed. One night, over wine and pizza with two of his colleagues, the conversation turned to Vietnam.

"There's no way out," Jenkins said. "That's the problem. We're in too deep, and nobody's come up with a way for getting out."

"I have a way," Hiroshi said. "We have to admit we're never going to win this war. If we do that, we'll find a way out."

"Kono," Caulfield said, "we can't lose. We'd lose face. You of all people should understand that."

Caulfield covered City Hall, one of the prime beats on the paper, and he was in line for a position at the London bureau. But for all of that, he came across like a prep school twit.

"Here's something else I understand," Hiroshi continued, undeterred. "Blacks are rioting all over the place—in Rochester, Philadelphia, Watts, San Francisco, Cleveland. Yet we've got a half-million troops in a piddling little country in Southeast Asia trying to beat back a revolution we should be supporting. Johnson's got his head up his ass. He can't see another revolution that's coming right under his nose, right here in the US of A. Which side are we going to be on when that happens? Which side are *you* going to be on?"

His colleagues, taken aback, remained silent. Hiroshi said no more. He drained his tumbler of wine, which was how they served it at Bellini's, and ordered another.

Hiroshi smoked Gauloises, a non-filtered, noxiously potent French import that blended dark Turkish and Syrian tobaccos. As bad as they smelled and tasted, it was unthinkable to be seen smoking anything else while sipping coffee at a Left Bank café. Gauloises were what intellectuals—writers and artists—smoked. While in Paris, Simone had smoked them too, but she had long since given up the habit. Meanwhile, Hiroshi had worked his way up to nearly two packs a day. His bronchitis was getting so bad he feared he was getting emphysema, lung cancer, or both. When he finally went to a pulmonologist to get checked out, he was prescribed daily doses of theophylline, a bronchodilator. The doctor put enough of a scare into him that he quit smoking cold turkey.

But the cure had a bad side effect. The sudden cutoff of nicotine to his system put Hiroshi in such a deep funk that Simone said he was becoming impossible to live with. He was restless, irritable, and quick to take offense at any perceived slight or neglect. Worse still, he found himself trapped in dark and morose moods. When Hiroshi mentioned all this to his doctor, he was told that he should probably see a psychiatrist, but that he might try a regular course of exercise first.

Hiroshi began getting up at five in the morning to jog. He would take Vodka along with him, and because it was still dark at that hour, he would let her run off leash. She took full advantage of this freedom, running in and out of yards, treeing cats, and knocking over trashcans. "Atta girl," Hiroshi would say. "Don't let the bastards grind you down!" She seemed to understand and would run up to Hiroshi and give his hand a flick of her tongue. In the shimmering glow of the street lights, it almost seemed as if she were giving him a conspiratorial wink.

A big problem with jogging so early in the morning was that Hiroshi's body rhythms were thrown out of sync. About fifteen minutes into his run, his bowels would begin to churn, and he'd have to duck into the woods or, in an emergency, behind a large rhododendron or a bank of azaleas. This bit of unpleasantness eventually had an effect on his feelings toward Vodka. He was already aware of Vodka's coprophagous leanings; he frequently had to jerk her away from dog droppings on their walks. But he was not prepared to see her going after his leavings. Once he saw her emerging from behind the bushes where he'd just been, licking her chops. He recoiled at the sight. This beautiful dog with her look of fine breeding was a shit-eating cur.

Gradually, over a period of two years, the late nights and heavy drinking began to take its toll. Hiroshi would often skip his morning runs with Vodka, and eventually he stopped them altogether. This meant that Vodka was chained to her run for long periods of time, sometimes for days on end. Simone did her part to keep Vodka fed and watered, but she was at the university most of the day, teaching and working on her dissertation. She didn't like walking the dog at night, so it was up to Hiroshi to take her out.

Vodka's leash was attached to a wheel that could roll the length of the 20-foot run, so she had a wide radius of mobility.

Nevertheless, even with those liberal constraints, the long periods of isolation produced a gradual change in her personality and character. She would snap and growl at any dog that came near her on their walks. She especially detested female dogs. Whenever she encountered one, it would take all of Hiroshi's strength to restrain her.

One Sunday evening, when Hiroshi was walking Vodka in the neighborhood, a yapping Yorkshire terrier named Mopsie, long ill-disposed toward Vodka, foolishly came too close and snapped at her. Hiroshi was not being as attentive as he should have been, because Vodka got Mopsie in her teeth and, with one violent jerk of her head, snapped the little bitch's neck. No wolf in the wild could have disposed of its victim with more dispatch. Hiroshi had difficulty suppressing a certain pride in her performance, but when Mrs. Greenberg, Mopsie's mistress, rushed out of her house, wildly waving both hands in the air and screaming, he went through the motions of scolding and beating Vodka, who, feeling betrayed, looked pitifully sad. He apologized profusely to Mrs. Greenberg who, inconsolable, said over and over, "What have you done? Mopsie, my poor Mopsie."

When the Greenbergs demanded that Vodka be put down, threatening to sue, Hiroshi got one of the lawyers who hung out regularly at the Court House to send a letter to them. Hiroshi dictated the letter, pointing out that it was Mopsie, not Vodka, who had been off leash and running free at the time, and that Mopsie was the one who had initiated the fight. The lawyer added a hint of a countersuit.

When Hiroshi offered to pay him for his time, the lawyer said, "Forget about it. Let's just say you owe me one."

The letter proved effective, and the Greenbergs backed off. But word of the incident quickly got around the neighborhood, adding to Vodka's notoriety

Working on the desk was a major promotion for Hiroshi. As a

rewrite man, Hiroshi retrieved calls from reporters in the field and wrote up the stories they reported about fires, train wrecks, muggings, burglaries, rape, or murder. Despite his misgivings about the intrinsic racism of the process, Hiroshi was good at making snap judgments. A shooting in the West Baltimore ghetto might get two graphs buried deep inside the paper; a similar incident in lily-white Roland Park would get front-page coverage.

Though Hiroshi kept up his daily visits to Bellini's, it didn't affect his work, which had become routine. The bigger problem was boredom.

Then Martin Luther King was assassinated in Memphis. Three days later, the desk called him at home. It was his day off, but rioting had broken out in East Baltimore and every available man was being sent out to cover the story.

When Hiroshi got to the site of the rioting, he found that the police had set up a roadblock on Eastern Avenue.

"I'm with the *Herald*," Hiroshi said.

The officer shrugged. "Okay. Keep your windows rolled up."

Hiroshi could smell smoke and see flames shooting up on Gay Street from five blocks away. He got as close as he could and parked his car. The pavement was a tangle of hoses, and police cars screeched in and out of side streets, lights flashing, sirens screaming.

The fires still raging on the next block had been extinguished here, leaving behind the charred hulk of a furniture store and an adjacent row house, its front door gaping open. Curious, Hiroshi picked his way through the rubble and into the house. Remarkably, a light bulb was still glowing in the front room; the electricity was still functioning. The air inside was heavy with the sour smell of water and soot. The windows had been shattered, probably by high-pressure hoses, and the furniture was overturned and soaked through. The kitchen, however, appeared to have been spared. An undisturbed bowl of fried chicken rested incongruously on a small table in the corner.

"What you doin' in here?"

He turned to see a woman holding a child on her hip with one hand and grasping another by the wrist.

"Oh, I'm sorry, ma'am. My name is Hiroshi Kono. I'm a reporter with the *Herald*."

"That don't give you the right to go pokin' into people's houses."

"You're right, ma'am. I'm sorry. I was just trying to see what the damage was like."

"Well, now you've seen it."

The woman followed Hiroshi back into the living room, where they both stood for a moment staring at the broken windows. There was a jagged hole in the ceiling where a large section of plaster had fallen off, and the carpet was sopping wet.

"Lord, have mercy," the woman said.

"I'm so sorry, ma'am," Hiroshi said.

The scene brought back memories for Hiroshi, but nothing as bad as this. His home had also burned down, but he'd been long gone when it had happened.

The woman looked at him for moment, then continued surveying the damage. "Oh Lord, Oh Lord," she murmured as if to herself.

"Sorry," he said again as he slipped out the door.

After the Mopsie incident, Simone told Hiroshi that some people in the neighborhood had started calling Vodka "the killer dog."

"It's George Hartmann," Hiroshi said. "He's had it in for Vodka and for me for a long time."

"That's not true," Simone said. "The Hartmanns are good people. It's Mrs. Greenberg. She's still upset. You can't really blame her."

"Are you taking their side now?"

"Oh Hiro, don't be silly. Just be careful with Vodka. That's all I'm saying."

Despite this admonition, late one night, when Hiroshi was taking Vodka for a walk after a bit too much wine, she got away from him again. When he got home, the phone was ringing. It was George Hartmann—Vodka was outside his house and upsetting his schnauzer. Not long after he hung up, his anonymous woman friend called to say that Vodka was howling outside her window.

In Hiroshi's inebriated state, the woman's accusatory tone touched a nerve. "What the hell do you expect me to do about it?" he shouted. "If you don't like it, call the authorities! Call the goddamn cops! Stop harassing me!"

Simone came out of the bedroom. "Who are you shouting at?" she said.

"Just one of our racist neighbors."

"There's nothing wrong with our neighbors, Hiro," she said. "And you really should go and fetch Vodka before she wakes all of Mount Washington."

Chastened, Hiroshi went out to retrieve Vodka. Afterwards, he sat most of the night on the living room couch with a bottle of bourbon. When he awoke the following morning, he was still on the couch, and Simone had already left for the university.

Simone was a woman both familiar and comfortable with complexities and paradoxes. Her father, the son of a prominent Parisian banker, had been a member of the Communist Party during his student days, and had met his wife, Simone's mother, in a commune. Her father had also struggled with alcoholism, even as he'd settled with great distinction into academia. Meanwhile, her mother was known for her salons, which were frequented by poets, writers, artists, and other denizens of the Rive Gauche. When Simone met Hiroshi, she said she saw in him a questing spirit like her father, someone willing to explore the unfamiliar, to learn and grow.

They had talked endlessly of this during their courtship and after their marriage. She saw him struggling and drinking excessively, but she was willing to wait it out. In the meantime, she buried herself in her dissertation, spending hours in the bowels of the university library, filling shoeboxes with tiny handwritten notes about the lives and works of 19th century French literati. She and Hiroshi were essentially leading separate, cocooned lives, but when Hiroshi was sober enough, they did have their moments of reflection, mutual affection, and physical intimacy.

Nearly a month had passed since the riots, but Hiroshi couldn't get them out of his mind. One scene he'd witnessed reminded him of the kabuki tales of his youth—horrifying at first, but emblematic and larger than life. He could still see the young man standing on the hood of a parked car at Ashland Avenue with a papier-mâché penis strapped to his waist, a foot long affair with testicles the size of grapefruits. As people surged around him, the young man had waved this grotesque appendage from side to side, cheering on the rampaging crowd. People were laughing as they threw bricks through plate glass windows and kicked in doors. In contrast to the Japanese, who'd marched meekly into camp, these people were fighting back, less with anger than with joy. Perhaps they had more right, he thought. He felt himself getting caught up in the almost celebratory air. He felt safe in it. It was only when the police came screeching around the corner in their squad cars that he'd felt threatened and afraid.

As Hiroshi recalled the scene at Ashland Avenue and the strangely joyous sense of release he'd shared with the rioters, he started to think there might be more answers for him in the inner city than behind a desk. Nobody ever asked to be placed back in the districts. Rookie reporters counted the days until they were brought inside—even writing obits was considered a promotion. The City Editor thought Hiroshi was crazy when he asked for the transfer, but relented when Hiroshi explained that he was tired of being stuck behind a desk when the real story was taking place on the streets. Hiroshi fully believed what he told his editor, but working the districts also gave him a certain amount of freedom. He carried a bottle of vodka in his car and a flask in his coat pocket.

In the winter of 1969, word came from France that Simone's father had suffered a stroke. She flew at once to his side. After a week, Simone wrote to tell Hiroshi that her father was well on his way to a full recovery, but that she'd decided to remain in Paris to take advantage of the resources at the Sorbonne and other research libraries there.

When, after a month, she still hadn't returned, Hiroshi began to feel abandoned. He wondered whether she was taking a first step toward leaving him entirely, but he couldn't bring himself to ask her to come back to him. Alone in their cottage, he ate TV dinners or nothing at all.

It was a hard time for Vodka as well. Hiroshi was often too drunk to take her for walks. She would make a mess in the house and get beaten for it. Though still able to manage at work, once at home, Hiroshi would enter a miasmic world that had only a tenuous connection to what he barely recognized as reality. Drunk one evening, he slipped on a dog turd in the middle of the bedroom. He found Vodka in the kitchen, cowering behind the refrigerator, and he dragged her yelping to the door before flinging her out into the snow. When he turned around, he discovered he had tracked dog shit all over the house. It made him weep. He took his shoes, socks, and clothing off piece by piece and wiped the floor with them. It might have been his drunken state, or it might have been an act of penance. In any case, the hard work of scrubbing the floors had a sobering effect. The smell made him retch, but he continued cleaning on his hands and knees, naked. He finished up by soaking his shirt and underwear in soapy water and giving the floors a final wipe down. Then he discarded his clothes, shoes and all, in a trash bag. He gulped more whisky from a bottle.

He was stirred out of this alcoholic funk by the ringing of the telephone. It was George Hartmann. Vodka had apparently attacked his schnauzer.

"Your dog," Hartmann said, "is a disgrace to the neighborhood."

Hiroshi was naked, shivering in the cold, and Hartmann's words sent him into a rage. "What the hell do you mean a disgrace to the neighborhood!" he screamed through chattering teeth. "Look, Hartmann, if you don't like us in the neighborhood, you move." With that he slammed the phone down.

The phone rang again and again, but he ignored it. He put on some clothes and went out to look for Vodka.

A full moon was out and fresh snow coated the ground, so the dog's tracks were easy to follow. Hiroshi could hear her howling not too far away, but in the heavy snow, getting to her was slow, plodding work. As soon as Vodka saw him, she would take off in the opposite direction. "Vodka! Bad dog!" he shouted, but she only ran faster. An image floated in his mind of a primitive hunter, spear in hand, tracking a deer until the animal dropped in exhaustion. He was that hunter. As for Vodka, the snow and the chill seemed to invigorate her. She would stand as if waiting for him, then bolt when he got close enough to grab her collar. Hiroshi had not put on heavy socks or boots, and his toes were getting numb. Wind was whipping snow into his face and down his collar and back. He was stiffening, the cold seeping into his bones, and he was afraid his knees would lock.

He had been tracking Vodka for more than an hour, and they were now more than three miles from home. His body was turning to stone. Vodka stood in the middle of the street looking at him, her underbelly matted with clumps of snow. She took a few wary steps toward him, then bounded away again.

"No. Vodka! Please!" he said.

She stopped and looked at him, tilting her head. When she

at last came to him, her tail drooping, there was a sad look on her face. He dropped to his knees to attach the leash, and she licked his face.

It was long, painful slog home for both of them. Hiroshi saw himself as a stiff-legged rheumatoid old man. Vodka, covered with ice and snow, also walked with labored steps, breathing hard. She, too, was a weary old dog now. When they got home, Hiroshi banged the kitchen door behind him, picked up a bottle of whisky, and drank it down.

When he awoke, he was lying on the kitchen floor, and Vodka was licking his face. The television was blaring in the next room. His watch read one o'clock. It took him a moment to realize it was the afternoon, and a little more thought to conclude it was either Saturday or Sunday. When he went to pour himself a drink, he found only empty bottles of bourbon and vodka. The liquor cabinet had also been ransacked; the bottles of Grand Marnier, Cointreau, and the champagne he'd been saving for special occasions were all empty. Checking the fridge, all he found was a half-eaten pot of rice covered with blue mold rings and fine white hairs like an extraterrestrial spider.

Vodka remained at his side, whimpering, and it slowly occurred to him that no one had fed her. An open fifty-pound bag of Purina Dog Chow that Vodka could easily have helped herself to was sitting on the kitchen floor, but the thought had never occurred to her. Hiroshi measured out her usual four cups into her food bowl. As he watched her eat, he became aware that he was hungry as well. He sat down beside her and, pushing her aside, took her bowl onto his lap. The food had the flavor of seaweed, like the Japanese senbei he had liked as a child. The hard nuggets made a crunching noise as he chewed. Vodka looked at him with a perplexed expression. She came to him hesitantly and licked his face, and Hiroshi gave her back her food.

On Monday, he called in sick; he stayed home for the rest of the week as well. During the day, he let Vodka run free outside.

Oddly enough, she never stayed out for long. After half an hour or so, she would scratch at the door and ask to be let in. In the evening, they would share a meal of Purina Dog Chow.

On Thursday, he went shopping. It was a life or death struggle to drive past the liquor store, but he managed. He went to the market where he bought food: steak, eggs, frozen vegetables, rice, and fruit juices for himself, canned dog food and ground beef for Vodka. The Purina Dog Chow had constipated him, so he bought laxatives and an enema kit to purge himself.

Simone had been gone for three months. When she finally returned to Baltimore, she found Hiroshi sober and Vodka sleek and well-nourished.

Some weeks after Simone returned, Hiroshi was sent to a nightclub on Pennsylvania Avenue to report on a shooting. In years past, the club had drawn big-name performers such as Billie Holiday, Cab Calloway, and Count Basie. It had once been fashionable for stylish young men and women to go slumming along the Avenue, but now the devilish allure of going to Negro night clubs had faded, and Pennsylvania Avenue was known mainly for its numbers racket and a growing drug trade.

Inside the club, a man was mopping the floor.

"Is this where a man was shot?" Hiroshi asked.

"Don't know nothin' about it," the man said and nodded toward the bartender.

The bartender was an elegant-looking man with shiny, pomaded hair and a meticulous, ultra-fine mustache. He looked like Duke Ellington. A dozen patrons sat around the bar, quietly drinking. The men were conservatively dressed in dark brown pinstriped suits, buttoned-down collars, and tie-pins. The women wore red, orange, and purple lipstick that matched their dresses and shoes. Two of them had blond hair.

"Excuse me," Hiroshi said to the bartender. "I'm Hiroshi Kono with the *Herald*. I understand there was a shooting here."

"They took him to Maryland General," the bartender said. "You'll find the police there. You talk to them."

"Did you see the shooting?"

"You go to Maryland General. Talk to them there POH-lice," he said and laughed.

"He means the fuzz," said a man sitting at the bar.

"Did you see the shooting?" Hiroshi asked him.

A man on the other side of him tapped his shoulder. "Hey, man, you Chinese?"

"Yeah," he said. "Did you see anything?"

"Man, look at that hair. So black and straight. You know, you Chinese gonna rule the world."

"Henry," the bartender said, "leave the man alone. Let him go about his business."

"I'm just complimentin' the man. That's all."

"Look," the bartender said to Hiroshi, "you're wasting your time here. Go to Maryland General. Talk to the cops."

At Maryland General, two detectives were talking just outside the swinging glass doors of the critical care unit. A curtain hid most of the gurney inside, so all Hiroshi could see were its wheels.

"I'm a reporter for the *Herald*," Hiroshi said. "That the shooting victim in there?"

"Yeah, that's him."

"Can I talk to him?"

The cops looked at one another.

"Not just yet," the older of the two said. "We're not through with him yet."

They went back inside, leaving Hiroshi to wait. He didn't have to wait long.

"He's all yours, buddy," the older cop said as the two re-emerged through the swinging doors.

When Hiroshi walked in, he saw that a sheet had been pulled over the victim's head, baring his feet.

It came to him that the cops were homicide detectives.

Feeling like a fool, Hiroshi pulled back the sheet.

The corpse was that of a light-skinned Negro, middle-aged, clean-shaven except for a small mustache, hair still neatly in place. The wound was little more than a small red spot on his chest. He seemed to have been shot through the heart, but there wasn't a trace of blood anywhere.

Hiroshi called homicide, but the detectives were unavailable. It didn't take long for Talbot, the *Herald*'s headquarters man, to get the story. Red-nosed and paunchy, Talbot had been covering headquarters for twenty years and knew every cop in the building from the commissioner on down. Hiroshi's contribution amounted to descriptions of the crime scene and the corpse, none of which, he knew, would make the paper. It was a colored shooting in a colored part of town.

At the end of the week, Hiroshi asked to be put back on the desk. The City Editor approved the move with a knowing smile.

After Simone's return, Hiroshi began a rigorous training program for Vodka. They went on long walks, twice a day, regardless of the weather, and Vodka seemed to enjoy it. After a year, he could walk her off leash for long stretches, and she would always come to him when he called. Looking after Vodka became the most important thing in his life. She was the pole star by which he set his compass; the day started and ended with her. At the *Herald*, he was assigned to cover City Hall, which meant regular hours. He no longer dawdled at the office or schmoozed at Bellini's after turning in his story, but would go straight home for dinner and Vodka's evening stroll. Simone began coming with them on these evening walks. "Un ménage à trois," she'd say with a soft laugh, putting her head on Hiroshi's shoulder and hugging his arm.

Two years later, the managing editor at the *Herald* told Hiroshi he was in line for the Paris bureau, so he and Simone decided to take an extended trip to France, in part to refresh Hiroshi's language skills. Previously, at Hiroshi's insistence, they had always taken Vodka on their vacations, but the impracticality of transporting a dog overseas for a few weeks was apparent even to him, so they put Vodka in an animal clinic instead. The facility assured him that she would be taken for frequent walks, but when they returned, they found that the month-long ordeal had left Vodka arthritic. Hiroshi doubted that she'd been taken out of her cage for more than ten minutes a day. He began giving her regular doses of aspirin, which seemed to help with her pain. A geriatric workup disclosed that she also suffered from chronic bronchitis. Dr. Fogel, the vet, prescribed theophylline, so Hiroshi was able to share his pills with her.

Perhaps because of the medications she was taking, Vodka started getting skin rashes, and at Dr. Fogel's recommendation, Hiroshi had her hair cropped. Vodka looked like a pup with her short hair. The neighbors thought they'd gotten a new dog and cooed over her. The change in Vodka was remarkable. She rubbed noses with George Hartmann's schnauzer, letting him sniff her hindquarters when they met.

The following year, the Hartmanns even attended the farewell party that friends and colleagues threw for Simone and Hiroshi.

Vodka never made it to Paris. She died the week they were scheduled to leave Baltimore. The vet said the proximate cause was a heat stroke, but it was old age that had claimed her.

In Paris, Hiroshi and Sabine lived in Montmartre, in the 18th arrondissement. The idea of living in the midst of artists, writers, and poets appealed to them. Their neighbors were friendly and scarcely seemed to notice that Hiroshi was Japanese. Nor were they surprised that he spoke French; they seemed to think it only natural. Best of all, the rents were reasonable, so they could afford an apartment with room enough for a nursery.

Simone was happy. Not only was she pregnant, a Parisian publisher had read her dissertation and wanted a book from her on the works of Rimbaud and Verlaine as a prelude to postmodernism. Simone was thrilled. It had been a long time since Hiroshi had seen her so content, so happy. And so beautiful—especially at night, when they sat on their balcony, her face illuminated by the street lamps and the soft light that reflected off of Sacré Coeur's distant, gleaming dome. It was true what they said about pregnant women.

Sometimes, when they walked on a summer's night along the narrow, winding streets of Montmartre—with its bars and cafés, flowerboxes overflowing with geraniums, diners noisily chatting and laughing around outdoor tables, whiffs of garlic sautéing in butter, and the pungent smoke of ever-present Gauloises—Hiroshi would think of Vodka. Before he had taken her in, she had probably been an inner-city dog. Montmartre would have been paradise to her.

UNCLE SAMMY'S ASHES

1981 - 1982

After entering Mickey's North Hollywood home, Hiroshi's glance fell on a small, unglazed ceramic urn. Although he couldn't remember the last time he'd seen it, he knew instantly that it contained Isamu's ashes.

"We can't leave Isamu here alone in the desert," Father had said as they were preparing to leave the camp after the end of the war. Father had arranged for Isamu's ashes to be disinterred and placed in a pickle jar that traveled with them first to Hacienda, then to San Pedro, and finally to North Hollywood. Father had been dead for nine years, and the urn that now contained Isamu's ashes was gathering dust on a shelf above a coat rack.

As Hiroshi headed for the dining room, he heard one of his nephews say, "Hey, look. There's Uncle Sammy." Hiroshi turned to see the others laughing. As the urn had been moved from place to place over the years, finding it had become a game among the younger generation. Hiroshi wanted to tell his nephews and nieces about Sammy, but their uncle had died long before they were born. What he could tell them about his older brother in a few words would have no meaning for them.

"Isamu's ashes are back there in the hallway," Hiroshi said, going up to Yukio, who was standing in the dining room, drink in hand, surveying the lavish spread of Asian delicacies that had been prepared by caterers from Mickey's restaurant. After the war, Yukio, who had stayed in Arizona with his in-laws, had found work as a gardener. He now owned his own nursery, but he had the burnt and leathery look of someone who labored daily in the sun. His hair was silvery, his nose sharp. Hiroshi thought he looked like an Indian chief.

"What do you mean?" Yukio said. "I thought he was buried in Arizona."

"He was," Hiroshi replied, "but Father had his ashes dug up."

Yukio looked surprised, but remained silent. He stared into his drink.

"We ought to give him a proper burial," Hiroshi said, "or at least spread his ashes somewhere. Maybe in the desert. You know, Isamu liked the desert."

"I can take him back to Arizona," Yukio said. "Bury him in the Kubota family plot."

"Mickey won't like that," Hiroshi said. "He'll want to bury him in Rolling Hills, where Father is."

"I don't care what Mickey wants. Isamu was a true brother to me," Yukio insisted. Then, seeing the look on Hiroshi's face, he added, "You were too, Hiroshi, but you were just a boy."

"Well, we don't have to decide right now," Hiroshi said.

The entire family had gathered at Mickey's home because Mother had just turned 88, a number associated with health, prosperity, good fortune, and, most of all, longevity.

Mother had recently undergone a course of chemotherapy and was emaciated and frail. To cover her baldness, Sachi had made her an elegant turban of white silk with a jade crane pinned to it. Seated in the middle of an overstuffed sofa and buttressed by mounds of foam cushions, she looked like an Oriental potentate.

As they came into the room, Mother's children and their spouses all made their way to the couch where she was sitting, bowing and uttering congratulatory words in an attempt to make the proper traditional Japanese obeisance. Yukio and Kazuko were the only ones for whom this came naturally. However, their Japanese manners did not extend to their children, nor to the rest of Mother's grandchildren, who spoke no Japanese. Instead, they simply said, "Happy birthday, Grandma," to which she would respond quietly with a soft smile.

Enfeebled as she was, Mother retained an aura of dignity and calm that struck Hiroshi, who had not seen her since he and his family had returned from France four years before. Orphaned at the age of 13, she had had only six years of education in Japan, and that much only because her father, an impoverished samurai, had refused to have an illiterate in the family. In his austere way, influenced by a mix of Zen and Confucianism, her father had instilled in her a deep respect for learning. Even during her difficult first years in America, she had snatched up to read whatever she could find—magazines and books from Japan, Father's joruri texts, books on ancient Japanese history.

After Father's death, Mother had lived in a senior residence in the Little Tokyo quarter of Los Angeles. It was less lonely for her there, where she lived with other Japanese, mostly widows of her age. Moreover, the facility was located next to a Buddhist temple that gave courses on flower arrangement, calligraphy, and even English. Mother took to reading books on Buddhism, which she said she found illuminating. She was amazed and delighted with the depth and richness of what she had previously thought was a simple devotional path to the Pure Land. At the end of her life, it seemed, her solitary readings and wrenching life experiences were coming together with a simple clarity that transcended karmic entanglements and complexities.

Throughout the afternoon, her children and grandchildren took turns attending to her, bringing plates of food and filling her teacup. Everyone was making a special effort because they all quietly understood that this was not so much a celebration of her longevity as it was a final farewell.

As Yukio looked at the bountiful display of food in the dining room of Mickey's spacious and luxurious home, his thoughts went back to a New Year's celebration he had spent with his brothers and sisters long ago in Hacienda, just before the outbreak of war.

The house had been prepared for visitors as was the custom. The traditional shogatsu foods had been laid out in black lacquered boxes on the claw-footed walnut table in the dining room. In the kitchen, Masako-san was pouring sake into small porcelain bottles for warming. Yukio would have preferred to celebrate the day with his Kibei friends, drinking Scotch and eating rice crackers at the Young Men's Association Hall, but Father was out making shogatsu visits of his own, so Yukio, the chonan, had resigned himself to spending a dreary afternoon with Mother entertaining tottering old men in starched collars and ill-fitting suits who emitted sake vapors with every exhalation. Other members of the family were free to do what they pleased. Sachi was at a movie with friends, and Isamu, Mickey, and Hiroshi were stuffing themselves with sushi and listening to Stanford play Nebraska at the Rose Bowl.

Later in the day, after the last guests had come and gone, Father had come home with Kubota-sensei. He'd asked for tea to be brought into his study, where the two men had secluded themselves. They were in the room for nearly an hour before Father asked Mother to join them. Masako-san was asked to bring sake.

Yukio was not included in the discussion, even though he assumed it concerned his engagement to Kazuko, who was at a teachers college in Japan. She was scheduled to return in the fall.

Theirs had been a "love match," one of those rare instances where a boy and girl found each other on their own. They had been corresponding the whole time she had been away at school, with the understanding that they would get married upon her return. When Kazuko had dutifully told her father about their liaison, he'd been delighted, so there was no reason for any concern on that end. The Kubota family was nearly equal to the Kono family in terms of social class and education—indeed, some would have said they were superior in standing. Both Kubotas were from samurai families, and Kubota was a graduate of the University of Kumamoto. The only reason he'd come to America, hoping to make his fortune, was because he was the second son.

As it turned out, Yukio was right; the toasting with sake did indeed signal the conclusion of an agreement. Kubota left with a broad smile on his face, and Father explained that he had agreed to allow Yukio to be adopted into the Kubota family. Since Kubota had no male heirs himself, he was reluctant to give away his eldest and most prized daughter in marriage unless he could adopt Yukio as a yoshi to carry on the male family lineage.

Yukio strenuously objected to this arrangement, but Father reminded him that he himself was just the son of a fish merchant, whereas Kubota and his wife both came from distinguished Kumamoto families. Besides, that was the only condition under which Kubota would agree to the marriage. In the end, not wanting to lose Kazuko, Yukio consented.

The war and internment had delayed the marriage, but the agreement had held. Even after all these years, the memory of it still left a bitter aftertaste. As he stood in Mickey's spacious home, which had been expanded to take up two lots—room enough for a kidney-shaped swimming pool—Yukio wondered if Father would have given away his chonan so easily had he been allowed to finish his studies at Tokyo University, or if Mickey had not been on the cusp of graduating from Stanford.

Beyond the living room window, the younger grandchildren, including Hiroshi's son and daughter, splashed about noisily in the pool, supervised by their older cousins. Their parents and assorted friends clustered about the dining-room table, drinks in hand, or took plates of food to the patio. Still another contingent, which included Mickey's son Ricky, were watching a Dodgers game that was being projected onto a screen that took up nearly half a wall in what Mickey called his "home theater." A college dropout, Rickey worked as a blackjack dealer in Las Vegas and was living with a blonde cocktail waitress. Hiroshi heard him boasting that he had "a couple of big ones" on the game.

Meanwhile, Mickey's wife Amy was helping Ricky's girlfriend Cindy select food from the buffet. Cindy was wearing skin-tight jeans and a t-shirt decorated with rhinestones that stretched thin over her ample bosom. She was what might be called a miniskirt in a kimono shop.

"Is that, ugh, raw fish?" Cindy was saying, "And what's that?"

"Sea urchin," Amy said. "But why don't you try the makizushi. This one's good, it has avocado and crab. We call it a California roll."

"What's that stuff around it?"

"Seaweed—but it's not the kind you find on the beach. It's specially grown and processed in Japan."

"I think I'll pass."

"Well, there's also crispy duck or lobster with black bean sauce. And these Szechuan noodle dishes are good, though they're a little spicy."

Cindy didn't respond.

"Our caterers are still in the kitchen," Amy said quickly.

"They can fix you anything you want—how about a sandwich or an omelet?"

"Gee, thanks, Amy," Cindy said, "but if you don't mind, I'll just have another bloody mary."

By way of contrast, Hiroshi's wife Simone handled herself like an Asian gourmet, expertly using her chopsticks to pick out special tidbits from the vast array of dishes.

"Simone," Amy said, "this probably isn't the kind of food you're used to."

"No, but I love it," she said. "We French still have a lot to learn about food."

Amy, who knew French cooking, suspected Simone was being patronizing, but she kept her smile in place.

Mickey stood by the bar observing the guests and what they picked from the buffet. As a restaurateur, this always interested him. Next to him, Cindy was pouring herself another drink with a generous portion of vodka.

"Can I help you with that, Cindy?" he said.

"No thanks, Mickey. Believe me, I know how to make a bloody mary."

Mickey had never given Cindy permission to address him by his first name, but there was nothing he could do about it; those were the kinds of girls his son brought home. Ricky, a star quarterback in high school, had been recruited by USC, but he didn't have the discipline to play at the college level, especially not in a top-flight program. So he'd ended up dropping out of school and drifting from job to job. At one point, he'd attempted to make a living as professional poker player, which is how he'd ended up in Las Vegas. Now he was living with a cocktail waitress. Mickey found himself imagining how appalled Father would have been by Cindy. He himself felt the same way. Not because Cindy was a hakujin. When Ricky had dated white girls in high school, Mickey had never raised any objections. But those had been nice girls from good homes—girls like Sue Wheatley, whom Mickey had gotten to know back when he played football at Santa Marguerita High. Watching Cindy teeter about unsteadily on her heels, he found himself wondering again, as he did from time to time, what had become of Sue Wheatley.

Being both Japanese and a football hero had been hard for Mickey, who was never invited to parties despite being the star of the team. Socially, he was an outcast among his teammates. At Monday practice, he would hear his teammates talking about their weekend dates—he knew which girls were easy and wanted "to do it" and who was a tease—but no one even thought to include him in these conversations. Out of all the hakujin girls in school, Sue Wheatley was the only one who, for reasons he could not fathom, went out of her way to be friendly with him. Their friendship never went beyond an exchange of smiles across a classroom or chats between classes or the occasional short walk together when they happened to meet in the hallway. Mickey was friendly with a lot of Japanese girls, but Sue was different, and not just because she was hakujin. Sue Wheatley was the leader of the cheerleading team and one of the most popular girls in school.

One Saturday afternoon, after a victory over an important rival, Sue impetuously invited Mickey to an after-game party at her house. But when he arrived, she rushed out to tell him that he couldn't come in. She had clearly been watching for him.

"I'm so sorry, Mickey, but my mother..." She began stammering, unable to finish. She didn't need to. Mickey could see two of his teammates looking at him through the large bay window, drinks in hand. They seemed to be smirking, as if enjoying his embarrassment. He walked away, forcing himself not to look back. He wanted to run, but he kept an even, steady pace. Every retreating step seemed to seal his shame.

The following Saturday, Sue threw her arms around Mickey at a victory rally and kissed his cheek. She wanted to make it up to him, but she shouldn't have done that, not in public. After that, they couldn't even talk in the halls anymore. Guys would bump into him and say, "Sorry," but he knew they'd done so on purpose.

After Sue's scandalous behavior, even the few friendly encounters they'd had in the past became impossible. Sue told him that her father, who owned an insurance agency in town, had received expressions of concern from his customers and business associates as well as anonymous warnings.

"I'm so sorry, Mickey," she said. "It's all my fault. Please don't be angry with me."

That was the last time they ever spoke.

Even though he'd never imagined anything more than a casual friendship between them, Sue Wheatley stuck in Mickey's mind. True, she was pretty, but it had been the friendship itself, a friendship with a nice, middle-class American girl, that had awakened in him a vision of participating fully in an American life. It was because of that vision that he'd joined Loyalty League, converted to Christianity, and fought in the American army.

After Mickey was mustered out of the Army, he'd gone with his buddy Kenji to Los Angeles, where Kenji's father was working to reopen his Little Tokyo restaurant. That was where Mickey had met Kenji's sister Amy. After a year's apprenticeship, he and Amy were married, and a year after that, the two bought a greasy, broken-down waterfront café in San Pedro. Now the owner of a small but successful chain of restaurants, Mickey felt he had achieved his goals. But as he looked at Cindy, one of three fast and easy hakujin women Ricky had brought home over the past few years, he wondered how he had failed his son.

He saw Simone talking to Cindy and was embarrassed. Simone was a university professor. What must she think? How could he command any respect from Hiroshi, or from Yukio, whose son was a writer and journalist. His own daughter Kathy at least had finished college and was married to a lawyer, a hakujin, Jewish, a good man. He smiled to see his two grandsons noisily splashing in the pool. They at least were his joy and consolation.

Hiroshi was sitting with Sachi and her husband Takashi when Simone, plate in hand, came to join them. Sachi taught math at a high school in Sherman Oaks, and Tak was a partner in a thriving dental practice in town. Sachi now called herself Alice, and at her insistence, her husband went by Harry. Hiro stubbornly insisted on calling his sister Sachi and her husband Tak, but Simone obliged them by addressing them as Alice and Harry.

When Simone joined the group, Alice was expressing her distress over her daughter, Susan, a senior in high school. "She insisted on bringing her tape recorder," Alice was saying. "She wants to interview everyone here."

"Really?" Simone said. "About what, Alice?"

Alice raised her eyebrows and clamped her mouth in exasperation. "The camps," she said. "She wants to interview everyone about their camp experiences."

"Well, seems like a good idea," Simone said. "Everyone's here."

"No," Alice said emphatically. "We're here to celebrate Mother's birthday and to have a good time. No one wants to be badgered about the camps."

"Actually, I had a good time in camp," Harry broke in. "Played cards, fooled around with girls..."

"Yeah, I'll bet," Alice said, jabbing an elbow into his ribs.

"Really?" Simone asked. "Did you really have a good time in camp?"

"Well, everybody had it tough," Harry replied. "There was a war on, you know. Plus, I wasn't in camp long because I volunteered for the Army the first chance I got. I finished college and went to dental school on the G.I. bill. So everything worked out."

"That's not how Hiro looks at it," Simone said. "Isn't that right, *cheri?*"

Hiroshi merely grunted.

"Hiro, you're never happy, never satisfied," Alice said. She turned to Simone. "He's always been like that. He was a cute baby, but as he grew older, he was always getting into trouble, making the wrong kinds of friends, rebelling. You know how he is."

"Yes," Simone said. "Believe me, I do."

Everyone laughed except Hiroshi.

"But, Harry," Simone persisted, "I'm still a little puzzled. You make it sound as if being interned during the war was almost a good thing. Hiro's father lost everything. Didn't your family lose a lot, too?"

"There was a war on, for God's sake," Harry said. "And you don't know what the Issei were like."

"Well, I know what my father was like," Hiroshi said, "and I'm guessing your father was probably the same. They were honest men, men with honest convictions. They were Japanese patriots. They knew who they were, and they weren't afraid to show it. That's a lot more than we can say for ourselves."

"Jesus, Hiro," Harry said. "I hope you don't go around saying that to hakujin."

"I'm not only saying it," Hiroshi said, "I'm thinking of writing a book about it."

"Oh, Hiro," Alice said. She looked around quickly to see where her children were. "Harry," she said, "we really should get going. We've got so much to do tomorrow."

After they'd taken their leave, Hiroshi turned to Simone. "I wonder what was so pressing that they had to leave."

"What was so pressing was for Alice was to get Harry away from you," Simone replied.

"I figured," Hiroshi said. "But I just can't keep my mouth shut when Tak talks like that." Then, glaring at Simone, he added, "And her name is Sachi."

Simone laughed. "I'll call her Sachi, if I can call you Pierre, Hiroshi-san."

Sachi never talked about her camp experience if she could help it.

As far as she was concerned, those years did not exist, even though they had arguably played a positive, if conflicted, role in her life. Like everyone else, she had endured the fear, misery, desolation, and hunger of the early months. But as it became clear that her family would survive, as life began to take on some primitive semblance of normality, she experienced a sense of liberation, as ironic as that might be. Like girls on the outside, she'd dressed in skirts and bobby sox; she'd jitterbugged with her girlfriends—and sometimes even with boys—to records by Glenn Miller, Tommy Dorsey, and the Andrews Sisters. She'd even pinned a photo of her movie-star crush, cut from *Silver Screen* magazine, onto the wall next to her bunk, something she would never have dared to do in Hacienda.

While in camp, she'd also finally been freed from that obsessive hag of a dance teacher, Osho-san, who, in her smarmy but cutting way, had found fault with everything about her—even the shape of her mouth and the size of her feet, as if there were anything she could do about them. She'd always hated the kimono ordered for her at great expense from Japan that forced her to walk in tiny mincing steps like the pitiful women in Japanese movies who would bow and drop to their knees at the very sight of a man. Best of all, there was no more talk of "when we return to Japan."

In Hacienda, it seemed as though everything she did—her attendance at Japanese school, her Japanese dance lessons, her rigorous training in Japanese etiquette, the constant correction of her spoken Japanese—was a way of preparing her for "when we return to Japan." Her parents were more easy-going with the boys; it was only with her that they became so stringent and demanding.

Sachi was not sure when she first began to realize what was going on, but it gradually became clear to her that her parents were grooming her for marriage. They wanted her to be like Mother, at the beck and call of her husband, attending to and anticipating his every need. No thank you, she thought. She was an American; she would never agree to that kind of life, and she had no intention of going to Japan. One way or another, she would find a way to stay in America.

In that sense, for Sachi, the war had been a blessing in disguise. It had blasted to smithereens any danger of her ending up as a demure and obedient Japanese wife. The scholarship she won to a college in Minnesota had been her ticket to freedom, and she had never looked back.

Still, the war that had freed her had also devastated her family, killed a brother, and destroyed her father's fortunes, reducing him to a penniless laborer. Her mother, a woman of grace and refinement, had become pathetic in camp, reduced to hoarding bread crumbs like a beggar woman. Returning to Hacienda that first summer break after the end of the war, she'd watched her parents return from the fields, weary and dressed in filthy rags, their faces covered in dirt. She couldn't bear it. She'd found an excuse to leave early and never again returned to Hacienda.

But how could she explain all of that to her daughter? Susan couldn't possibly understand what it had been like—and why should she ever have to. The war, the camps, and their aftermath were dirty, ugly secrets best kept locked forever in some dark corner of her mind.

Susan didn't leave with her parents. Much to her mother's distress, she made her brother Mark promise to give her a ride home, and free from her mother's angry scowl, she latched onto Hiroshi as the person most likely to be open to talking with her.

Finding a quiet corner in Mickey's big house for an interview with Susan would have been easy enough for Hiroshi, but seeing Mother, Yukio, Mickey, and Sachi together after so many years had stirred thoughts and feelings that he had long ago laid aside. While arguing with Tak, he had felt his throat beginning to constrict. And seeing the urn with Sammy's ashes had brought back memories of that terrible night when Sammy had vanished in the storm. Hiroshi scarcely knew what to do with such memories. He didn't trust himself to talk candidly with Susan without embarrassing her and himself by breaking down in tears.

"Susan," Hiroshi told her, "Call me in Baltimore. You can call collect. Next week. I'll talk to you as long as you want then."

He offered to show her how to tape record a phone conversation, but she looked annoyed and said she already knew how.

"Tell me, Uncle Hiro, why don't any of you want to talk about the camps?"

Susan was slender and petite, with straight black hair tied back in a ponytail. She was seventeen, but to Hiroshi she looked even younger. Her look of earnest inquiry touched him.

"I do want to talk about it, Susan," he said, "and I will. I promise. Just not today. Today we're here to celebrate Grandma's birthday, and I don't want to bring up unpleasant things."

"But I don't mean just today," Susan said. "My mom and dad never want to talk about the camps. All my dad ever says about it is that he had a good time, and Mom says it was all such a long time ago that we should just forget about it."

"Susan, if I could forget about it, I would. But I can't, so I promise I'll talk to you about the camps. Just call me next week."

"And wasn't it wrong, Uncle Hiro? I mean, you were American citizens. Mr. Ferguson, our social studies teacher, says it was unconstitutional."

"Yeah, there's that too," Hiroshi said.

Susan looked around and spotted Yukio's son Seiji talking to her brother Mark by the swimming pool.

"Come on, Uncle Hiro. I want you to hear what Seiji says about you Nisei."

Seiji had once come to visit Hiroshi and Simone in Baltimore, and Hiroshi had offered to help him get a job at the *Herald,* but Seiji had wanted to stay in New York where he did freelance work, mostly for left-wing publications.

Seiji had a cockiness that appealed to Hiroshi. "Thanks, Uncle Hiro," he'd said to the prospect of working for the *Herald,* "but I'm not ready to retire yet."

While in college, Seiji had been described by some members of the family as a "pot-smoking, anti-war hippie," which had only further endeared him to Hiroshi. Now, joining him by the swimming pool, Hiroshi found that the young man had not lost any of his feistiness.

"You want to know why the Nisei won't talk about the camps?" he said to Susan. "I'll tell you why." Turning to Hiroshi, he said, "Excuse me, Uncle Hiro, but the Nisei—not you or my dad maybe—but most Nisei want to believe that they're one hundred percent, unadulterated Americans. That's why they can't talk about the camps. You don't put Americans in concentration camps. The camp experience doesn't jive with their self image."

Mark objected. "Why shouldn't they think of themselves as Americans?" Susan's brother was a medical student at UCLA. "Hell, they fought in World War II," he said. "My dad did, at least. So did Uncle Mickey. They're as American as anybody else."

"You know," Seiji said, "you're right. They did fight in the war. But they were in the 442nd, a segregated, all-Jap unit. They were the spearhead of every attack. That's why they got so many Purple Hearts, more than any other unit in the war. That didn't make them Americans. That only made them expendable."

Hiroshi was amazed by the clarity of Seiji's comprehension.

"You're right, Seiji," he said. "You've got it mainly right. But try being a little more gentle with us old guys. Things weren't so simple in those days."

"I know," Seiji said. "I get carried away sometimes."

The subject of Isamu's ashes didn't come up until late that evening, after all of the young crowd had dispersed

Yukio said he would take the ashes back with him to Arizona

for burial in the Kubota family plot. When Mickey objected, Yukio was firm. "You had Isamu's ashes hidden in a closet here for more than twenty years. Why don't you let me bury him?"

"That's not true. We had the urn on the mantel while Father was alive," Mickey said. "And it's not in a closet. That's an alcove."

"You never liked Isamu," Yukio said.

There was bitterness in his voice. It was as if fifty years of pent-up anger and resentment was bursting out. Yukio had left for Japan when he was six and had been called back to the US when twenty. Isamu might have been crippled by fortune, but Yukio had been turned into a foreigner in what should have been his own country by the whims of his father. Being cast out of the family had been the final indignity for him. Now, more than forty years later, he lashed out at Mickey, saying, "You were ashamed of Isamu because you were a football star and he was in a wheelchair. It was more important for you to put your football trophy on the mantel instead of Isamu's ashes."

"That trophy's not mine," protested Mickey. "It's Ricky's. I never got a trophy."

"You blamed Isamu for that."

"Don't be ridiculous," Mickey said, but he too was trapped in the past. The truth was he never wanted the ashes in his house, and resented having to hear Father say that Sammy was the brightest of his sons, even after he and Amy had taken him and Mother into their tiny home, supporting the family by slaving away night and day in a tiny, rundown café that served drunks, whores, johns, and the other scum who would come in from the sleazy bars and strip joints on Beacon Street. He had endured with a smile what passed for witticism with that crowd—"Ching, Chong, Chinaman" and shouts of "chop chop" when they wanted faster service. They'd worked twelve hours a day, fourteen on weekends He would get up at four in the morning twice a week to get fresh vegetables at the produce markets in Los Angeles.

Late at night, he'd make deliveries to greasy fat men smoking cigars around a poker table or to dangerous looking characters in shiny sharkskin suits who would peel twenty dollar bills from a roll to impress women who looked a lot like Cindy. In their macho way, they usually waved off the offer of change, so it was good business, but it was unpleasant—even humiliating—work nevertheless. He and Amy had endured all this for five long years until they were able to sell the business for twice what it was worth to a bar owner who had no idea what it took to keep a café such as theirs profitable, much less how to make cheap and tasty Chinese dishes they sold as chop suey.

When Mickey had overheard Yukio's son's Seiji disparaging the Nisei who'd fought in the war as "cannon fodder," he'd gritted his teeth and remained silent. The tangled story of the war and its aftermath was not something he trusted himself to revisit. He'd come through the war virtually unscathed, but he'd had friends who'd died and others who were maimed for life. The worst wound he ever got during the war was a fractured skull caused by some of Yukio's friends, men who were now benefitting from the sacrifices made by those they had attacked as *inu,* spies, traitors, sellouts. Their children were going to colleges and universities, going into professions that had been closed to Japanese before the war. What's more, Yukio, the chonan, had fled to Arizona after the war, leaving his parents to scratch out a living as field laborers. It was he, Mickey, who had rescued them.

And now they were quarreling over Sammy's ashes, which meant less than nothing to him. Mickey was absolutely sincere, but his words were cutting and filled with bitterness, when he said, "Look, I really don't give a damn. If you want to take the ashes to Arizona, go ahead. It makes no difference to me."

Hiroshi, caught up in his own thoughts, barely heard what the others were saying. "Look," he said at last. "I think I knew Sammy better than any of you. I was just a kid, but we talked a lot in camp. We talked about loyalty—not loyalty to Japan or to

America, but loyalty to who we are as individuals. And you know, he thought all of you were crazy. He thought the Loyalty League was just as crazy as the back-to-Japan nuts."

"I never wanted to go back to Japan," Yukio said.

"I know. I'm not talking about you. But there were some nutty guys in camp. Sammy thought the whole world was crazy, and that's why he liked the desert. He liked the quiet, the space. He never wanted to leave. I think he fell into the canal on purpose. He never wanted to be found, just like Mr. Nakashima. Remember him? I think he wanted to join Mr. Nakashima in the desert."

"What happened to Nakashima?" Yukio asked.

"This was after they sent you to Tule Lake. He wandered off into the desert and was never found. We kids thought he was crazy, but Sammy told me he was a highly intelligent man, maybe even a great man."

"Hiro," Mickey said, "sometimes I think you're crazy. Like I said, I don't give a damn about Sammy's ashes. But ask Mother before you do anything."

Mickey and Amy had convinced Mother to spend the night, so she was in the guest room reading in an armchair when her three sons entered. She had an orange knitted shawl over her shoulders and a cream-colored woolen blanket on her lap. She'd taken off her turban, exposing her bald head. She looked like a Buddhist nun. When Mickey patted his own head, silently offering to put the turban back on for her, Mother smiled. "No, Mikio, I don't need my helmet on at night." She called it her "kabuto," the ornate steel helmet that samurai warriors wore into battle. "I only wear it during the day for your sake," she explained.

Yukio gently introduced the subject of Isamu's ashes. He explained how he and Isamu had been close after he'd returned from Japan, and how it would be a comfort to him, and no doubt to Isamu as well, to have him nearby. Hiroshi then made his case, explaining how he and Isamu had gone out into the desert, and how much Isamu had loved the wilderness and the freedom of the open space.

Mother listened, keeping her eyes closed. After Yukio and Hiroshi finished, she remained silent. Everyone thought she had fallen asleep. She opened her eyes and looked at Mickey. When he remained silent, she said: "It doesn't matter where Isamu is. Our Lord Buddha tells us we are all impermanent. We are all in a state of Being and Non-Being. From Being we inevitably return to Non-Being. We are one, and we are nothing."

Mickey and Hiroshi thought their mother had fallen prey to a sudden bout of senility. Mother was frail and tired easily, but she had been mentally alert and coherent earlier in the day. Only Yukio recognized the vein of Buddho-Taoism their mother had touched upon.

"Yes, Mother," he said. "Ultimately we all return to nothingness. But in the meantime, what should we do with Isamu's ashes?"

Mother smiled. "Yes, you are right," she said. "There's always the here and now to deal with. You can do what you think is best, but Father would have wanted Isamu buried next to us. He died suddenly and could not attend to it himself, and I, in my forgetfulness, put the matter entirely out of mind. That was neglectful of me."

In early summer of the following year, Hiroshi and his family went to Arizona. Hiroshi was writing a magazine article on the 40th anniversary of the internment and needed to revisit the site of the now vanished camp. Simone wanted to see it too, so they had decided to make a trip of it, taking their children: Kai, their son, was nine years old, and Dani, their daughter, was seven.

When they got to the former site of the camp, Hiroshi found the place even more desolate than he had remembered. The barracks were gone; only crumbling concrete foundations remained, marking the location of the former mess halls. And even those weren't easy to find amongst the sagebrush that had crept back to reclaim its domain.

It was midmorning, and the searing heat of the desert sun was already beginning to assert itself. "We should have brought hats for the children," said Simone. "We can't stay long in this heat."

Dani said, "This is not such a good place to camp, Papa. Did you have tents?"

"No, Dani. It wasn't like that. There used to be barracks here—big wooden buildings, lots of them. And mess halls where we ate, and shower houses, toilets, stuff like that."

Kai was walking along the broken edges of what had once been a concrete foundation. "Is this where you lived Papa?" he said, "Is this where the barracks were?"

"Actually no, that used to be a mess hall. All the barracks are gone now," Hiroshi said. "I don't think there's anything left of them."

"Yes there is. Look, here's some nails and pieces of wood," Kai said as he squatted in the dirt and began stuffing his pockets with the debris.

"Be careful where you poke around," Hiroshi shouted.

"Why Papa? Are there snakes?"

"I'm afraid of snakes," Dani said.

"They usually don't come out during the day. But still, be careful, okay? Stay clear of the sagebrush. And don't stick your hands into holes or cracks."

"Oh, look," Dani exclaimed, excited. "A lizard!"

She pointed to what was in fact a horny toad, a harmless creature Hiroshi used to catch with his bare hands as a child.

"Just leave it alone, Dani," Hiroshi said. He didn't want the children running off and chasing after things. He stomped his foot, which sent the lizard scurrying off into the desert.

"Where's the river, Papa?" Kai asked. "You said there was a river."

"It wasn't really a river, Kai. It was a canal. And it used to be over there on the other side of the butte, that little mountain there. But it doesn't seem to be there anymore."

Kai wanted to climb the butte to see for himself, but Dani was content to stay with Simone looking for colored rocks that she put into her mother's handbag.

As Hiroshi led Kai up the butte, poking under rocks and boulders with a stick, he wondered why he was being so cautious. As a child, he had wandered all over the desert, clambering up and down this very butte without a second thought. He'd never worried about rattlesnakes back then.

"Kai," he said. "Don't go climbing around there. Come here. Stay close."

"Why Papa? I want to find a Gila monster."

"Never mind Gila monsters, you hardly ever see them. Don't go scrambling around," he called out as Kai disappeared beyond a rock. "It's dangerous!"

At nine, Kai was the exact age Hiroshi had been when he'd been thrown into this prison camp surrounded by barbed wire. Over the years, Hiroshi had convinced himself that he'd grown to love the desert wilderness, that its very remoteness had made him feel safe. Like Tak, he had focused on the "good times." Now, looking out over the vast, unending wilderness, Hiroshi realized that his nephew Seiji's analysis had been only partially correct. The Nisei couldn't talk about the camps, not only because it disturbed their self-image as Americans, but because it reminded them of a fear that ran too deep to probe. Somewhere at the core of their being, they were still terrified—afraid for themselves and afraid for their children. For all he or his family knew, they'd been brought to the desert to die, to starve in a barren wasteland crawling with snakes, lizards, scorpions, and other unknown dangers. Hiroshi recalled the war propaganda: the Japanese were an evil race; they were subhuman, snarling apes, rats, vermin. Mother and many of the Issei had been convinced that they would all be killed out here in the wilderness. And though the site had turned out not to be the extermination camp they had feared, the terror and the sense of their helplessness had remained. At its most primitive level, that terror had been the unspoken shame of being Japanese. But the real threat—the worst degradation, not existentially, but spiritually—was the shame itself.

Hiroshi put his arm around his son and held him tight.

"What's the matter, Papa?" Kai said.

"Nothing, Kai. But we need to go down now. We need to get back to Mother and Dani."

When they came down from the butte, Simone was holding Dani's hand. "I think we should go now," she said. "The children are very hot."

Hiroshi saw that her eyes were tearing.

What's the matter?" he asked.

"I don't know," she said. "There's so much here. So much sadness."

"I know," Hiroshi said.

"I was thinking of your mother," Simone said. "How it must have been for her. You were the same age as Kai."

"I was thinking of that, too. I didn't fully understand that at the time. But it must have been hard for her. I think I'm beginning to understand my father better, too."

They stood quietly for some moments, Simone clutching Dani's hand and Hiroshi still holding Kai close.

"And there's sadness for me, too," Simone said.

"I know. It was worse for you, the war."

"Yes, but it wasn't so complicated."

When they got to their hotel, a message from Yukio was waiting for them. When Hiroshi called, Yukio said they'd just gotten word that Mother had died. The news came as no surprise. Mother had been in a hospice for nearly a week, and Hiroshi and Simone had planned to visit her before returning to Baltimore.

Mother's funeral was held in the Buddhist temple next to the senior residence where she had lived. Hiroshi was amazed at the large number of mourners who turned out for the service and the magnificence of the ceremony and rituals. In part, all this was a tribute to Father, who had once been a major contributor to the Buddhist mission in America. But in her final years, Mother had herself been a regular presence at the temple, and so was well known to the people there.

In her coffin, Mother looked much as she had when Hiroshi had last seen her, serene and at peace. She was dressed in her white silk turban, the one with the jade crane that Sachi had made for her.

Five priests, dressed in purple and gold brocade, stood before the coffin chanting a sutra to the mournful throbbing of the prayer gong. Bouquets set on easels were massed on both sides of the coffin and strung out along the walls. The burning smell of incense cut through the scent of flowers with a pungent fragrance that, for Hiroshi, recalled his childhood. Mickey had no doubt paid for most of the flowers, but many of them were from old friends, some of whom had come from as far away as Hacienda, Santa Marguerita, and even out of state. Many occupants of the senior residence were there as well.

Following the ceremony, the Kono siblings and their children and grandchildren gathered at Mickey's restaurant for lunch. There they were told that another ceremony would take place later that afternoon at the Rolling Hills Cemetery, where they'd just buried Mother. Everyone was invited to attend.

The plan had been to bury Sammy's ashes during Mother's interment, but in the morning rush, no one had remembered to bring the urn. So Hiroshi had volunteered to take the ashes to the cemetery later that afternoon.

As it turned out, most of the family members had already made their travel plans, and so were either unable or unwilling to return to the cemetery. In the end, only six people were able to make it out to Rolling Hills for the second burial of the day: Yukio and Kazuko, and Hiroshi and Simone with Kai and Dani.

As they waited at the grave site, a workman in gray coveralls with a matching baseball cap came by in an electric cart. He took the urn from Hiroshi and set it in a pre-prepared cavity in the ground. After filling the remaining space with dirt, the man nodded politely to them and drove off again in his cart. There was as yet no grave marker.

The six of them stood there silently before Sammy's grave, feeling inadequate and empty. Hiroshi turned his head and looked off into the distance. The cemetery was built on a hillside overlooking the Pacific Ocean. Instead of traditional gravestones, the plots were marked with flat bronze markers, so the only interruption to the rolling carpet of green that stretched down to the sea were occasional clusters of white alder, cottonwood, and maples. Looking out toward the ocean, Hiroshi thought that this was in fact where Sammy belonged, next to Mother and Father. It had only been in his own imagination that Sammy had wanted to remain in the desert. Father was right to remove his ashes from the camp graveyard. And he was right about Isamu being the brightest of his sons. Sammy had seen clearly what the desert was for them—little more than a prison.

They all stood there for some time, not knowing exactly what to do, until Simone, struck by inspiration, said that it was an old Jewish tradition to put a stone on the grave of a loved one. She opened her handbag.

"Dani," she said. "Can we give one of your stones to Uncle Sammy? That will remind him that we are thinking of him."

Dani readily agreed, and after carefully examining each of her specimens, she chose a very small triangular piece of pink sandstone. "This is the prettiest one," she said.

Kai dug into his pocket and pulled out a nail. "Uncle Sammy can have this, too."

Kaz went to Mother's grave and plucked a white rose from

one of the bouquets. "Isamu liked roses," she said.

Yukio opened his mouth as if to say something, but instead remained silent and placed his palms together in prayer. Hiroshi was surprised; he had never known Yukio to be religious.

Collecting the stone, nail, and rose, Hiroshi carefully placed them on the dirt that covered Sammy's ashes. He stepped back alongside his family and said, "The stone is Uncle Sammy's character, the nail, his truth, and the rose, the love of his family." Placing his palms together, he too bowed his head, as did Simone and Kaz. Kai and Dani, looking up to see what their parents were doing, smiled inquiringly at one another, then hunched their shoulders and did the same.

They stood together silently for a while. When they lowered their hands, they were able to leave. Isamu was at peace finally. He was where he wanted to be. He was home.

ACKNOWLEDGEMENTS

Much of this novel began as short stories first written or rewritten in 1990 when I was enrolled in the Writing Seminars of the Johns Hopkins University under the tutelage of Stephen Dixon and John Barth. I owe much of this completed work to their critiques and steady guidance. I also thank Madeleine Mysko, novelist, poet, teacher and a dear friend who read the short stories that later formed this novel many times over with great care and patience, never ceasing to offer words of encouragement. I thank my daughter Elisabeth and my son Peter for their love, patience, and support during the difficult years this book was in the making. My daughter Eve, a writer and scholar, has through the years been a loving critic and an invaluable pillar of support. My good friend Greg Robinson, a distinguished scholar and author of Japanese American histories, was instrumental in introducing my work to Kaya Press. Arthur A. Hansen, long a dedicated scholar in Japanese American history, provided invaluable advice and support. I am especially indebted to Sunyoung Lee, Publisher and Editor of Kaya Press, for her gracious acceptance of my manuscript and the thoughtfulness, creativity, and energy she brought to its publication. Her careful and astute editing, her advice and suggestions, her firm grasp of the art of fiction were essential for converting a collection of short stories into what I hope is a coherent novel.

And finally, to Sabine, my beloved wife and dear friend of fifty years, to whom this work is dedicated, I owe my everlasting gratitude. Many years ago, she read the first four pages of what was to become the first chapter of this novel, and never ceased to push, prod, and cajole me to keep on writing.

AFTERWORD

In Search of Hiroshi, my memoir published in 1988, started out as a novel, but it was so strongly fettered to my own life and memories that I had to give up the pretense that it was a work of fiction. *Fox Drum Bebop,* I will admit, is also autobiographical and made of scraps of personal memories reimagined and reconstituted to form stories—pieces of fiction that have a deliberate narrative structure, giving them an element of universality in much the same way fairy tales can depict the human condition. My desire to write a work of fiction has always been a wish to tell a story that was bigger than myself, to tell a tale about the Japanese in America.

Born in 1933, I grew up at time when Japanese communities in America were still intact and culturally alive and vibrant. My first language was Japanese. Growing up, the first songs I heard and sang, both nursery rhymes and pop tunes, were Japanese. We saw Japanese movies and kabuki plays performed by our friends and neighbors. Buddhism and Shinto in their various manifestations were a constant presence, and although I did not realize it at the time, so was Confucianism and, in the culturally defined ways my parents responded to the beauty and wonders of nature, perhaps Taoism as well.

Of course, as I grew into school age, I became American. How could I not, surrounded as I was by the culture of American public schools, by movies, by TV and radio shows, newspapers, magazines, comic books. I didn't speak English when I entered kindergarten, but when I think back on that time, I am amazed at how quickly English became my first language, and how easily Japanese language and culture began fading into a secondary and later vestigial role.

This would have happened eventually even without the Pacific War, as the Japanese call World War II, but for the Japanese in America, Pearl Harbor and the war that followed were the cultural equivalent of the Big Bang—it sent us as a people and each of us as individuals flying off into the vast space that is America. Some say that this was ultimately a good thing. Perhaps in some important ways it was. But it also shattered our communities and our identities. It left us not knowing—or insecure about—who we were. It caused us to scramble to hide ourselves in a communal masquerade that some white observers would later call "the model minority."

As an adult, when I began thinking more about personal identity, I concluded that Japanese Americans, the Nisei in particular, had cut off and discarded the Japanese part of their upbringing and were mentally crippled. At one point in my quest to write this novel, I tried to make my protagonist a polio survivor who was confined to a wheelchair, his physical state a metaphor for the crippled mental state of Japanese

Americans generally. I eventually gave up on that idea, and relegated the character, now named Isamu or Sammy, to an important but secondary role—that of a detached and clear-eyed observer of the drama being played out before him. His physical disability became a metaphor for Japanese American political impotence. I was sad to see him die, but in my mind, at least, Sammy's spirit hovers over the whole of the novel.

What made the writing of both *In Search of Hiroshi* and *Fox Drum Bebop* challenging is that both struggle against a headwind of popular opinion—stereotypes that are well intentioned and positive, but at bottom demeaning. These were popularized views of Japanese Americans which the Nisei were loath to contradict, for they grew out of an understanding that the Japanese in America were grievously wronged during Word War II, were not the spies, saboteurs, and genetically determined monsters that war-time propaganda made us out to be. This perceptual rehabilitation, however, eventually went overboard, making us out to be uniformly good, strong, enduring, comic-book people. Put on such a delicate perch, we were denied our humanity and our freedom to be ourselves or to speak for ourselves.

When reading a chapter from *Fox Drum* in a writers' workshop, a woman objected to the 12-year-old Hiroshi shouting, "That's bullshit," to his friend. A nice Japanese boy would never use such a word. At another workshop, readers objected to a depiction of a raunchy Japanese couple in the camp. When someone the next compartment over complains of the sexually explicit noises coming through the walls, the man says, "What else but nookie in this goddamn place." Would a Japanese American be so coarse and common? Another reader was upset because Hiroshi's father did not pay a Mexican woman for cleaning out his stable. A Japanese would honor his debts. Others thought the father's patriotic love of Japan made him a zealot. Reverence for the Emperor, flying the Japanese flag from a mountain top, a leftist radical Sansei who calls the revered 442nd Regimental Combat team cannon fodder—these were nothing short of blasphemy. In my private life, a Sansei writer with whom I was corresponding was shocked when I wrote in one of my letters that I loved Japan. He thought I was insane, and our correspondence ended shortly thereafter.

So focused were we, as were others who supported Japanese Americans, on showing that we were just as American as anybody else, we ended up digging a deep hole somewhere in our psyche in which we kept hidden all that was uniquely Japanese about ourselves. What was left was what could be called faux Americanism. How can any literature of any worth emerge from such a cramped and narrow space? Japanese Americans are real people with all the virtues and vices, strengths and weaknesses, wisdom and foolishness, intelligence and stupidity that are common to all of humanity. At the same time, most of us are different in unique ways from other Americans, and there is nothing wrong with these differences; they make us who we are.

My hero Hiroshi is a tormented soul who has not learned this valuable lesson and is caught between the opposing forces of the *Fox Drum* and *Bebop*. For him, these are the two extremes of the American experience. He is pulled by the one and pushed by the other. It is probably not an uncommon predicament for ethnic Americans, perhaps even for those in the mainstream, to be caught in the pull of tradition and the push of the new and liberating. But for Hiroshi, the flight from his tradition is a form of self-betrayal that he scarcely understands, and the escape to jazz and beatnik bohemianism is rife with dangers and existential dread. Even the safe harbor he eventually finds in his own family is haunted by ghosts from the past, leaving him in search of his basic essence, or, as I put it elsewhere, in search of Hiroshi.

As a final word, I want to say something about the postwar Sansei generation. Nisei rarely, if ever, spoke to their children about the war years, about the incarceration, the breakup of their families, about the fear, humiliation, and shame they endured. They hoped to protect them from the trauma of that experience. But the historic event that imprisoned Japanese Americans because of their race was never a secret. Excellent, well-documented books were written on the subject soon after the war that the Sansei could read if they wanted. What they could not learn from these historical works, however, was how their own families and they themselves were affected. Quite apart from its literary aspirations, *Fox Drum Bebop* is, as was *In Search of Hiroshi,* an attempt to add to the canon of individual experiences that began to emerge later in the form of novels, poetry, plays, and documentaries. It is my hope that my works, along with others, will encourage a more open and differentiated discussion of our experiences to help free ourselves, our children, and their progeny from the crippling emotional baggage many of us still carry.

—G.O.

Gene Oishi, former Washington and foreign correspondent for the *Baltimore Sun*, has also written articles on the Japanese American experience for *The New York Times Magazine*, *The Washington Post*, *Newsweek*, and *West Magazine*. His memoir, *In Search of Hiroshi*, was published in 1988. Now retired, he lives in Baltimore, Maryland with his wife Sabine.